P9-DHJ-295
MYTH-O-MANIA
I

UNDERWORLD LIBRARY
ANCIENT GREECE

AUTHOR
Kate McMullan

TITLE
Have a Hot Time, Hades!

DATE DUE	BORROWER'S NAME
XXVII	Lord Hades
XXXI	Lord Hades

Myth-O-Mania is published by Stone Arch Books
A Capstone Imprint
151 Good Counsel Drive, P.O. Box 669
Mankato, Minnesota 56002
www.capstonepub.com

Library of Congress Cataloging-in-Publication Data is available on the Library of Congress website.

Library binding: 978-1-4342-2136-0 • Paperback: 978-1-4342-3437-7

Summary: Hades sets the record straight on how he became King of the Underworld.

Cover Character Illustration: Denis Zilber
Cover, Map, and Interior Design: Bob Lentz
Production Specialist: Michelle Biedscheid

Image Credits:
Shutterstock: Animyze, B. McQueen, Cre8tive Images, Eky Studio, Natalia Barsukova, NY-P, osov, Pablo H Caridad, Perov Stanislav, Petrov Stanislav Eduardovich, Selena, VikaSuh. Author photo: Phill Lehans.

Printed in the United States of America in Stevens Point, Wisconsin.
082011 006341R

HAVE A HOT TIME, HADES!

BY
KATE McMULLAN

STONE ARCH BOOKS
a capstone imprint

N
THESSALY
ITALY
GREECE
AEGEAN SEA
Delphi
Thebes
PELOPONNESE
Athens
Olympia
SICILY
IONIAN SEA
Sparta
MEDITERRANEAN SEA
CRETE
ANCIENT
Greece!
IF YOU LIVED HERE, YOU'D BE HOME BY NOW!
UNDERWORLD · MAP · CORPORATION
Mount Olympus
Cave Headquarters
Mount Ida
Olympic Stadium
Mount Etna
Hades's Underworld Entrance

TABLE OF CONTENTS

PROLOGUE 7

CHAPTER I: Hothead Dad 11
CHAPTER II: Ultrabright Mom....................................20
CHAPTER III: He's Toast! 31
CHAPTER IV: Sun Spot 37
CHAPTER V: Family Fireworks 45
CHAPTER VI: Hotfooted Gods......................................54
CHAPTER VII: Olympic Torch..63
CHAPTER VIII: Bright Idea...72
CHAPTER IX: Hot Dog!...83
CHAPTER X: Shiner and Co. 91
CHAPTER XI: T-Bolt Attack! 101
CHAPTER XII: Red-Hot Olympians..................................106
CHAPTER XIII: Great Balls of Fire! 113
CHAPTER XIV: Fire Escape 124
CHAPTER XV: Star Wars 132
CHAPTER XVI: Smokin' Granny 141
CHAPTER XVII: Have a Hot Time, Hades!...................... 149

EPILOGUE 156

KING HADES'S QUICK-AND-EASY
GUIDE TO THE MYTHS 160

Prologue

Call me Hades.

My full name — His Royal Lowness, Lord of the Dead, King Hades — is a bit of a mouthful.

I rule the Underworld. The ghosts of the dead travel down to dwell in my kingdom. If they were good in life, they get to go to an eternal rock concert, where really great bands play on and on forever. The ghosts of the not-so-good? They have to wander around, trying to memorize an endless list of really hard spelling words. And the ghosts of the wicked? You *don't* want to know.

It's my job to make sure everything in the Underworld runs smoothly. After a hard day, I like to go home to the palace with my dog. Don't I, Cerberus? Yes, that's my good old boy, boy, boy.

(He has three heads, and he hates it when I leave one out.) I had my palace totally wired millennia ago with all the premium stuff. Plus Channel Earth and HB-Olympus, so I can keep an eye on what's happening up above.

I have a great library, too. You think the Big-Fat-Book-of-the-Month Club doesn't know how to find me down here? Last month their featured selection was *The Big Fat Book of Greek Myths*. I knew all of the stories, of course, but I thought it might be a fun read. So I sat down in my La-Z-God, shifted into recline, and started in. I couldn't believe the nonsense I was reading! Take a look for yourself — go on, read it!

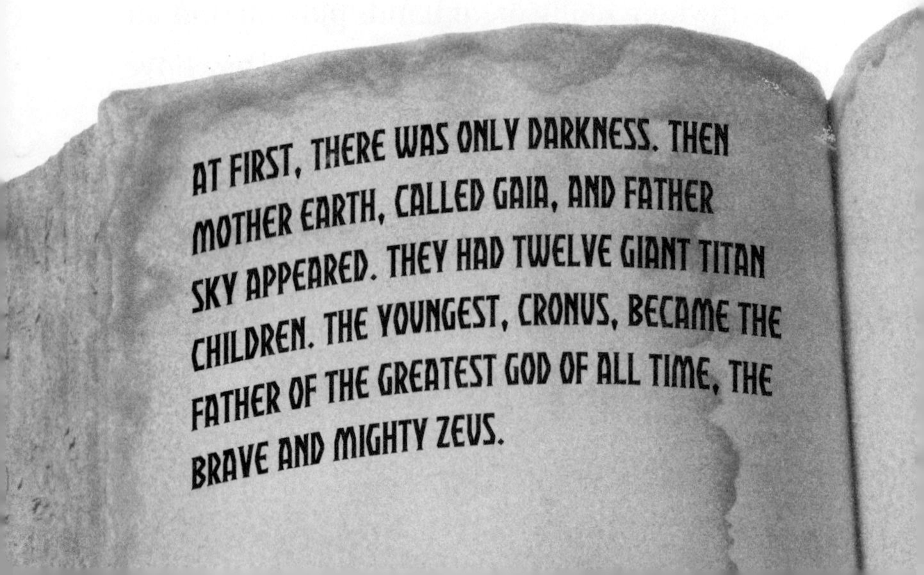

AT FIRST, THERE WAS ONLY DARKNESS. THEN MOTHER EARTH, CALLED GAIA, AND FATHER SKY APPEARED. THEY HAD TWELVE GIANT TITAN CHILDREN. THE YOUNGEST, CRONUS, BECAME THE FATHER OF THE GREATEST GOD OF ALL TIME, THE BRAVE AND MIGHTY ZEUS.

Brave and mighty Zeus? Ha! Chicken-hearted Zeus is more like it. Okay, he *is* officially Ruler of the Universe, but that's only because he cheated at cards.

The more I read, the madder I got. The stories were all wrong. Not a single one was told the way it really happened.

But I knew what the problem was. My little brother Zeus had been messing with the myths. He'd scratched out all the parts that didn't fit with his own overblown idea of himself as Supreme Thunder God, Ruler of the Universe. He'd added things, too. Lots of things! All the stories about him hurling lightning bolts? The guy is so out of shape he couldn't hurl a lightning *bug*. And the bit about him being so great that he was crowned with a laurel wreath? Trust me, he only wears that thing to hide his bald spot. What a myth-o-maniac! (That's old Greek speak for "liar.")

Finally I slammed the book shut. There was only one thing for me to do. I had to write a book of my own to set the record straight.

Writing a book was harder than I expected. But I was lucky. My kingdom is loaded with ghost writers! Once I put them to work, the whole thing was a snap.

Now, for the first time ever, you can read the myths the way they *really* happened.

So move over, Zeus.

Make way for me, Hades!

CHAPTER 1

HOTHEAD DAD

Way, way back — so long ago that time and space and triple-digit division problems had only just been invented — a race of giants called Titans ruled the earth.

They were so big that their Mama Gaia, also known as Mother Earth, made mountains as their thrones. Where do you think the word "titanic" comes from, anyway? Right — from the immortal Titans.

Cronus was the youngest Titan, and Mama Gaia was just crazy about him. After he was born, Mama Gaia decided that she and Sky Daddy would never have a more perfect son, so she declared that no more Titans would be born.

Mama Gaia loved giving young Cronus presents. She gave him a golden girdle (old Greek speak for "belt"). She gave him a silver sickle (old Greek speak for "weedwacker"), which he hung from his golden girdle. And she gave him his very own kingdom on top of Mount Olympus, a mountain which was one hundred times taller than the other mountains on earth.

Mama Gaia spoiled him rotten.

From the top of Mount Olympus, Cronus ruled over all the other Titans. He ruled over all the beasts and the mortals on earth at that time, too. Cronus was the Ruler of the Universe, the Big Enchilada. Everyone called him "O Mighty Cronus!"

I called him Dad.

My mom, Rhea, was a Titan, too. She was tickled pink to be married to the Ruler of the Universe. Because no more Titans were to be born, Rhea knew that her children would be little gods. Well, not as little as mortals, but not too much bigger. Still, she couldn't wait to start her own royal family. Everything might have worked out fine if it hadn't been for that prophecy.

It seems that Dad was not content to be Ruler of the Universe. He also wanted to know the future. So he went to visit a seer — an old, blind fortune-teller. He sat down on a hill and asked the seer to tell him about his future children.

"O Mighty Cronus!" the seer said. "You shall have six children!"

"Ah, six!" said Dad. "That is good!"

"O Mighty Cronus!" said the seer. "Three of your children shall be sons. And three shall be daughters!"

"Ah, three of each!" said Dad. "That is good!"

"O Mighty Cronus!" said the seer. "One of the children shall be mightier than the father and one day shall overthrow him!"

"Ah, mightier!" said Dad. "That is — wait a minute, *I* am the father. What are you saying? That one of my children shall overthrow ME?"

"The future grows cloudy," the seer muttered. He knew better than to answer *that* question.

"I'll slay them all!" Cronus shouted. "No one shall be mightier than mighty Cronus!"

"Your children shall be immortal," the old seer pointed out. "You cannot slay them."

“Humph,” said Cronus. “Well, I’ll think of something.”

Not long after that, I was born. I was tiny — not much bigger than Mom’s fist. Mom wrapped me up nice and tight in a swaddling blanket with my name stitched on it, as was the custom. Only my face stuck out. She proudly carried me to my father.

“Behold, O Mighty Cronus!” Mom said. “Here is Hades, your firstborn son! Is he not a handsome little baby god? Look at his teensy dimples!”

Mom handed me to Dad. Dad held me up close to his face. Mom thought he was going to kiss me. Wrong! Dad opened up his giant mouth, shoved me in, and — *GULP!* He swallowed me whole.

I half remember sliding down a slippery tunnel, then *THUMP!* I landed in a huge dark space. Somewhere outside, I heard Mom shrieking. Dad started laughing, which bounced me all over the place inside his stomach. He couldn’t get over his clever plan to keep me from becoming mightier than he was. And there was nothing Mom could do about it.

So it was that I spent my early days inside the cave of Dad's stomach. It was dark, as I said. But after a while my eyes adjusted to it. The thing I never got used to was how damp and sticky it was, especially at mealtimes.

Like all immortal beings, Dad needed to eat ambrosia and drink nectar in order to stay peppy and strong. Ambrosia is sort of like angel-food cake with orange frosting. Nectar is like ancient Greek apple juice. So when I say sticky, I mean *sticky*.

But the worst of it was, there was nothing to do down there. So I thought up ways to make Dad miserable. I kicked him. I punched him. I jumped up and down for hours. If I jumped hard enough, I gave Dad the hiccups. But I'm not sure who suffered the most, Dad or me. I got tossed around with every *hic*.

Then one day — or was it night? Impossible to tell, down in that gut — I was taking a little snooze when, *THUMP!* Something landed beside me. It was a wrapped up little bundle. I picked it up and undid the wrappings. Inside was my baby brother, Poseidon.

Dad was up to his tricks again.

For Poseidon's sake, I was sorry that Dad had swallowed him. But I was happy to have company. I taught Poseidon to kick and punch and jump along with me. We tried our best to give Dad some really serious stomach problems. But Cronus was just too big and too tough. Nothing bothered him.

One day — or it could have been night — Dad chugged down lots more nectar than usual. Talk about a flood! The whole place turned into a lake.

"Come on, Po!" I grabbed my brother's arm and tried to pull him to high ground.

But Po yanked himself away from me.

"Ye-hoo!" he cried as he leaped, grabbing his knees tight to his chest, and plunged into Lake Nectar.

KER-SPLASH!

I got soaked.

Po's head quickly popped out of the lake.

"Did you see that, Hades?" he yelled up to me. "I call it 'the cannonball'!"

"I call it disgusting." Nectar dripped from my hair into my eyes. *Yecch!*

Po started paddling around in the sticky stuff. "And I call this the 'doggie paddle'!"

He stayed in and swam until all the nectar had been digested.

In the years that followed, my three sisters slid down Dad's throat.

First Hestia. *THUMP!*

Then Demeter. *THUMP!*

And finally, Hera. *THUMP!*

Every time a new baby came down the chute, I heard Mom out there, screaming and yelling. Clearly she was not one bit happy with Dad's plan to keep his children from overthrowing him.

Dad's gut was so big that it wasn't crowded, even with five of us down there. Of course, every once in a while, we got on each other's nerves. Po was always trying to organize swimming meets. Hestia was always tidying up the place. Hera ordered the rest of us around, nonstop. We started calling her "The Boss" — but not to her face. Even then it didn't pay to get on the wrong side of Hera. But Demeter was definitely the weirdest. She was always going on and on about wanting to plant a little vegetable garden.

But, hey, we five were family. We grew up in Dad's belly together.

Then one night — or possibly day — *THUMP!*

"A new baby!" cried Po.

We all rushed over to where the baby had landed.

Po picked it up. He began unwrapping its swaddling blanket.

That's when I noticed something odd.

I didn't hear Mom outside, crying and yelling.

Suddenly, Po gasped. "This is no baby!" he cried. "Dad has swallowed a stone!"

Sure enough, in his arms, Po held a big, smooth, baby-size stone.

"You know," I said, as I looked at that stone, "I think Mom has finally come up with a plan of her own."

"Yes!" cried Demeter. "She wants us to plant a rock garden!"

"Uh, not exactly," I said. "Mom's fooled Dad. He thinks he's swallowed another baby. But really Mom switched the baby for this stone."

My brother and sisters nodded. And we all understood that somewhere out in the world, a baby god was growing up.

At the time, I was glad for the baby. Glad that one of us had escaped Dad's big gulp.

But that was before I'd met my little brother Zeus.

CHAPTER II

ULTRABRIGHT MOM

That stone became our plaything. Hey, when you have no toys, no TV, no bikes, no scooters, no dogs, no cats, not even a gerbil, you'd be surprised at how much fun you can have with a stone.

Po liked to throw it into Lake Nectar, then dive in and pull it out again. Hestia enjoyed polishing it. Demeter could often be found trying to find a way to plant it. And all of us, except Demeter, liked to kick it around. We invented a game we called "kickstone," where we divided into teams and tried to kick the stone into the other team's territory.

That's what we were doing the day — and it was day — we heard *GLUG, GLUG, GLUG!*

"Dad's hitting the nectar again," Hera called. "Places!"

My sisters and I backed up against Dad's stomach wall. We braced ourselves for the flood of sticky liquid we knew would soon come rushing down his throat. As usual, Po ran over and assumed a bodysurfing pose under Dad's esophagus. He loved trying to catch that first big nectary wave.

I sniffed. "What's that awful smell?"

"Ew!" said Demeter. "Rotten nectar!"

Hestia started whimpering about how hard it would be to get rid of a foul odor in a closed up space.

The smell turned quickly to a major stink. Then — *WHOOSH!* A torrent of the nastiest liquid imaginable cascaded down Dad's gullet. In no time, we were up to our necks in the stuff.

The glop didn't just sit there, either. It foamed and bubbled. Then it began churning, spinning around faster and faster, turning Dad's stomach into a giant whirlpool. It started sucking us down!

"Scissor kick! Scissor kick!" Po yelled. "Tread water! Heads high!"

We all fought to keep our heads up as the smelly fluid sloshed over us. The whole place shook with Dad's moans and groans. Then the walls of his stomach started clenching like a giant fist. With every clench, a wave of the sour juice flew up Dad's throat. I don't know what happened next because the whirlpool sucked me down. It spun me around. And then suddenly, *SPURT!* I was catapulted up, up, up, up, up Dad's slimy gullet and — *BLECCHH!* — spat out into the world.

I landed on a pile of my brother and sisters. We all blinked and squinted in the daylight, the first we'd seen since our births. As we tried to untangle ourselves from each other, I figured out what had happened. Dad had just barfed. The big lug was lying above us on a hilltop, holding his stomach and wailing.

As soon as the five of us had sorted out whose feet were whose, we stood up. Demeter picked up the stone, and we ran down the hill, away from

Dad. None of us wanted to take a chance on being swallowed again.

"Where are we?" asked Hera when we reached the bottom of the hill.

"You're in Greece!" came a voice from above us.

We looked around. Standing on a hill behind us was a young god. He wore a white tunic and a bronze breastplate. A sword hung from his girdle.

The guy was grinning.

"I am Zeus, your brother!" he said as he walked down the hill toward us.

Ah, so this was the god Mom had saved when she gave Dad the stone. I noticed that Zeus was bigger than the rest of us. All those years down in Dad's gut must have stunted our growth.

"It was I who rescued you," Zeus said. "You may thank me now."

We all muttered our thanks.

But really, couldn't Zeus have waited a few minutes before asking us to thank him? Here we were, newly thrown up into the world, stinking to high heaven, blind as bats in the blazing sunlight, and wearing only the tattered remains of our swaddling clothes. We needed a few minutes to pull ourselves together.

"Look!" Po cried suddenly. "A stream! Last one in is a rotten egg!"

Po cannonballed into the cool, clear water. The rest of us were right on his heels. Ahh! Unless you've spent a few thousand years down in someone's belly, you have no idea how good a clear, clean stream can feel. Or how fine it is to breathe fresh air. And did it ever feel great not to be eternally sticky!

Zeus kept calling, "Get out! Come hear the tale of how I saved you!"

But we ignored him and stayed in that stream until we were good and ready to climb out. Then we lay in the sun to dry. Dry — what a concept! It was paradise, until Zeus ran over and started yakking about himself.

"See, Mom fooled Dad into swallowing a wrapped-up stone," Zeus said. "Then Mom rushed me to a cave on the island of Crete and hid me there where I was raised by a Fairy Goat and a band of nymphs who did whatever I told them to. They gave me this sword."

Zeus held up his sword and started banging it on his breastplate, which he called his aegis. It made a loud clank.

"The Fairy Goat gave me this aegis," Zeus continued. "No sword or arrow can pierce it. So nothing can ever hurt me as long as I have on my aegis."

"Cool," said Hera. "Can I try it on?"

"Not a chance," said Zeus. "Now, here's how I rescued you. First, I found all these stinky herbs. When Dad sat down on a little mountain this morning to have his nectar tea, I snuck the herbs into his cup. He drank the tea, and *URP!*"

"Nice work," said Po. "Thanks!"

"Yeah." Zeus nodded. "You guys owe me, big time."

As we sat there, a huge ball of bright light appeared suddenly in front of us. And out of the glow stepped a giant raven-haired Titaness.

"Mom!" we cried, all at the same time.

"Oh, my little godlings!" Rhea clasped her

hands to her heart. "I knew you'd know me, even after all these years!"

Talk about a family reunion. Hugs. Kisses. Tears. The works.

Mom rummaged around in a shopping bag she'd brought and pulled out five clean white robes and five pairs of sandals.

"Fresh clothes, godlings!" she began handing out the robes and footgear.

The sandals and the robes were way too big. But Mom said that if we always ate everything on our plates, we'd soon grow into them.

We sat down in the shade of an olive tree then and had our first picnic. Mom was too big to sit under the tree, but she sat close by. She'd brought a basket of yummy ambrosia sandwiches and nectar punch for our lunch.

"Eat all your ambrosia," Mom told us. "That's what makes healthy ichor flow through your godling veins."

Ichor — that's what we gods have instead of blood.

We all dug in. It was a long, slow feast.

Demeter ran up the hill every once in a while to check on Dad, but he was out cold.

"Now," said Mom, when we'd all finished eating, "let me tell you how you came to be rescued."

"We know that already, Mother," Hera said. "Zeus told us how he put powerful herbs in Dad's tea."

Mom's eyebrows went up. "Zeus . . ." she said in a warning tone of voice.

"Okay, okay. You found the herbs," Zeus admitted.

"And who told Cronus that the herbs would make him unconquerable?" Mom asked. "Who gave them to Cronus to drink in an herbal nectar tea?"

"You did, Mom," Zeus muttered. "You did."

Mom shook her head. "What did those nymphs in that cave teach you, Zeusie? That it's all right to lie? To be a myth-o-maniac?"

"No!" cried Zeus. "I figured that out for myself!"

Mom took a deep breath. "Anyway, the main

thing is that I have my godlings back!" And there was more hugging and kissing.

After that, Po talked everyone into taking another dip. But Mom waggled her finger at me. "Come here, Hades. I need a private word with you."

I felt very special with Mom singling me out this way. I sat back down under the olive next to her.

"Hades, my firstborn!" she said. "Let me tell you why your daddy swallowed you godlings." And she told me about the old seer and his prophecy.

"He'll do anything to keep you kids from taking over," Mom said. "So it's important for the six of you to stick together, and be on the lookout for Cronus. You're the oldest, Hades, so you have some extra responsibilities."

Uh-oh. I didn't like the sound of that.

"I want you to keep an eye on the others," Mom went on. "Make sure they stay out of trouble."

"They won't listen to me, Mom!" I said.

"Besides, they're all gods. They're immortal. Nothing can happen to them."

"Ha!" Mom said. "You don't know the ways of the world, Hades. There's plenty of mischief a young god can get into without half trying. Zeus in particular worries me. Those nymphs spoiled him terribly, and now he thinks he can get away with anything. And his myth-o-mania —" She shook her head. "That could get him into big trouble one day."

Just then Dad moaned. We saw that he had lifted his head.

"I have to scoot." Mom hopped up and started gathering her things. "I don't want to be around when Cronus remembers who gave him that tea."

"Bye, Mom," I said, hoping she'd forget about the responsibility thing.

I should have known better.

"Not so fast, Hades." Mom pawed around in that bag of hers again and took out a small vial. "This is filled with water from the River Styx in the Underworld."

I didn't have a clue what she was talking about.

"Put your left hand on the vial," Mom said. "Raise your right hand. Now swear an oath that you will look after your brothers and sisters, Hades. Especially Zeus. Make sure no harm comes to him."

I sighed. "All right. I swear."

Mom smiled. She tossed the vial back into her bag. "Oaths sworn on the River Styx are unbreakable, you know." She began to glow.

"They are?" I said. Her glow grew brighter and brighter. "You mean for my whole, long eternal life I'm doomed to —"

"Ta-ta, Hades!" Mom cut in. "Tell the others goodbye for me, will you? I'll be in touch!" Then her glow went into hyperdrive, and *ZIP!* She was gone.

CHAPTER III

HE'S TOAST!

Dad was waking up, and gone seemed like a good place to be. I ran over to the stream to warn the others. Po was holding some sort of class.

"Run in place!" Po instructed. "Knees high!" He waved to me. "I call this 'water aerobics,' Hades!" he shouted. "Come on, Zeus! Get your heart rate up!"

"We're immortal, you ninny," Zeus growled. "We don't have to exercise!"

"Dad's waking up!" I called.

My sibs stopped running in place and ran for real to the shore. They threw on their robes.

"Let's get out of here!" cried Zeus. "We can hide in my old cave!"

"Wait!" I said. "I have an idea."

"Make it quick, Hades," Hera said. "I, for one, have no wish to get swallowed up again."

"Quick?" I said. "Okay. An old seer told Dad that one of us will be mightier than he is. That's why he swallowed us in the first place and why he'll never leave us alone. He'll keep trying to catch us and swallow us again or lock us up to make sure we don't overthrow him."

Zeus scratched his head. "What are you getting at, Hades?"

"That maybe we should go after Dad now and try to overthrow him while he's weak and sick."

"Fat chance!" cried Zeus.

"Wait!" said Hera. "Hades is right. Once Father starts to feel better, we'll never be able to overpower him. But if we strike now, we might have a chance."

"Last one to Dad is a rotten egg!" said Po.

And we charged up the hill.

Dad had managed to push himself up to a sitting position. But he swayed as he sat, looking none too steady. His eyes were half closed. His face was red and blotchy. His mouth hung open. He smelled so awful that, without saying a word, the six of us shifted as we ran so that we approached him from upwind.

Dad's eyes were half closed, as I said, but they were half open, too. He saw us coming. He reached for his silver sickle.

"Be gone, spawn!" he growled.

"You won't be rid of us that easily, Father!" cried Hera.

"Shhh!" Dad said. "Not so loud. Ooooh, my pounding head."

"LOUD?" I yelled. "WE CAN DO LOUD!"

We all began yelling and shouting. Zeus banged his sword on his aegis.

Dad put his hands over his ears. "Have mercy!" he cried.

"Why should we?" shouted Po. "You're a bad dad! All those years we spent trapped down in your belly, did you show us any mercy?"

"NO!" the five of us shouted.

And with that we all began running around him, whooping and shouting and making as much noise as possible. Zeus kept up his banging.

Dad groaned and struggled to his feet. He flung his sickle at Zeus. It hit the aegis and bounced off.

"Nonny, nonny, nee-jus! You can't pierce my aegis!" chanted Zeus.

Demeter quickly bent down and picked up the sickle. She held it up over her head. "I shall use this to harvest wheat!"

"Stay on task, Demeter!" scolded Hera.

"Uh . . . sorry," mumbled Demeter.

Zeus grabbed the sickle from her. He waved it in the air. "I am mightier than mighty Cronus!"

Dad roared. He lunged at Zeus.

"Yikes!" Zeus cried, jumping out of the way.

And before Dad could catch himself, he tripped over the root of an olive tree and went tumbling down the hill.

The six of us ran to the edge of the hill and watched him as he rolled. Faster and faster he went, down, down, and down. As he rolled, he picked up soil and gravel and even a bush or two. He went so fast that sparks began to fly, and near the bottom of the hill, the whole thing burst into flames. Seconds later, he splashed into the sea, steaming and hissing. Looking very much like a huge, smoking, cigar-shaped island, he drifted off toward a spit of land that we later learned was Italy.

"He's toast!" yelled Zeus.

"Bye-bye, big, bad Dad!" called Po.

"So long, Age of Titans!" called Hestia. "Hello, Age of Godlings!"

"Not godlings." Hera frowned. "We need a name as strong as *Titan*."

"I think I've got one," said Po. "Let's be the Aqua Gods!"

"Don't try to think, Po," said Hera. "Leave that to me. Now, we need to get organized. Zeus, the first thing you have to do is —"

Suddenly the ground beneath our feet began to shake. I grabbed on to the nearest olive tree and held on tight. Those who didn't grab on to anything got bounced all over the place. It was an earthquake!

After a while the quaking stopped and we all looked around. No one was hurt, so at the time we didn't think too much about that quake. Or wonder why Mother Earth, our own Granny Gaia, might be trying to shake us up.

Chapter IV
Sun Spot

"I know this great place where we can live," Zeus said.

"It's not your cave, is it, Zeus?" asked Hestia. "Because Dad's stomach was like a great big cave, and we're sick of caves."

"We want fresh air and sunshine — and soil!" cried Demeter.

"And privacy," said Hera. "No more living on top of one another."

"Something with a water view," said Po.

"Mount Olympus has it all," Zeus said. "Dad used to live there."

"So why did he move?" asked Hestia.

"Maybe he got sick of the commute down to Greece every day." Zeus shrugged. "It is sort of a hike. But it's not hard for me. I've moved into Dad's old palace. The chairs and tables were titanic, but I hired some Carpentry Nymphs to saw them down to size. I look really cool sitting on Dad's old throne. Come on! I'll show you. And you can see the stable where I keep my winged steeds!"

So we trotted after Zeus, uphill and down, all across Greece. Demeter insisted on lugging the stone from Dad's belly, so she quickly fell behind the rest of us. After a while, the journey became mostly uphill and hardly any down. At last we found ourselves trekking straight up a mountain. The mountain was so high that the top of it was hidden in the clouds.

Zeus ran without breaking a drosis (old Greek speak for "god sweat"), but the rest of us were huffing and puffing and drosissing like crazy. There hadn't exactly been a jogging track down in Dad's belly, and we five were sadly out of shape.

Finally, Hera yelled, "STOP!"

I, for one, was grateful. We all stood there,

breathing hard, until Demeter caught up with us. She was drenched in drosis.

"We're gods, Zeus," Hera said. "We have powers. There has to be a better way to get to a mountaintop than jogging up like mere mortals."

"Oh, you want to instantly transport yourselves to the top of Mount Olympus?" asked Zeus.

"Take a wild guess," said Demeter. Dragging that stone halfway up the mountain had given her a scary, desperate look.

"Hey, no problem," said Zeus. "All you have to do is close your eyes and spin around one foot, chanting, 'Fee fie fo fum! Mount Olympus, here I come!'"

The five of us closed our eyes. We started spinning and chanting all together: "FEE FIE FO FUM! MOUNT OLYMPUS, HERE WE COME!"

I opened my eyes. I didn't see Mount Olympus. I saw Zeus, doubled over laughing.

"Gotcha!" he cried, slapping his knee. "Fo fum! Oh, that was a good one!"

"Myth-o-maniac!" Demeter cried, raising the stone over her head as if she meant to hurl it.

"Hey, back off!" yelled Zeus. "Can't you take a joke?"

"Not really," said Demeter, but she lowered the stone.

"Sorry," Zeus muttered. "I don't know of any quick way to get there."

And so we hiked the rest of the way to the top of Mount Olympus.

When we got there, we saw that for once, Zeus hadn't been lying. Mount Olympus was as great as he'd said it would be, with acres and acres of rolling green hills, burbling brooks, and a clear, sparkling lake.

"Whoa!" said Po, looking around. "Great lake!"

"Home, sweet home," said Hestia.

"I see the perfect spot for my palace," said Hera, never one to waste time simply admiring the scenery.

A Welcome Nymph flitted over to where we stood. "Welcome to Mount Olympus," she said, "where there's never any wind, it only rains at night, and every day is sunny."

After all that time down in Dad's belly, we were ready for sun. We'd have privacy, too. Mortals couldn't see what we were up to because the top of Mount Olympus was separated from the earth by a thick blanket of clouds.

"On top of the highest hill over there?" Zeus pointed to a compound of stone buildings. "That's my palace." He glanced at the setting sun. "The Kitchen Nymphs usually have supper ready about now."

"You'd better not be lying about that," Demeter said, and we godlings ran the rest of the way to the palace.

That night we feasted in the Great Hall, sitting together at a long table. There was plenty of ambrosia, and the nectar flowed freely. The palace was gigantic, with dozens of rooms, so we all slept over that night and for many nights to come. Dad's old home became our new home, and our lives quickly settled into a pattern. Each morning, five of us were awakened by: "WAH-

HOOOOO!" Then *SPLASH!* as Po cannonballed into the lake for his morning skinny-dip. The rest of us threw on our robes and strolled to the Great Hall for the breakfast buffet. Ambrosia with melon, scrambled ambrosia, ambrosia pancakes with maple-ambrosia syrup, and freshly squeezed nectar — what a spread! With all that good, fresh ambrosia and nectar, we godlings quickly grew into full-size gods and goddesses.

After breakfast, the six of us went our separate ways. Zeus liked to ride around in his storm chariot all day, lying and bragging about his great deeds to anyone who'd listen. He started wearing Dad's silver sickle on his girdle. I guess it made him feel big and powerful. Po liked to swim laps in the lake. Hera was always rushing off to supervise the construction of her palace. Hestia took over looking after Zeus's palace, making sure things ran smoothly. She could often be found sitting by the fireplace, making endless "to do" lists for the nymphs. Demeter, as you might have guessed, got into gardening, big time. She planted acres and acres of corn. But her crowning achievement was a rock garden, centered around the stone from Dad's belly.

Me? I took long walks beside the river. I sat on high hills and took in the scenery. I followed Mom's orders and checked on the others. But to tell you the truth, I grew restless up on Mount Olympus. The sameness — all sun and blue skies — made life a bit boring. Okay, I wouldn't have traded it for Dad's gut. But at least down there, you never knew when Dad might get the hiccups. Or when something might tickle him so he'd burst out with a big belly laugh and we'd get tossed around. Life back then had been unpredictable. It had kept us on our toes.

Zeus's bragging soon turned into a problem. We all learned to duck out of sight when we heard his steeds coming. He got very cranky if he couldn't boast a good part of each day, so he took to driving his storm chariot down to earth. Mortals are easily impressed, and this suited Zeus perfectly. He began staying down on earth for years at a stretch. After a while, rumors reached us that he'd gotten married. Then we heard that he'd gotten married again, this time to a Titan. The next we heard, Zeus was engaged to a mortal. And then to someone else. Before long, we started hearing about Zeus's children. Lots of them were immortal, too, and he began sending them up to live on Mount Olympus.

Most of us didn't mind.

But Hera wasn't one bit happy about it.

CHAPTER V

FAMILY FIREWORKS

Athena was the first of Zeus's children to arrive. She came all decked out in a helmet and a shiny suit of armor. She'd hardly set her metal-clad foot on Mount Olympus when she announced that she was the Goddess of Wisdom.

Hera freaked out. "We don't divide up our powers like that," she told Athena sternly. "We all dabble in any area we want to. Including wisdom."

Athena's gray eyes flashed haughtily. "Let's just see what happens."

Next, Hermes flew up by means of his winged sandals and his winged helmet. He was small and looked far younger than his years. And talk about sneaky! No sooner did Hermes arrive than things started to disappear. Little things at first: an urn, a goblet, Po's nose clips and goggles. Once, Hera discovered that her favorite girdle was missing. Then she spotted Hermes wearing it and hit the ceiling. But Hermes only laughed and tossed the girdle back to her, and even Hera couldn't stay mad at the little thief for long. He was just too charming.

Golden-haired twins Apollo and Artemis came next. Apollo had a lyre made out of a tortoise shell slung over his shoulder, and from the moment he arrived, there was always music on Mount Olympus. Apollo was a mellow guy, which is why we were all caught by surprise when he began talking about how he saw himself as the future Sun God.

Apollo's twin sister, Artemis, had golden braids. She claimed this kept her hair out of the way when she shot her bow. Artemis was crazy about hunting. After a few days on Mount Olympus, she complained that there weren't enough unspoiled woods for her tastes, and soon she started slipping down to earth to go on hunts.

Dionysus showed up next, toting seedling grapevines. He and Demeter bonded instantly over planting them. Before long there were grape arbors all over Mount Olympus, and Dionysus set himself up as the God of Wine.

Then Aphrodite appeared. She was flat-out gorgeous, so nobody was surprised when she said she hoped to be the Goddess of Love and Beauty.

After a while, Zeus's children began coming in bunches. The three Seasons. The three Graces. All these kids with their big talk drove Hera wild. But she managed to cope until the day the nine Muses showed up.

"Hi! I'm Clio, Muse of History!" one sang out. "The wheel was invented in 32 B.C. — that's 'Before Cronus.'"

"Call me Terpsi!" another said. "Muse of the Dance." She did a few steps of what we would later come to call the polka.

"I'm Thalia!" said a third. "Muse of Comedy. Here's a good one. Why did the chicken cross the road?"

"To be sacrificed to the gods, of course," Hera said.

"Wrong!" said Thalia. "To get to the other side!"

All the other Muses cracked up.

But Hera was not amused. That night, she called a meeting of the "belly bunch," as Po called the five of us, in the Great Hall of the palace.

"Something has to be done about Zeus's brats," she said. "If they keep coming in these numbers, it'll get so crowded up here we'll all have to convert our palaces into high-rise condos. It isn't right. And they have all sorts of high-and-mighty ideas about being god of this and goddess of that. Especially that Athena. Goddess of Wisdom, indeed! Who do these kids think they are, anyway?"

"The children of Zeus!" boomed a voice from the doorway. We all turned, and there was Zeus, standing with his hands on his hips, grinning like a maniac.

"My children are gods," he said as he strode into the Great Hall. "They're family. They belong up here with us."

Hera sighed. "Have it your way, Zeus. But you'd better stick around and deal with them. You don't know what they're like, always squawking about who has power over what."

"I'll be here," Zeus declared. He marched to the head of the table and sat down. "I've been thinking about how we gods ought to rule the universe, and I've come up with a plan."

The fact that the universe had been doing just fine for thousands of years while he ran wild down on earth didn't seem to have occurred to Zeus.

"You're not talking dictatorship here, are you, Zeus?" asked Hera. "That was Father's thing, and it didn't work out too well."

"Not exactly." Zeus shrugged. "But somebody has to be CEO."

"C-E — what?" said Hestia.

Zeus grinned. "Chairgod of Everybody on Olympus."

I sat up straighter when I heard that. If anyone was going to be in charge, it should be me. I was the eldest, after all. And hadn't Mom asked me to keep an eye on the others? Plus I was thoughtful, kind, hardworking, that sort of thing. I felt I had CEO written all over me.

So it came as a nasty surprise that I wasn't the only one who felt this way.

"How do we pick the CEO?" asked Hera. "Because if it's organization you're looking for, I'm your goddess."

"What am I, diced clams?" said Po. "I can rule the universe PLUS the seas, lakes, rivers, streams, creeks, and puddles."

Hestia leaned over and whispered. "Those are *parts* of the universe, Po."

"No kidding?" said Po.

"I know you call me 'The Boss' behind my back," Hera added. "Make me CEO, and you can call me 'The Boss' to my face!"

Hestia turned to Zeus. "I've been taking care

of things the whole time you've been away," she said. "It seems to me that I'm already acting CEO."

"I *am* the firstborn," I put in. "That should count for something."

"I see the universe as a garden!" Demeter shouted out. "With me as the landscape architect."

Zeus smiled. "I guess we'll have to put it to a vote."

"That won't work," Hera pointed out. "We'll each vote for ourselves."

"Then we'll need tiebreakers." Zeus cupped his hands to his mouth and shouted, "Kids! Time to vote!"

The rest of us watched in amazement as Zeus's children burst into the Great Hall. Athena, Hermes, Apollo, Artemis, Dionysus, Aphrodite, the Seasons, the Graces, the Muses — the whole pack showed up.

Hera gasped. "They must have been standing right outside the door. Just waiting to be called!"

The kids squeezed in at the long table.

Now I understood what Zeus had been doing down on earth. He hadn't just been fathering children. He'd been fathering VOTES! Ooh, why had I promised Mom to make sure nothing happened to him? I wanted to be the one to MAKE something happen to him. Something awful!

"Close your eyes, and put your heads down on the table," said Zeus. "No peeking. I'm talking to you, Hermes. Okay, all for Zeus as Supreme Thunder God, Ruler of the Universe, Chairgod of —"

CLANG! CLANG!

A loud noise drowned out Zeus's voice. We raised our heads. There was more clanging and what sounded like battle cries. We jumped up and ran to the entrance of the Great Hall.

From there we could see, marching up the mountain toward us, an army of giant Titan warriors! They shouted and beat their swords against their bronze breastplates.

And who was leading them?

You guessed it.

"Dad!" we all cried.

"That's right, you little ingrates!" Cronus roared. "Big Daddy's back!"

He thumped his breastplate with his fist. "I'm over my stomachache, and I'm here for revenge. Me and my army of one hundred Titan warriors are taking back Mount Olympus! Once more shall Mighty Cronus rule the universe!"

Chapter VI

Hotfooted Gods

"Back off, Titans!" cried Zeus. "Or we shall destroy you!"

"You tell 'em, Dad!" said Athena, her gray eyes flashing.

"*How* are we going to destroy them, Zeus?" said Hera. "Think about it! You're the only one of us who has a weapon!"

But Zeus kept on. "Mount Olympus is ours, now!" he shouted. He yanked the silver sickle off his girdle and waved it at Dad. He thumped his fist on his chest, but it didn't make the usual booming noise. Zeus looked down at his chest and gasped. "Hey! Where's my aegis? My impenetrable shield? Hermes? HERMES!"

"Yo, Pops!" Hermes waved. He had the aegis buckled around his own scrawny chest.

Zeus looked back at the Titans. His eyes grew wide.

They were almost upon us now.

"Oops!" Zeus cried. He turned and started running. Athena was right behind him. The rest of us sped after them.

I'm not proud of this, but the truth is, we gods fled in terror. We ran helter-skelter down Mount Olympus. Except for Demeter, who made a little detour to the rock garden first to pick up her beloved stone.

As we ran, we gods heard big Titan feet pounding behind us. At last we broke through the blanket of clouds. We kept running until we reached level ground. Then we hotfooted it across Greece. Mortals stopped to stare openmouthed as we rushed by.

"Gods on the run," Hera said. "How embarrassing!"

"Mortals will stop sacrificing to us if they think we're scared," Hestia pointed out.

Hera waved to the mortals. "Just warming up for the big marathon!" she called to them.

I looked back over my shoulder. I didn't see any Titans. I didn't hear any battle cries. Or pounding feet.

"They've stopped chasing us," I called to the others. "I guess Dad just wanted to run us off Mount Olympus."

And so at last we stopped. We stood there, gasping for breath and wiping the drosis from our brows.

"Now Dad will move back into the palace," Zeus moaned. "It won't be mine anymore!"

"Win some, lose some," said Hera. "Come on. Let's find ourselves a roomy cave where we can hide for the night, just in case."

We hunted around, and at last we found a cave beside a lake. It was big and deep, with lots of separate rooms. We scurried inside.

The next morning, I woke everyone up and asked them to meet outside of the cave.

When we were all gathered I said, "We need to —"

"Yes!" cried Zeus, who never could stand to let anyone else run a meeting. "We need to come up with a plan for taking Mount Olympus back from the Titans. Raise your hand if you have an idea."

Of course no hands went up.

"I was going to say," I continued, "we need to find a new place to live."

"No!" cried Zeus. "Mount Olympus is our home! We have to take it back. Think harder! How can two dozen gods defeat a hundred giant Titan warriors?"

"We could take turns smiting them with your sword, Dad," Athena said.

Zeus nodded. "Okay. That's a start. Anyone else?"

But no one else had any ideas about how to drive the Titans off Mount Olympus, or about finding a new place to live. So that cave became our home. Hera, who could put a positive spin on anything, started referring to it as "Headquarters."

Hermes's son, Pan, who lived on earth, heard

about us holed up in that cave. He came to visit us one day, and stuck around. Pan was a pretty strange fellow. He had goat horns and ears and a little goatee. He had hooves and hairy goat legs, too, and a goat tail. And talk about nervous! One day Zeus dropped the silver sickle onto a stone. The clatter startled Pan, and he screamed.

Pan's scream was the loudest, most horrible sound that any of us had ever heard, and it scared the girdles off us. We jumped up and started running around, yelling and shouting, and no one knew what was going on. In short, we were in a *panic*. It took a long time for us to get used to Pan's crazy shouting.

Weeks went by. Zeus never stopped badgering us to think up a way to boot the Titans off Mount Olympus. But no one ever had any ideas.

One day Hera called us all together. "I have a plan," she said. "We can play games against the Titans for the right to live on Mount Olympus."

"What kind of games?" asked Apollo.

"All different kinds," said Hera. "Kickstone, for one."

"Kick-*what*?" said Zeus.

"It's a game we used to play down in Dad's belly," I explained.

"We can run races, too," Hera said. "And have jumping contests and wrestling matches. Whoever wins the most games gets to live on Mount Olympus."

"The Titans already live on Mount Olympus," I said. "Why would they agree to play?"

"Because games sound like fun," Hera said. "And because the Titans will think they're unbeatable."

"They probably *are* unbeatable," Hestia pointed out. "They're titanic!"

"Size won't matter in the games I make up," said Hera. "And besides, we're a talented bunch. Hades spent all his time down in Dad's belly jumping. Carrying that stone has given Demeter amazing upper-body strength. And Po is a great swimmer."

"Yes!" cried Po. "Plus, I invented the doggie paddle, the frog kick, the swan dive, and the cannonball!"

"You mean you're going to make up games based on what we're good at?" I said.

"Exactly," said Hera. "And since we're playing for Mount Olympus, we'll call them . . . the Olympic Games."

"I'll do weight lifting," Zeus said. "I'm as strong as an ox. No, make that *ten* oxen."

Hera nodded. Then she turned to Hermes. "You can sell anybody anything. How about flying up to Mount Olympus and talking the Titans into this?"

"No problem." Hermes jumped into his winged sandals, put on his winged helmet, and off he flew.

While we waited for Hermes to come back, we taught Zeus and his kids to play kickstone. We played game after game of it in a field not far from the cave. Apollo was a natural dribbler. Aphrodite had a kick like a mule. And Dionysus proved to be a fearless goalie. Nothing got by him. The Muses were duds on the field, but they discovered a talent for standing on the sidelines and inspiring some amazing plays. Hera watched everyone and made notes.

Two days later Hermes plopped right down in the middle of a game.

"We're on!" he said. "When the Titans stopped laughing, Cronus agreed to play games for Mount Olympus. He gave me a list of a few games the Titans want to play, too." He handed the list to Hera. "We're to meet them in Olympia Stadium a week from today."

Hera raised a megaphone to her lips. "Listen up, gods. Intensive training starts at dawn. The games I've invented will use your strengths —"

"Hold it!" said Zeus. "Who made you team captain?"

Hera shot him a look.

"Uh, for Olympic team captain I appoint Hera!" Zeus said quickly.

Hera handed a list of her games to Hermes, and he flew it up to the Titans. Then she drew a chart with the events she'd made up so far on the wall of the cave.

EVENT	GOD
Archery	Artemis
Badminton	Athena
Doggie Paddle	Po
Goat-Footed Race	Pan
Kickstone	Team Gods
Long Jump	Hades
Rhythmic Gymnastics	The Muses
Synchronized Swimming	The Graces
Weeding	Demeter
Weight Lifting	Zeus
Wrestling	Hades

"Now wait a second," said Athena. "What's badminton?"

Hera smiled. "You'll love it."

Chapter VII

Olympic Torch

Zeus stared at the chart. "Hades is in *two* events," he whined. "And I'm only in *one*?"

"The idea is to win, Zeus," said Hera. "And get Mount Olympus back."

Zeus muttered under his breath and stomped off. He didn't show up at a single practice all week. Hera threatened to take him out of weight lifting, but he wasn't worried. He was bigger than anyone else. He knew Hera couldn't replace him.

The three Graces spent hours in the water each day, practicing their synchronized-swimming routine. By the time Hera said they could get out of the lake, their fingertips were as wrinkled as dried figs.

I practiced the long jump in the mornings.

My best was 16.5 dekameters — not too shabby. In the afternoons Po and I wrestled. I got better at both events.

The only dud on our team was Athena. She swung the badminton racket fiercely, but she just couldn't hit the birdie. And all that armor made it hard for her to run around the court. But Hera just kept saying, "You can do it, Athena!"

The morning of the games dawned. We put on our competition robes, lined up by height, and marched into Olympia. Hestia had the bright idea of running ahead of us carrying a lighted torch.

Outside the stadium, vendors hawked demi-robes with GODS RULE! printed across the chest. And others that said TITANS RULE!

The games made the headlines of the morning edition of the *Olympia Oracle*:

OLYMPIC GAMES

TO BE PLAYED IN OLYMPIA

MAYOR SAYS, "GAMES ARE A FAD. THEY'LL NEVER LAST!"

We made our entrance into the stadium with Hestia running, carrying the torch. Ahead of us, the place was packed. In those days, there was nothing mortals loved more than a good contest between immortals.

"Who we gonna beat?" yelled the muse Euterpe. "Who we gonna defeat?"

"The Titans!" the other Muses yelled back. "Yeah, the Titans!"

We paraded once around the stadium and sat down on our bench.

A Titan in a black-and-white striped robe walked onto the field.

"That's Themis," Hestia told me. "You know, the one they call Justice? She's the referee."

"A Titan referee?" I said. "Oh, great. She'll be really fair."

Now the Titans marched into the stadium. The crowd roared.

It was hard not to notice that the Titans were titanic. Okay, we gods had grown up, but we still only came up to the average Titan's knee. How could I ever beat a Titan in the long jump?

The Titans sat down on their bench — and it collapsed under their tremendous weight. The whole team ended up milling around on the sidelines.

Themis put two fingers in her mouth and gave a mighty whistle.

The fans quieted.

"The first event is archery," Themis announced.

A pair of nymphs ran onto the field carrying a target and set it up.

Artemis and a Titan carried their bows and arrows onto the field.

The Titan strung his bow. He put in an arrow and shot it.

"Bull's-eye!" said Themis.

Now it was Artemis's turn. She pulled back her bowstring and shot.

"Bull's-eye!" said Themis.

After a dozen perfect shots each, Themis made the archers back up. They still got bull's-eyes. Themis had them shoot standing on one foot. And then on the other. But it wasn't until she blindfolded them that the Titan shot an arrow just left of center.

"The gold medal for archery goes to the gods!" Themis announced.

The mortals cheered as Artemis proudly took her medal.

The scoreboard showed one medal for the gods. And for the Titans? Zip.

"The next event is badminton," called Themis.

Athena walked sullenly to the middle of the field, where the nymphs had laid out a badminton court.

Her Titan opponent threw the birdie up and slammed it over the net. Athena ducked. The birdie hit her armor and bounced off. The Muses tried, but they couldn't inspire Athena. In no time, Themis was handing the gold medal for badminton to the Titans. Again, the mortals cheered.

Now each team had one gold medal.

After that, the Muses won rhythmic gymnastics, no drosis, and we pulled ahead.

Then the Titan Ocean killed Po in the doggie paddle. Tied again. Demeter cleaned up in the weeding event, which put us up by one. Next came weight lifting.

The Titan went first. Then Zeus stepped up to a barbell.

"You call these weights?" Zeus laughed. "I call them baby rattles!"

He put his hands around the bar and gave a mighty tug. The barbell didn't budge. He tugged again. And again. He grunted and made awful growling noises. But he couldn't lift the barbell off the ground.

"The gold medal for weight lifting goes to the Titans," Themis said.

"Strong as ten oxen, huh?" Hera said when Zeus came back to the bench. "You and your myth-o-mania!"

"Aw, that thing was nailed to the ground," Zeus said.

The score was tied again.

The games went on for days. The Titans took breath holding — an event they'd made up to draw on their titanic lungpower. Then Pan medaled in the goat-footed race. I got pinned in wrestling, but Hermes cleaned up in the frisbeus throw. Dad had made up an event called "push me." Contestants stood on a greased iron disk and challenged anyone to push them off. It was a crowd-pleaser, and it put the Titans ahead by one medal. Then Po medaled in high-board belly flop.

The score was tied again. And so it went. We'd win a medal, then the Titans would win one. Neither team could pull ahead. At last, with only two events left, the score was Titans: XXXVI gold medals, Gods: XXXV gold medals.

"The next event is the long jump!" said Themis.

I started drosissing as I ran over to the sandpit. If I lost this event, we'd lose the Olympics! And how could I win against a Titan jumper?

Then I saw my Titan opponent.

"Dad!" I said.

Dad sneered. "Give up now, Hades."

I ignored him and stepped to the starting line. I took a deep breath and started running. I hit the toe mark and leaped into the air. I landed, pitching myself forward. I held still while the Measuring Nymphs ran to see how far I'd jumped.

"Nineteen dekameters!" a nymph announced.

My best jump yet!

But Dad burst out laughing. "Nineteen?" he cried. "A *frog* can jump farther than nineteen!"

Dad kept laughing as the nymphs raked the sand.

Then it was his turn. He stood in starting position. But he kept cracking up. He was laughing when he started running. He stepped on the toe line, still howling over my pitiful jump, and his foot slipped. That slip threw him off, and he lurched to the left. He jumped — *a lot* farther than nineteen dekameters — but he missed the sandpit entirely.

"The gold medal for long jump goes to the gods," said Themis.

"WHAT?" roared Dad. "I jumped ten times farther than he did!"

"That's true," said Themis, "but . . ."

"Re-jump!" cried Cronus. "I demand an immediate re-jump!"

"Uh . . . that seems fair," said Themis. "Okay with you, Hades?"

"No!" I said. "I won!"

"Keep the medal, Hades!" Hera yelled. "Don't let them cheat you!"

I held tight to my medal. The score was tied again, XXXVI medals each.

Dad gave me a terrible look. "You'll pay for this, shortie," he said. Then he turned and strode off the field.

Chapter VIII

Bright Idea

"The last Olympic event is kickstone," Themis announced. "If the score is tied at the end of the game, we will go into a sudden-death overtime. The first one to score wins the game. Okay, team captains to the field."

Hera jogged out to where Themis stood. Atlas, the biggest Titan of them all, did the same. Standing between the two Titans, Hera looked very small.

"We'll flip to see which team kicks off," said Themis. "Atlas, call it." She flipped a gold coin into the air.

"Gold coin!" called Atlas.

"She means call heads or tails," Hera said.

Themis flipped the coin again.

"Heads or tails!" Atlas called.

"Uh . . ." said Themis. "Atlas, your side can kick off."

I groaned. Themis was so unfair!

Both teams ran onto the field. I took up my defense position close to our goal. Themis put the stone down on the fifty-dekameter line. Our team backed up and got ready to receive the kick. Dad was kicking off for the Titans. He had a sneaky look on his face. What was he up to now?

Themis gave a whistle, and the game began.

Hermes and Pan were too small to play kickstone, but they found ways to help. Pan kept score. And Hermes borrowed Hera's megaphone and set himself up as the announcer.

"The Titans are running for the stone, mortals," said Hermes. "Cronus kicks off! Ooh! The stone just missed the gods' goal. Now Dionysus picks it up. He kicks it to Aphrodite. She boots it to Apollo. Will you look at that god dribble? He's taking the stone deep into Titan territory. Now Cronus is — holy cow! He's pulled a sword out from under his robe! The other Titans are pulling out swords, too!"

So this is what Dad meant when he said I'd pay for winning the long jump! This wasn't kickstone. This was war!

"Cronus takes a swing at Apollo!" Hermes cried. "Apollo jumps back — he's safe! But the Titans have taken possession of the stone!"

Every time we got close to that stone, the Titans tried to whack us.

"Themis!" cried Zeus. "They're cheating! Call a foul! Do something!"

But Themis only shrugged. Titan Justice was no justice at all for the gods.

The score at the end of the first quarter was Titans: IX, Gods: I.

But luckily we had a smart coach, and we were fast learners. The next quarter, Zeus brought his sword onto the field too. Apollo figured out how to duck under the Titan swords and keep dribbling. Aphrodite sharpened her aim. She knocked the sword out of many a Titan hand with a well-placed kick of the stone. Those of us on defense body-blocked dozens of near goals.

By the end of the third quarter, we were only three points behind. And when the clock ran out on the game, the score was Titans: XXIV, Gods: XXIV. A tie!

Now the game went into sudden-death overtime. The first team to score would get to live on Mount Olympus — forever!

We gods redoubled our efforts. So did the Titans. We played all day. But we couldn't score on them, and they couldn't score on us.

At last the sun sank low in the sky, and it got too dark to see the stone. Themis whistled and declared the game over for the day.

"Report to the field tomorrow morning to finish the game," Themis said.

But the next day, neither team scored the final point. There was no score the following day either. Days turned into weeks. Weeks turned into months, and still no one scored a point.

Mortals stopped coming to the stadium. You could pick up a GODS RULE demi-robe for next to nothing. And without the mortals there watching, the Titans played ugly. They started chopping down trees and flinging them at us. Whole forests quickly disappeared. When that didn't stop us, the Titans hacked boulders out of mountains and threw them at us. They ripped up the earth as the game raged on. But we gods gritted our teeth and kept playing. We didn't let them score.

Every evening, we retreated to our cave, bruised and ichoring. But every morning, we showed up at the stadium again. And so did the Titans. The game dragged on for ten long years.

Then one morning, Hera shouted the usual through her megaphone: "Up and at 'em, gods! We've got a game to win!"

And I knew I couldn't take another day of the kickstone war. I slipped out of the cave. I took off down the road. I didn't know where I was headed, but I kept walking for miles. The sun was blazing, and when I came to a stream, I sat down to cool my feet in the water.

I was so wrapped up in trying to think of some way to end the endless game that I never heard footsteps. The first I knew that I had company was when someone sat down next to me and put his feet into the stream. Big feet. Titanic.

I looked up and saw a Titan with blond hair and a blond beard. A pair of very cool blue sunglasses rested on top of his head.

"Howdy," he said.

"*What?*" I said.

"Say, you're one of those little gods, aren't you?" the Titan said. "The ones who gave ol' Cronus such a bad time."

I nodded, hoping he wasn't big on revenge. "Who are you?"

"Hyperion's my name," the Titan said. "And light's my game. You know Sun, Moon, and Dawn? They're my kids. A bright bunch, too. If only they'd take some responsibility! Most mornings, I have to drag Dawn out of bed and get her glowing. Sun always wants to stay up late. You should see what I go through to get him to set. And Moon?" he sighed. "She puts on weight, and then goes on a crash diet. Gets so thin you can hardly see her. Boy, howdy! Being in charge of light, day and night, can wear a fellow down."

"You don't talk like the other Titans," I said.

Hyperion nodded. "Don't rightly know why," he said, "but the day I bought me that cattle herd, I just up and started talking this way."

I didn't think I'd seen Hyperion around Olympia Stadium, but I had to ask. "Do you ever play in the Olympic games?"

"No, sir, I don't." Hyperion shook his head. "Cronus and those boys are a bad bunch. I hear they ran y'all off Mount Olympus."

I nodded. "If only we could win at kickstone, we'd get it back."

Hyperion stroked his beard thoughtfully. "I know some fellows who just might help you beat those Titan thugs," he said at last.

I jumped up. "Will you come with me back to our cave — er, our headquarters — and tell that to all the other gods?"

Hyperion glanced at the sky. "I can't stay past sunset," he said. "So if we're going, let's skedaddle."

He led the way to an old flame-scarred chariot. We jumped in, and he drove us back to the cave. We got there just as the rest of the gods were dragging home from the stadium.

Hera saw us coming and shot me a nasty look for skipping the game.

I hopped out of the chariot and said, "Hera, this is Hyperion, Titan Ruler of Light. He's Dad's brother, but he doesn't like Dad any more than we do. And he has an idea about how we can get some help and win the Olympics."

"Announcement!" Hera called through her megaphone.

Everyone gathered round. Hera introduced Hyperion.

"Howdy," Hyperion said. "I'm thinking that my little brothers might like to play on your kickstone team."

"But you're a Titan," Hera said. "So your brothers are Titans too."

"Not all of 'em," said Hyperion.

We looked pretty blank, so Hyperion explained. "After Mama Gaia gave birth to us Titans, she had triplets called the Cyclopes. Each Cyclops had one big eye in the middle of his forehead."

"Gross!" said Hestia.

"That's just what Sky Daddy said," Hyperion continued. "He thought the Cyclopes were beyond ugly. He couldn't stand the sight of 'em. But Mama Gaia loved her Cyclopes children. She kept saying, 'Sky Daddy, honey, they're family!' And Sky Daddy kept saying, 'Mama Gaia, honey, they're revolting.'"

"In time, Mama Gaia had another set of triplets," Hyperion went on. "And this batch was *really* strange. Each one had fifty heads and one hundred arms. No kidding! Mama Gaia loved each little head, of course, but Sky Daddy? Uh-uh. He took one look at them and went, 'Yeeech!' He scooped them up, and the Cyclopes, too, and he flung them down into Tartarus, a deep, fiery pit in the Underworld."

"Wasn't Mama Gaia mad at Sky Daddy?" asked Demeter.

"You betcha." Hyperion nodded. "She was so mad that she helped Cronus overthrow Sky Daddy, and she set him up as top Titan. After he took over, Cronus was supposed to spring the

Cyclopes and the Hundred-Handed Ones from jail. He went down to Tartarus to get them, but he took one look at them and left them where they were. He was shaking-in-his-sandals scared they'd overpower him one day. So those ol' boys have been in jail all this time, locked up and guarded by Campe, the Underworld Jail Keep. They'd be mighty grateful for a rescue."

"But would it be fair to have them play on our team?" asked Hestia.

"Fair?" snapped Hera. "Are the Titans playing fair? I don't think so."

"Rescuing those boys might not be any picnic," Hyperion added. "Campe is huge, second only in size to Typhon, the terrible donkey-headed monster. And I hear she has some ugly tricks up her sleeves. But, hey. It's worth a try."

Hyperion glanced up at the sun. He took his blue sunglasses from the top of his head and slid them on. "Duty calls," he said. "Good luck!"

Apollo ran quickly over to Hyperion's chariot and handed him the reins. It looked as if the wanna-be Sun God had found his role model.

Hyperion clucked to his horses, and they galloped off toward the west.

"Okay! Let's get organized!" Hera said. "Hermes? Take a message to the Titans. Say we call a three-week time out. Hades? You, Zeus, and Po go down to the Underworld and get the Cyclopes and Hundred-Handed Ones out of jail. The rest of us will stay here and —"

"Plant corn!" Demeter cried.

"Clean the cave!" Hestia said.

"Work on our kickstone skills," said Hera firmly.

Not one bit sorry to be missing that, I packed up a cooler of ambrosia sandwiches and Necta-Colas for the journey, and then my brothers and I took off for the Underworld.

Chapter IX

Hot Dog!

After a nine-day hike, Zeus, Po, and I found ourselves standing on the banks of a dark Underworld river.

"This must be the River Styx," I said. "Mom told me about it."

"You mean the River Stinks," said Po.

"Pee-yew!" Zeus agreed.

The smell was strong, but to me it just smelled like an old auntie who'd put on too much perfume.

From our spot on the riverbank, we could see the place where night met day. And one of the huge pillars, where the vault of the sky anchored so that it bent over the earth in a perfect blue arc. The pillar was badly cracked.

An old boatman with a shaggy white beard poled toward us from the far shore. A sign on his boat read CHARON'S RIVER TAXI.

"Ahoy!" Charon called out. "One-way or round-trip?"

"Round-trip!" Zeus called back.

"That'll be two gold coins," Charon said. "Each!"

"What?" Zeus cried. "Why, that's robbery!"

"If you're a living god, you can hand the coins directly to me," Charon said. "If you're a dead mortal, have a relative slip them under your tongue. I'll find them."

"We are immortal gods, and we demand that you take us across!" Zeus boomed. "We aren't paying!"

"So stay put." Charon shrugged. "I don't care one way or the other."

Po eyed the river. "No way I'm swimming across this sludge."

As the three of us stood there trying to figure out what to do, I heard a growl. I turned and saw a little three-headed pup crouched down on the riverbank. All six of its glowing red eyes were fastened on Zeus.

"Beat it, dog!" Zeus said.

The dog growled louder.

"Scram! Vamoose!" Zeus kicked at the dog. "Be gone, I say!"

"Hey! Take it easy, Zeus. This little guy is still a puppy." I squatted down and held out my hand. Instantly, the pup stopped growling and started sniffing me.

"That's a good pup." I patted what seemed to be his friendliest-looking head, and the other two heads started pushing in, trying to get some of the action. "Why, all he wants is love. Isn't that right, pup?" He wagged his tail.

"Lose the dog, Hades," Zeus said. "We're on a mission, here."

The pup pulled its lips back in a vicious triple snarl. He didn't like Zeus — obviously this pup was an excellent judge of character.

Zeus reached for the handle of the silver sickle that hung from his girdle.

I quickly scooped the pup up in my arms. All

three of his tongues started licking my face like crazy. What a bath!

"Sorry, pup," I said, jogging away from Zeus. "You'd better go back to wherever you came from. You don't want to stay around here, bothering Zeus. He's a little short on patience. Short on a lot of things, actually." I put the pup down. "Go on, now. I don't want you to get hurt."

The pup picked up a scent, and off he charged, one nose to the ground and two mouths howling.

I went back to my brothers, who had stepped into Charon's boat. Zeus was signing an I.O.U. He winked at me. I knew he had no intention of paying.

"This is a binding I.O.U. Signed while standing over the waters of the River Styx," Charon said while rolling up a piece of parchment and tucking it into his tunic.

"Yeah, whatever," said Zeus. "Just take us across."

After I hopped aboard, Charon did just that.

My brothers and I stepped out of the boat and onto the far shore. We found ourselves standing beneath a pair of bronze gates. The inscription on them read:

WELCOME TO THE UNDERWORLD!

MORTALS EVERYWHERE ARE DYING TO GET IN

We pushed open the gates and entered a gloomy land lit by a mysterious silvery glow. Ghosts of the dead wandered aimlessly as far as the eye could see.

"You there!" Zeus called to a pair of them. "Which way to the jail?"

But the ghosts didn't answer. They glided by, talking to each other.

"*Epilogue,*" the little ghost said.

"E-p-i . . ." The big ghost let out a moan. "Oh, I can't spell it! I don't even know what it means!"

"An epilogue is a short bit at the end of a

book," the little ghost said. "It often deals with the future of the book's characters. Try it again. You can do it. *Epilogue.*"

"The jail!" Zeus shouted at them. "Where's the jail?"

But the ghosts made no reply.

"I don't think they can hear us," I told Zeus.

And so we wandered aimlessly for a while ourselves. Zeus and Po complained the whole time.

"What a dreary swamp!" said Po.

"Disgusting!" said Zeus.

"There's no sunlight," I put in. "But it's not so bad."

When our stomachs started growling, we sat down under some black poplars and broke out the sandwiches and Necta-Cola.

A lone ghost wandered by, chanting, "I before E except after C. I before E except after C . . . ."

I had just split my sandwich in two pieces, and the smell of it seemed to attract the ghost. He came closer, and I held out half the sandwich to him.

The ghost took it and gobbled it greedily. A faint color rose to his cheeks.

On a hunch, I broke off another piece of my sandwich for him. He ate it and turned positively rosy.

"Do you know where the jail is?" I asked before he faded.

"East of Tartarus." The ghost pointed. "This side of the flames."

Then he drifted off, losing color as he went.

We ate quickly and headed in the direction the ghost had pointed. We walked down a steep hill. The further we walked, the hotter it got. The sky overhead turned orange, reflecting the flames from the lower region. At last, we came to a tall stone structure built into the side of the hill. Its top was studded with nasty-looking spikes.

"This must be the place," said Zeus, wiping drosis from his brow. It was blazing hot in this part of the Underworld.

Sounds of hammering echoed from inside the building.

"And THAT must be Campe," said Po.

The Jail Keep of the Underworld sat on a stool just outside the great iron jailhouse door, fanning herself. She was huge, twice the size of a Titan. She had big hands and big feet. But for her size, she had a rather small, knobby-looking head covered with thinning brown hair. Around her neck she wore a gold chain, and from her girdle hung a large brass ring with dozens of keys dangling from it.

Campe watched our approach with watery blue eyes.

Zeus put a hand to his chest, checking to make sure his aegis was in place. Then he drew the silver sickle from his girdle and cried, "We have come to rescue the Cyclopes and the Hundred-Handed Ones!"

CHAPTER X

SHINER AND CO.

Campe smiled. She was missing all but three of her teeth.

"Come to rescue them, have you now?" Her voice was deep and hoarse. Slowly, Campe stood up. She towered over us. "Well, come ahead."

"Hades! Po!" Zeus cried. "Charge her! I'll back you up!"

"Oh, puh-lease!" Campe laughed. She held up her key ring and jangled it. "I'll make you a deal. You can each take one shot at finding the key that fits the jailhouse lock. Pick the right one, and you can take my prisoners. But if you pick wrong . . . you're my new cleaning crew."

We eyed that jail. It was a pretty good bet that it had never been cleaned.

Campe held out the keys.

"Me first!" Zeus said. He took the ring and walked toward the door. He sorted through the keys, saying, "One potato, two potato, three potato, four." On "four," he chose a key, fitted it into the lock, and tried to turn it.

"Uh-oh," said Zeus.

"My turn!" said Po. He took the key ring from Zeus. He peered at the lock. Then he spread all the keys out on the ground and studied them for a long time. "Got it!" he said at last. He, too, fitted a key into the lock. But when he turned it, nothing happened.

I started drosissing. Now it was up to me to find the right key, or my brothers and I would end up scrubbing down the jailhouse — forever! I took the key ring. It weighed a ton. I examined the keys. They all looked the same. Then I thought, *Campe opens the jail door all the time*. She had to have a quick way to find the right key. An idea popped into my head. I took a chance.

"The key isn't on this ring, Campe," I said. "It's on the chain around your neck."

Campe smiled. "Well, well, well — a thinker." She drew the end of the chain out of her robe. Sure enough, dangling from it was a single golden key.

She put it into the lock.

Click!

She pulled the door open and disappeared into the jail. We heard more clicking as she unlocked the cell doors.

"Thunderer! Lightninger! Shiner!" she bellowed. "You've been sprung, Cyclopes!"

The hammering stopped. Heavy footsteps sounded, and soon three giant Cyclopes appeared at the jailhouse door. They were as tall as Titans, but much skinnier. They stood looking out at us, each blinking one great eye.

Campe turned and went back into the jail.

"Fingers! Highfive! Lefty!" she called.

Again, we heard footsteps. Then a crowd appeared at the jailhouse door. It was really just the three Hundred-Handed Ones, but with fifty heads apiece, they looked like a crowd. These guys were even thinner then the Cyclopes. They, too, looked out at us questioningly.

"The little gods here have rescued you," Campe told them.

"Are you releasing us then?" asked a Cyclops.

Campe nodded.

"Let's pack up, bros," said a Hundred-Handed One. "Don't run off, little gods. Be back in a flash."

They all ducked into the jail again, and we heard much banging and shuffling. A few minutes later, the six reappeared. The Cyclopes wore huge backpacks loaded with what looked like a blacksmith's forge and blacksmithing tools. The Hundred-Handed Ones carried small suitcases in many of their many hands.

"Drop me a postcard every now and then, boys," said Campe. "Let me know how you're getting on."

"Will do," said a Hundred-Handed One. "But what about you, Campe? You'll be lonely without us!"

"Oh, don't worry about me," Campe said with a grin. "This jail is never empty for long. Farewell, boys!"

With that, the nine of us started hiking. We were all glad to leave the flames of Tartarus behind.

We got to know our uncles pretty well on that trip up to earth. The Cyclopes were big, hairy, scruffy guys who smelled strongly of sheep. Thunderer and Lightninger didn't say much. But Shiner was a talker.

"We three are excellent blacksmiths," he told us. "We shall prove it to you when we reassemble our forge."

The Hundred-Handed Ones pretty much yakked nonstop. With one hundred and fifty heads among them, they could carry on up to seventy-five one-on-one conversations at a time. It turned out that Fingers, better known as Sticky Fingers, was an accomplished pickpocket. He managed to pick Charon's robe pocket when we crossed the Styx, then paid our fare with Charon's own gold coins. He gave him a handsome tip, too. Highfive was a famous prizefighter. And Lefty was an ace at throwing a fast-breaking curve-rock.

On the trip, we filled our uncles in on what was going on with the kickstone game. They promised to help us because we all had one important thing in common: we were all really, really, really mad at Cronus.

To our surprise, when we got back to the cave, Mom was there. Talk about a family reunion! She'd never met her non-Titan brothers before, and when your long-lost relatives each have fifty heads and a hundred arms, a simple kiss and a hug can take hours.

At last everyone settled down, and Mom brought out of one of her amazing picnic lunches.

"Eat, eat, my long-lost brothers!" she said, beaming. She was never happier than when she was feeding her family.

Our weird uncles ate as though they hadn't eaten in centuries, which, in fact, they hadn't. Not ambrosia or nectar, anyway. Mom said this was why their immortal selves had shrunk down to nothing but derma and skeletos (old Greek speak for "skin and bones"). As they ate, our uncles grew bigger and healthier and stronger before our very eyes.

When we'd all eaten our fill, Hera stood. "I hate to bring this up," she said, "but we're due back on the field in Olympia Stadium tomorrow morning."

Shiner jumped to his feet. "Lightninger, arrange the tools!" he ordered. "Thunderer, commence reconstructing the forge!" He turned to Hera. "We shall create weapons and other items to assist you on and off the field!" And the Cyclopes got to work.

We gods spent the rest of the afternoon teaching the Hundred-Handed Ones the basics of kickstone.

As the sun went down, orange sparks from the Cyclopes' forge lit the sky. At last Shiner called, "We are prepared to bestow your gifts!"

We gathered around the forge.

"Time is scarce," Shiner began. "So we have

made only three gifts. They are for the three gods who journeyed bravely to the Underworld to free us. Step forward, Zeus!"

Zeus did.

Thunderer held out a great bronze pail.

"A bucket?" Zeus cried. "What sort of weapon is —"

"It is the Bucket o' Bolts," Shiner said.

Zeus reached into the bucket and drew out what looked like a long, zigzag spear. It gleamed with yellow light.

"Nothing can withstand the force of a thunderbolt," Shiner told Zeus. "Hurl it, and your enemies will experience dire consequences."

"Dire consequences," Zeus murmured as he tested the weight and heft of his weapon. "Not sure what it means, but I like the sound of it."

"We Cyclopes swear by the waters of the River Styx," said Shiner, "that the Bucket o' Bolts shall never be empty."

"What do you say, Zeusie?" said Mom.

"Thank you, Uncle Shiner," said Zeus.

Shiner nodded. "Step forward, Poseidon!"

Po eagerly stepped up.

Lightninger reached out and handed him a large, three-pronged spear.

"No fair!" cried Po. "Zeus gets thunderbolts, and I get a fish fork?"

"A trident," said Shiner. "A most powerful weapon. It can be hurled at your enemies or, for a more extreme effect, you may strike the earth with its shaft."

Po pounded the shaft of his trident on the ground. Instantly the earth began to shake.

Po smiled. "Nice," he said. "Thanks, guys."

"Step forward, Hades!" said Shiner.

I did, although I had mixed feelings about getting a weapon. I wasn't big on fighting. And so when Shiner held out my gift — a shiny iron-and-bronze helmet — I felt as if he'd been reading my mind.

"The Helmet of Darkness," Shiner said, setting it on my head. I was thinking what a nice snug fit it was when everyone started oohing and aahing and going, "Where's Hades?" and, "What has befallen him?"

"Nothing has befallen me," I said to Shiner. "What are they talking about?"

"We can no longer see you," Shiner explained. "The Helmet of Darkness renders you, and all that you hold, invisible to gods and mortals alike."

I smiled a big invisible smile. For me, it was the perfect gift.

"All right, that's over with," Hera said testily. Her nose was out of joint because she hadn't gotten a gift. "Let's get a good night's rest. And tomorrow, we're going to win this game!"

The next morning, we put on our competition robes and lined up by height behind our uncles. Zeus and Po hid their weapons under their robes the way the Titans had. I hid my helmet inside my robe, too.

Off we marched for Olympia Stadium.

Chapter XI

T-Bolt Attack!

We marched into the stadium. The Titans were already on the field. We quickly jogged out and took our positions.

The Titans all stared at our uncles in surprise.

"I know you," growled Cronus, eyeing Uncle Lefty.

"Yes, you do, bro," said Uncle Lefty. "You came to visit us in jail."

Cronus narrowed his eyes, trying to remember.

"You had vowed to release us from prison when you became Ruler of the Universe," Uncle Shiner reminded him. "But you broke that vow."

"You left us to rot in jail," said Uncle Highfive.

At last the light dawned for Cronus. These were his ugly brothers that Sky Daddy had tossed down into Tartarus.

"Well, so what?" Cronus cried. "I'll toss you down to Tartarus myself when I'm finished with you here!" He turned to Themis. "Let's get started!"

Hera and Atlas jogged over to Themis.

"Hera, heads or tails?" asked Themis. She flipped the coin.

"Tails!" called Hera.

"What do you know?" said Themis. "It's heads."

As always, the Titans kicked off.

There weren't any fans around to hear a play-by-play, but Hermes took his place in the announcer's box anyway.

"The Titans will kick off," he said. "There they go! Cronus put some muscle into that kick. Nice stop by the gods' team. That Cyclops really kept his eye on the stone, folks! Now he's passed it to Aphrodite. She's dribbling toward the Titan goal.

Intercept! Intercept! Titans gain possession! The stone is headed back toward the gods' goal. Atlas is lining up a shot. Oops! Another intercept! This time by a Hundred-Handed One. He's kicked the stone into the air. He's bounced it off one of his heads. Now off another. And another! Ow! That has to hurt! The stone is ricocheting from head to head while the Hundred-Handed One runs! He's taking the stone up the field. Amazing play here, just unbelievable!"

But every time we got close to the Titan goal, the Titans started uprooting trees and heaving them at us. They grabbed chunks of mountains and flung them at us too. They did everything they could think of to keep us from scoring.

Now, at Hera's signal, Po went into action.

"Po's pulled something out from under his robe!" announced Hermes. "It looks like a giant fish fork. He's pounding the earth with it. It's causing an earthquake! Everyone's falling down on the field. Po's down, too. He looks . . . shaken. Now the Titans are up again. They're taking the stone down the field."

Hera signaled me. I took out my secret weapon.

"Cronus is running at Zeus with his sword drawn!" cried Hermes. "Look out, Zeus! And — what's this? Cronus's sword just flew out of his hand. There goes Atlas's sword! What's going on, folks? Is there an invisible player on the field?"

Well, you know the answer to that one. I did what I could, but even with my best efforts, I couldn't grab all the Titan's swords fast enough.

Now Hera signaled Zeus.

"Still a scoreless game here in Olympia Stadium," said Hermes. "But wait. Zeus has just pulled something out from under his robe. Why, it looks like a bucket, folks. Now he's pulling something out of the bucket. It looks to be a thunderbolt. Yes! That's it! He's hurled it at Cronus! Whoa, is Zeus ever a lousy shot. That bolt is going to miss by a dekamile! Oh, no! It's headed right for my boy! He's hit! Pan's been hit on the hoof!

"YAAAAAAAAAAAAAA

AAAAHHHH!!!"

screamed Pan.

We gods had heard Pan shout before. But the Titans hadn't. They must have thought that the universe was coming to an end. They panicked, running in all directions, screaming and yelling and smashing into each other.

Hera saw our chance.

"After them!" she shouted. "After them!"

Chapter XII

Red-Hot Olympians

We took off running after those panicked Titans. We chased them out of Olympia Stadium. We chased them across Greece. We chased them to the very edge of the earth and all the way down to the Underworld.

The Titans were so big and they ran so fast that they didn't need Charon to ferry them across the Styx. In their panic, they leaped over the river. Campe stood on the far bank, waiting for them. The Cyclopes and the Hundred-Handed Ones quickly splashed across the river and helped her cuff the Titans.

Once the prisoners had been secured, Uncle Shiner threw his arms around Campe. Thunderer and Lightninger did the same.

"How we have missed you!" the Cyclopes said.

"I've missed you, too," Campe said, patting their hairy backs.

The Hundred-Handed Ones got in on the act, then. All hundred and fifty mouths started saying how much they'd missed Campe, and all three hundred arms hugged her.

"Me, too," came her muffled voice from the center of the hug. "It's just not the same down here without you boys."

As we gods stood on the bank of the Styx, watching this odd reunion, I felt something cold and wet on my ankle. I looked down and saw a shiny, wet doggy nose. Three of them, actually.

"Hey, there, little pup," I said, stooping down to pet his heads.

"Hold him there, Hades!" cried Zeus, pulling a bolt out of his bucket. "I'll zap him!"

"Back off, Zeus!" I reached down to pick up the pup, but he ran off on his own.

Zeus hurled a bolt at the dog as he ran, but I deflected it with my helmet.

"Aw, Hades," Zeus whined. "You fun wrecker!"

Campe lined up her prisoners. "Titans!" she said. "Who is your leader?"

Cronus quickly pointed to Atlas. "He is!"

"I was kickstone team captain," Atlas admitted, "but technically, Cronus is —"

"The captain is in charge." Cronus folded his arms over his chest. "And Atlas was captain."

"What a slimy guy Dad is," Hestia said.

We all nodded in agreement. Zeus nodded, too, though it seemed to me there was quite a bit of Dad in Zeus.

"The way you played kickstone was a disgrace, Captain Atlas," said Campe. "All that hurling of trees and boulders. You cracked one of my sky pillars. Take a look at the sky, will you? It's tilting! Come over here." She beckoned to Atlas. "Now turn around. Back up, back up . . . ."

She reached over and grabbed the top half of the cracked pillar. Grunting from the weight of it, Campe slid it over until it lay across Atlas's broad shoulders. She let go.

"Ugggghhhh!" said Atlas. "This is heavy!"

"Ought to be," said Campe. "It's the sky. This

is what you get for playing dirty and breaking my pillar."

Campe turned and walked away, leaving Atlas holding the vault of the sky on his shoulders.

"Hey!" Atlas called after her. "Wait a second! How long do I have to hold this thing?"

"Oh, I'm thinking . . . forever," Campe answered. Then she led the rest of the Titan army off to Tartarus and the Underworld jail.

We gods looked at each other. Only then did it dawn on us that the games with the Titans were finally over.

"We won!" said Zeus. "Mount Olympus is our turf again! We rule!"

We ran around slapping hands and hugging. We yelled, "What teamwork!" and, "Together, we can do anything!"

I found Pan in the crowd. Some First-Aid Nymphs had wrapped his right hoof in bandages and said he'd be fine in a week or so. I thanked him, because without his yell, we'd still be up on earth playing an eternal game of kickstone.

"Announcement, gods!" Hera cried.

Everyone stopped talking.

"I've thought of a name for us," Hera said. "It's even stronger than *Titan*. No longer shall we be called godlings or gods. We won the Olympic Games, so henceforth, we shall be called Olympians!"

We all clapped and cheered. The name fit. We were the Olympians!

"Mount Olympus, here we come!" said Zeus.

"Delay a moment, little gods!" Uncle Shiner called. He came splashing back across the Styx.

"No wading in the Styx!" Charon shouted at him. But he didn't try to stop him. He only poled his boat down river a bit, grumbled loudly about how hard it was for an honest river-taxi driver to make an honest living.

"We Cyclopes and Hundred-Handed Ones have made a momentous decision," Uncle Shiner told us. "We appreciate your rescuing us, and we are deliriously happy not to be in jail anymore. But in truth, we've missed Campe. And we've missed the Underworld. After inhabiting it for so many centuries, it feels like home. We've decided to stay."

We Olympians thanked our weird uncles and bid them goodbye. Then we made our way back up to earth. We felt great. With a little help from our uncles, and a lot of help from Pan, we had defeated the Titans!

We hiked back to the base of Mount Olympus. We had just started up it when the ground began to shake beneath our feet.

"Po?" said Hera. "Are you doing that earthquake thing with your trident?"

"No!" said Po.

"Why does it always *do* this?" cried Demeter.

Now the earthquake started for real. This one was a hundred times worse than the last one. We were tossed and thrown around so much that by the time the quake was over, we were bruised and battered.

"Look!" cried Zeus. "I'm ichoring!"

Then the earth stopped shaking, and everything was still.

Too still.

I had a feeling that something BAD was about to happen.

Of course right then, I didn't have a clue how bad BAD could be.

Chapter XIII

Great Balls of Fire!

We hiked back to Mount Olympus and started climbing. It wasn't easy. But however bad it was for most of us, it was worse for Demeter, lugging that stone. I had to hand it to her. When it came to pure, dogged will, she had the rest of us beat cold.

"Are we there yet?" whined Po. He'd tried using his trident as a walking stick, but he kept causing minor earthquakes, so he'd had to stop.

"Shhh!" said Zeus. "What's that noise?"

We all listened.

"It sounds like wings flapping," whispered Hera.

The sky grew dark then, as if some gigantic

winged monster was flying past the sun, blotting out its light.

Which is exactly what it turned out to be.

We all stared in horror as the monster appeared above us in the sky. It had the head of a donkey. A mean, vicious donkey. It had a silver-scaled dragon's body. Its arms and legs ended in paws. Instead of claws, each paw sprouted huge, writhing serpents.

"It's Typhon!" cried Hera. "That monster Hyperion told us about!"

Hissing and roaring, Typhon swooped down on us. Hot black smoke shot from his nostrils. As we coughed and sputtered, Typhon opened his mouth wide and spewed red-hot lava down at us.

All the teamwork bonding and the good togetherness feelings we had after we beat the Titans? Gone. Now it was every terrified Olympian for him — or her — self. There wasn't even time to wonder why the monster was attacking us.

Before Typhon, none of us knew that we had the power to change ourselves into other life forms. But with red-hot lava pouring down from the skies, our godly powers kicked into high gear. Hera instantly changed herself into a white cow and galloped off toward Egypt. (Leave it to Hera to turn into an animal that was worshiped there.) Apollo morphed into a crow and flapped off after her. Artemis became a wild cat, Aphrodite, a boar, and Dionysus, a goat. One by one, the Olympians all turned into beasts and ran away as fast as they could.

And the brave and mighty Zeus? Do you think he turned into a lion? A ram? A bull elephant maybe? Wrong, wrong, wrong! Zeus turned himself into a chipmunk and dove down the nearest hole.

I didn't change into anything, but I did put on my helmet. Wouldn't you? Imagine that the world's biggest, meanest, lava-spewing-est monster was hot on your heels. A monster that makes Godzilla look as helpless as a day-old kitten! I think you'd put on the helmet too.

Invisible, I dodged splashing lava as I ran over to the chipmunk hole.

"Zeus!" I called down the hole. "We have to drive Typhon away! He can't kill us, but if we get covered in lava, it will harden into rock, and we'll be stuck inside it *forever*! Forever is a long time, Zeus. Come out! We have to fight this monster!"

"Nothing doing," Zeus squeaked from inside the hole.

BLAM! A flaming lava blob hit the ground behind me.

When the coast was clear, Athena ran over to the chipmunk hole too. She alone of the gods had bravely kept her form. She knelt down beside the hole.

"Dad?" she said. "You are *so* embarrassing!"

Zeus didn't say a word.

Typhon swooped down and wound his snaky coils around a great boulder. He flew up in the air with it and let it go.

THUD!

The boulder landed inches from Zeus's hiding hole and covered us with a thick cloud of dust. That was it for Athena. She quickly changed herself into an owl, hooted a farewell, and winged away.

As I watched her disappear into the distance, I heard that squeaky voice again, coming from the chipmunk hole: "Helmet."

I sighed. "Okay. I'll trade you my helmet for the Bucket o' Bolts." Zeus was useless in battle, so I figured it was up to me to get rid of Typhon.

Zeus stuck his little chipmunk nose up out of the hole. I took off my helmet and put it down on top of the hole. It quickly rose up and vanished, and I knew that Zeus's invisible head was inside it. A few seconds later, the Bucket o' Bolts dropped mysteriously at my feet.

I gazed up at the sky. Where was Typhon? He wasn't circling overhead. Had he gone back to whatever deep crack in the universe he'd come from? That seemed too good to be true.

It was.

Typhon flew into view. His body was ten times the size it had been before! The bloated monster had flown to the sea and sucked up half an ocean. Now he blew it down at us in a terrible torrent. Zeus and I were caught in a swirling flood that swept us from the side of Mount Olympus. I couldn't see Zeus, but I heard him screaming.

I seized an uprooted tree and held on tight.

"Grab on, Zeus!" I cried.

"Got it!" came a disembodied voice.

Waves broke above our heads as the flood carried us out to sea. Typhon circled overhead. With one hand, I gripped that tree. With the other, I managed to grab a T-bolt from the bucket. I hurled it at Typhon.

ZAP!

The T-bolt bounced off the monster's leg.

Typhon howled in fury. He angled his wings for a dive.

I grabbed another T-bolt. I took aim at the creature's belly. I fired.

BAM! Got him!

A river of lava erupted from the monster's throat. Hot molten rock poured down on all sides of us, hissing horribly as it splashed into the water. But the great storming sea made us a moving target. Typhon could not score a direct hit.

At last our tree ran aground on an island that I later learned was Sicily. I ran frantically around the base of a huge mountain, looking for a crevice, a cave, any place to hide. I heard Zeus panting behind me.

Typhon flew after us. He hovered, getting ready to take a shot.

I quickly grabbed another T-bolt. I took aim.

THWACK!

"Take that, you fiend!" I cried.

The monster swayed crazily in the air, then plunged to earth. The ground shuddered as he hit. He lay still.

Typhon's eyes were closed. The monster was barely breathing.

"I think he's —" I began.

"Dead!" cried Zeus.

"I was thinking *hurt,*" I said.

But Zeus wasn't listening. He grabbed back his bucket. Then he ripped the Helmet of Darkness from his head. He tossed it in my direction, but it hit the ground before I could catch it. I picked it up and heard something rattle inside. I hoped it wasn't broken.

"T-bolts rule!" Zeus cried. "I have felled the mighty Typhon!" He strode over to the creature, and planted a foot in his back paw.

BIG mistake.

Typhon's serpent toes whipped themselves around Zeus, and faster than you can say *uh-oh*, he was caught in the monster's coils.

"Uh-oh," said Zeus. He dropped his Bucket o' Bolts. "Hey, let go!"

This capture seemed to revive Typhon completely. He managed a jagged-tooth smile.

"Not so tight!" Zeus gasped. "I can't breathe!"

Now Typhon let out what must have been a laugh. It bounced off the mountain, echoing in the air.

I jammed on the Helmet of Darkness and rushed to help Zeus. But when I came near, Typhon sensed my approach and spat a fireball my way.

Typhon held his captive in the air. Quicker than a flash, his serpent fingers unhooked the sickle from Zeus's girdle. Then, with its needle-sharp tip, he began to pluck out Zeus's sinews.

Okay, raise your hand if you know what *sinews* are.

Take a wild guess.

Give up? No one who hasn't had the word assigned for a weekly vocabulary quiz has a clue what it means.

But here, take a crack at it. *Sinews* are:

a) bushy eyebrows
b) rotten molars
c) rubber-band-like things that connect your muscles to your bones
d) little prickly hairs on the back of your neck

If you picked c), bingo!

I know what you're thinking. Most monsters eat their victims. Or maybe they bounce them around for a while and *then* eat them. Or they breathe fire on them and toast them like marshmallows. But this sinews thing — that's a new one.

Well, Typhon had a thing for sinews. He pulled out every one of Zeus's. For a monster of his gigantic size, he had excellent fine-motor skills. He threw the sinews into a bearskin bag and drew the drawstring tight.

Without his sinews, Zeus couldn't move a muscle. His head slumped down on his chest. His arms hung limply at his sides. His feet swung in the breeze. He was as limp as a rag doll.

Satisfied with his work, Typhon hooked the sickle back on Zeus's girdle and tucked the helpless Zeus under one arm. With the other arm, he scooped up the Bucket o' Bolts. Then, flapping his great wings, he rose into the air.

I could almost hear Zeus crying, "Help! Help!"

But without his jaw sinews, he couldn't even do that.

I stood watching Typhon soar over the mountain and bank to the right. Part of me, I'll admit it, was glad to see them go. Both of them — I was sick of Zeus!

But then I heard Mom's voice in my head: "Look after your brothers and sisters, Hades. Especially Zeus. Make sure no harm comes to him."

I'd sworn on the waters of the River Styx.

I didn't have much choice, did I?

It was up to me, Hades.

And so I took off in search of Typhon's lair.

Chapter XIV

Fire Escape

I ran after Typhon as he flew around the side of the huge mountain. I saw that he was headed for a large cave just south of it. He flipped rag-doll Zeus over his shoulder and ducked into the cave. He called, "Honey, I'm home!"

I crept closer to the mouth of the cave. A terrible damp smell came from inside. I took a last breath of fresh air and plunged in after Typhon.

In the dim light I spied a second monster. She was big, but nowhere near Typhon's size. Her body was that of a serpent — long, thick, and speckled. But she had the shoulders, arms, and head of a woman. A beautiful woman! Even in the dim light of the cave, I could tell that she was a knockout. Six or seven junior monsters romped around her coiled body. One looked like a baby lion. Another had a girl's head on a winged lion's body. Still another seemed to be a goat with a lion's head. Definitely a strange brood.

Typhon hung Zeus neatly on a peg by the cave entrance. Then he tossed the bag of sinews to his wife. "Don't let this out of your sight, Echidna."

"As if I haven't got enough to do, tending our young," Echidna grumbled.

"Give me a break, Echidna," Typhon said. "Look! I've been hit by T-bolts!" He poked a serpent finger into a little hole in his gut.

"Ow!" he whimpered. "I'm going to Mount Nyssa to see the Wound-Tending Nymphs. I'll bet I need a tetanus shot." And with that, he ducked back out of the cave and flew away.

"The least little scratch and he's off to see those nymphs," Echidna muttered. "All right, kids," she said. "Nap time! Chimera, stop that butting. Sphinx, zip it up. I mean it. One more riddle and you get a time-out."

At last the little ones settled down and snuggled up to their monstrous mama. Echidna sighed and closed her eyes.

Now was my chance to grab the bag of sinews. I edged invisibly toward Echidna. The bag rested against her shoulder. I reached out and took hold of it. Slowly, slowly I began to slide the bag away from her. I was patient. I took my time, keeping the bag moving almost imperceptibly along the cave floor.

Then suddenly, *WHAP!*

Something slammed into me. I pitched forward. The Helmet of Darkness flew off my head. Instantly, I became visible.

"Gotcha!" Echidna said. She wound her serpent's tail around me. "Name?"

"Hades," I managed.

"Hades." She picked me up and studied me with a pair of very pretty brown eyes. "I was just wondering what to have for lunch!"

I tried to smile, but Echidna wasn't so easily

charmed. She began to put the squeeze on me. I couldn't breathe. And I shuddered to think that if she swallowed me, I'd spend eternity inside another gut. Somewhere below, I heard dogs barking.

"Down, Cerberus!" Echidna ordered. "Be good, and I'll give you his bones to gnaw on."

But the barking didn't let up.

"What, Cerberus?" Echidna asked.

The barking took on a more frantic pitch.

"Cerberus," said Echidna, "are you trying to tell me that one day when you were playing on the bank of the River Styx, a mean god kicked at you and threatened to blast you with a thunderbolt and would have, too, only *this* god saved your life? *This* god? The one whom I am now squeezing so hard that his face is turning purple?"

"*YIP!*" answered the pup.

Echidna quickly set me down on the floor of the cave and began uncoiling her tail. As I fought to get my breath back, Cerberus ran over and began licking me with all three tongues.

"That was a close one, huh?" Echidna smiled, and her whole gorgeous face lit up. She picked up the bag of sinews and tossed it to me.

"Take it. And the guy on the peg, too. I don't know what Typhon was thinking, bringing him here. The last thing I need is another mouth to feed. Take your buddy and beat it before Typhon comes home."

I didn't have to be told twice. I quickly tied the bag of sinews onto my girdle. I scooped up my helmet, vowing to fasten on a chinstrap so it could never fall off again. Then I ran over to Zeus. I jumped up on a table to reach him and lifted him off the hook. Oof! He was dead heavy. But I managed to hoist him over my shoulder the way Typhon had done. I jumped down from the table.

I took a quick look around for the Bucket o' Bolts, but it was nowhere to be seen. I gave Cerberus three fast pats on the heads. Then with a wave, I called, "Thanks, Echidna! I won't forget this!" and I rushed out of the cave.

I stopped for a second to put on the Helmet

of Darkness. It sputtered, and I flickered from visibility to invisibility a few times before I disappeared for good. Then I toted Zeus to the seashore. Invisible as we were, it wasn't hard to catch a ride on a boat back to Greece, and from there I headed straight for Mount Olympus.

I carried Zeus the whole way up Mount Olympus. I felt like Demeter, lugging that stone from Dad's belly. Only Zeus weighed about twenty times more than the stone.

I climbed until I reached the bank of clouds covering Mount Olympus. Then I took off the Helmet of Darkness to let the Cloud Nymphs see it was me, Hades. They quickly parted the clouds. I stepped out of them and onto Mount Olympus. Home at last!

Hera was the first to spot me. "Hades!" she cried, running to greet me. "Where have you been? Everyone was so worried!"

"It's a long story," I told her. I lowered the blob of jelly formerly known as Zeus to the ground.

"AAAACH!" Hera cried. "What happened to *him?*"

"A *very* long story," I said. "Help me with him, will you?"

Hera picked up Zeus's arms. I picked up his legs. Together we carried him to his palace. As we went, I told Hera all about Typhon, Echidna, and the sinews.

"Very strange," said Hera, shaking her head. "I'll call Hermes. He's clever. If anyone can put Zeus's sinews back in place, Hermes can."

We laid Zeus out on the dining table in the Great Hall. I opened the bearskin bag, and while I was taking out the sinews, Hermes showed up.

"Step aside," said Hermes, "and let me at him."

Hermes rolled up his sleeves and got to work. He managed to thread each of Zeus's sinews back into place, reconnecting muscle to bone. The only mistake he made was to start with Zeus's jaw sinews. Once they were reattached, Zeus could move his mouth again, and he began crying and screaming like the big baby he is.

By the time Hermes got Zeus up on his feet again, the sky overhead was growing dark.

"Can night have fallen so soon?" Hermes asked, glancing out at the sky.

Hera thumped an hourglass that stood nearby. "Has this thing stopped? It can't be this dark this early in the day."

That's when I started to get a bad feeling in my stomach.

CHAPTER XV

STAR WARS

I hurried to the door of the Great Hall and looked up at the darkening sky.

Typhon was circling overhead.

I groaned. Why hadn't I thought of this? Of course Typhon would come looking for us!

The beast folded his great wings, preparing to dive.

"Zeus!" I yelled. "Get your storm chariot! We'll fight him in the sky!"

Zeus stood frozen to the spot. He had that chipmunk look in his eyes. I ran to him and grabbed him by the elbow. His muscles were weak from being de-sinewed, so he couldn't put up much of a fight. Still, he kicked and screamed as best as he could while I pulled him to the stables. Hera and Hermes were two steps ahead of us. They'd already harnessed Zeus's steeds to his chariot.

I jumped in and yanked Zeus in beside me. I picked up the reins. I gave those horses a slap, yelling, "Giddyup!"

The startled horses spread their wings and took off into the sky. In no time, we were high above Mount Olympus.

Then all of the sudden, *ZWACK!*

A thunderbolt whizzed by us.

"My T-bolts!" cried Zeus. "Typhon's got my T-bolts!"

The lightning flash startled the horses.

I pulled on the reins and cried, "Whoa, steeds!"

But they didn't whoa. In their panic, they raced up, up into the high heavens.

I heard Typhon's horrible growl behind us. I braced myself for another T-bolt. I wasn't disappointed. *ZWACK!* It came so close I heard my hair sizzle. The horses whinnied, winging their way higher and higher. Soon we were flying through the heavens, home to all the star-made creatures of the deep night sky.

Typhon raced on behind us, hurling T-bolts.

Suddenly, the Great Bear constellation rose up on his hind legs, furious at this invasion of his sky. Beside him, the Bull bellowed and pawed the air. The Ram lowered his head. The three charged Typhon.

But Typhon only grinned. He grabbed the Great Bear by one leg and hurled him across the sky. He drew back his arm and swatted the Bull as if he were a housefly. The Ram managed to butt Typhon, but Typhon grabbed him by the horns and dropkicked him high into the stratosphere. All the while, Typhon kept up the barrage of thunderbolts, filling the sky with an awful flashing. Other star creatures panicked, galloping wildly in all directions.

Our only hope was to get the Bucket o' Bolts away from Typhon. I pulled at the reins with all my might and at last regained control of the horses.

"Turn, mighty steeds!" I called. "Onward for

the Olympians!" We began to circle Typhon then, going around behind him.

The horses obeyed. Closer and closer we came to the monster, speeding straight towards his back.

"Zeus!" I cried. "See how Typhon is holding the bucket out with one arm? When I get close enough, grab it from him."

"Me?" cried Zeus. "Why me?"

I didn't bother to answer. It took all my effort to keep those horses on course. Closer we came, and closer still. The bucket was right before us.

"Ready, Zeus . . . NOW!"

Zeus made a halfhearted lunge for the bucket. He managed to knock it out of Typhon's snaky grasp, but he didn't manage to catch it.

The bucket spiraled through the sky, dropping down, down.

Typhon whirled around to see what had struck him. His huge face hovered before us like a giant donkey mask.

Typhon's snaky fingers reached out to grab us. If he caught us, I feared he'd fling us into the outer skies, where we would orbit the earth for eternity.

But just before he grabbed us, the starry Goat butted in between his serpent fingers and our chariot. Caught on one of her horns was the handle of the Bucket o' Bolts. The Goat galloped close, then tilted her head, dropping the bucket onto Zeus's lap.

"I caught it!" cried Zeus.

"Start hurling!" I yelled. I wheeled the horses around for a frontal attack.

Zeus reached into the never-empty bucket, pulled out a bolt, and hurled it.

PLIP!

Typhon caught the T-bolt and flung it back at us.

ZWACK!

"We're hit!" cried Zeus.

The chariot swayed crazily. I glanced over my shoulder. The back half of the chariot had been vaporized.

The horses whinnied and broke into a wild gallop. I lost my grip on the reins. The horses headed down now, out of the starry heavens, past the moon, past Mount Olympus, through the clouds, down toward the earth.

Typhon flew after us, spitting burning hot lava at our backs.

The horses touched down in a field, never slowing for a second.

Behind us, Typhon hit the ground too. He threw his long arms around a whole forest and uprooted it. He started hurling trees. We dodged one and then another as we galloped on. But it was only a matter of time before one of the huge timbers crashed down on our heads.

The terrified horses turned again and headed out to sea. We skimmed over the water. Our wheels touched down on the island of Sicily. We headed for the highest mountain on the island.

Typhon zoomed over our heads and landed in front of us. He opened his arms wide, encircling the entire mountain in his grip. Hugging it to him, Typhon gave a mighty pull. With a horrible sucking sound, the mountain came up out of the ground, trailing rocks and boulders.

Now Typhon threw back his head and let out a long, ichor-curdling laugh.

The awful sound panicked the horses. They bucked hard, snapping the reins and breaking free. They flew furiously away, leaving us sitting helplessly in the charred chariot.

Typhon raised the mountain over his head and hurled it at us.

"We're history!" whimpered Zeus.

In desperation, I plunged both hands into the Bucket o' Bolts. I grabbed as many bolts as I could and flung them with all my might at the hurtling mountain.

The bolts whizzed through the air and slammed into the mountain. Their force stopped it dead in its path. For a moment, the great mountain hovered in midair, frozen in space.

Then, with Typhon's laughter still echoing, the mountain began to fall back the way it had come.

THUD!

It slammed into the earth with tremendous force. It jolted us out of what was left of our chariot and sent us flying through the air. By the time we hit the ground, the earth had stopped shaking. All was still.

The silence was eerie.

"Typhon's a goner!" Zeus cried. "I did it!"

But I had an awful feeling that the battle wasn't over yet.

Then — *KABOOM!* The top of the mountain shot off. Red-hot lava and orange flames exploded into the sky. Thunderous roars came from deep down in the ground. The once peaceful mountain was now a raging volcano.

Zeus and I stood there, watching the fireworks. It was quite a show. After a long while, the fire didn't spurt so high. The roars quieted down. And at last the lava merely bubbled and boiled inside the mountain.

"He's toast!" said Zeus. "Typhon will never trouble us again!"

But personally, I had my doubts. After what I'd just seen, I thought Typhon might find a way to escape.

But to this day, he hasn't. Nope, Typhon

is still trapped under that mountain, raging and roaring. If you don't believe me, go to Sicily yourself. Go to Mount Etna. You'll see an enormous mountain belching smoke, fire, and molten lava.

Who else could it be under there but Typhon?

Chapter XVI
Smokin' Granny

"We have stopped the monster!" Zeus proclaimed.

"Right," I said, even though I didn't exactly agree with his definition of the word *we*. My stomach was growling like a beast. "So what do you say we head back to Mount Olympus? Get cleaned up and have a bite to eat?"

Zeus only kept up his bragging. And his lying. "I have felled the biggest monster ever! Never again shall Typhon —"

But he said no more, for once again, the earth beneath our feet began to tremble. The tremble quickly turned into a major quake, throwing Zeus and me to the ground.

There weren't any trees to grab on to.

Typhon had uprooted them all. So Zeus and I bounced around like corn in a popper while the earth bucked and cracked and seemed to change from solid to liquid form.

"Now what?" I moaned.

"NOW WHAT?" a voice boomed. "I'LL TELL YOU NOW WHAT!"

It wasn't Typhon's voice. It was a hundred times louder and scarier than that. Zeus and I looked around, expecting to see yet another monster with a grudge against us.

"Zeus? I don't see any monster," I said. "Do you?"

The shaking stopped suddenly.

"YOU CAN'T SEE ME," the voice boomed. "I'M TOO BIG FOR THAT."

Oh, great! A monster too big to be seen! This was curtains for sure. But somehow I managed to say, in the most respectful tone possible, "And who might you be, oh, mighty shaker of the ground?"

"I'M YOUR GRANNY!" the voice snapped. "GRANNY GAIA!"

"Mother Earth Gaia?" I said.

"THAT'S ME," Granny Gaia said. "I'VE BEEN TRYING TO SHAKE YOU LITTLE GODS UP FOR A LONG TIME!"

"Like after we fought Dad?" asked Zeus.

"THAT WAS ME," said Granny. "I WAS ANGRY! HOW COULD YOU HAVE SHOVED MY SWEET LITTLE CRONUS OFF THAT HILL?"

"We didn't really shove him," I said. "He tripped over a root."

"SILENCE!" shouted Granny Gaia. "I'LL DO THE TALKING HERE. I AM NOT HAPPY WITH THE TWO OF YOU. NOT HAPPY AT ALL. LOOK WHAT YOU'VE DONE TO *ME*, MOTHER EARTH!"

She had a point. In the kickstone games against the Titans and in the battle with Typhon, many forests and mountains had been destroyed.

"But it wasn't our fault!" Zeus said. "It was Typhon's!"

"TYPHON!" wailed Granny Gaia. "OHHH! MY YOUNGEST! MY SWEET, PRECIOUS, DONKEY-HEADED BABY! PINNED UNDER THAT MOUNTAIN!"

Hyperion had been right. Mother Earth really did love all her children, no matter what they looked like.

"YOU'VE DONE AWFUL THINGS TO MY OFFSPRING!" Granny Gaia said. "NOW MY CRONUS AND MY OTHER TITAN CHILDREN ARE LOCKED UP IN THE UNDERWORLD JAIL!"

"But what about the Cyclopes and the Hundred-Handed Ones?" I asked quickly. "They're your children too. And we got them *out* of jail."

"THAT'S TRUE," said Granny.

"And we're your grandchildren," I pointed out. "Most grannies are fond of their little grandkids."

"SO THEY ARE," Granny Gaia admitted. "WELL, MAYBE YOU'RE NOT SO BAD. BUT THERE WILL BE NOTHING LEFT OF ME IF THIS FIGHTING KEEPS UP. I WANT PEACE NOW, DO YOU HEAR ME? YOU SIX CHILDREN OF CRONUS CAN BE IN CHARGE OF THINGS. I'LL DECLARE THIS THE AGE OF THE OLYMPIANS. BUT YOU MUST RULE IN PEACE. GOT THAT?"

"No problem!" cried Zeus.

"HERE'S HOW IT WORKS," said Granny Gaia. "EACH OF YOU SHALL HAVE DOMINION OVER A CERTAIN AREA OF THE COSMOS."

She sounded like Zeus's children, wanting each god to be in charge of something.

"ONE OF YOU CAN BE GOD OF FRENCH FRIES, FOR ALL I CARE," Granny Gaia went on. "SOMEONE ELSE CAN BE THE GOD OF STANDARDIZED TESTING. YOU SIX GET TOGETHER AND FIGURE IT OUT. BUT NO FIGHTING. GOT THAT? NO MORE FIGHTING, AND, OF COURSE, ONE OF YOU WILL HAVE TO BE IN CHARGE OF IT ALL. YOU KNOW, BE THE RULER OF THE UNIVERSE?"

"No problem!" Zeus exclaimed again. His eyes gleamed as he turned to me. "Let's go tell the others!" And with that, he took off running.

"STOP!" ordered Granny.

Zeus stopped. "Huh?"

"HAVE YOU NO SENSE OF DIGNITY?" asked Granny.

Zeus shrugged. "Not that much, I guess."

Granny Gaia harrumphed. "I CAN'T HAVE THE GODS IN CHARGE OF THE UNIVERSE TROTTING AROUND THE EARTH LIKE A PACK OF WOLVES, CAN I?" she said. "LET ME TELL YOU A LITTLE SECRET."

And so it was that Granny Gaia told us how we could travel from one end of the universe to the other quicker than the blink of an eye. It's simple. I wish I could tell you how it works. But I can't reveal the secrets of the gods. If I did, mortals everywhere would be clogging up the skies, astro-traveling nonstop all over the globe. All I can say is that it does not involve spinning on one foot and chanting.

In any case, *ZIP!* Zeus and I found ourselves standing on top of Mount Olympus.

We quickly headed to the stables, where we were happy to see that Zeus's steeds had galloped safely back home. Then we went to Zeus's palace. I got cleaned up, and Zeus disappeared for a while. I hoped he was in the kitchen, letting the Cooking Nymphs know that fighting Typhon had given us a monstrous appetite.

In a while Zeus showed up and started banging his gong to summon everyone to a meeting in the Great Hall. All the other Olympians came running. We hadn't seen each other since most of them had changed into animals and fled to Egypt, so there was a certain amount of hugging and slapping of backs.

After a while, Zeus's kids went off, and Zeus, Hera, Po, Hestia, Demeter, and I took seats at the long table.

"Listen to me!" Zeus said to start the meeting. He began by telling everyone how we'd battled Typhon and trapped him under Mount Etna. The old myth-o-maniac took a lot more credit than he deserved, of course, but as he talked, the Kitchen Nymphs showed up bearing trays of ambrosia chips and ambrosia salsa and ice-cold mugs of foamy Nectar-Lite beer, and I stopped listening. I only tuned in again when Zeus said, "Granny Gaia says we must choose one of the six of us to be the Ruler of the Universe."

I brushed the crumbs from my robe. I tried to look modest yet noble. Humble yet worthy.

I felt sure that Zeus was going to announce to everyone that I, Hades, should rule the universe. After all, hadn't I just risked my neck to save rag-doll Zeus from Typhon and Echidna's cave? Hadn't I hurled the T-bolts that pinned Typhon under the mountain? And I'd medaled in the long jump, fulfilling the prophecy that one of us would become mightier than Dad. In every way, I deserved the top spot.

"Voting won't work," said Hera.

"That's true," said Zeus.

"Whoever grows the best garden can rule!" said Demeter.

"But we have to choose now," Zeus said. "We can't wait until harvest."

"Pick me," said Po. "I'll be top god, no drosis."

"No volunteering," said Zeus.

"Then what do you suggest, Zeus?" asked Hestia.

A crafty look came over Zeus's face.

Chapter XVII

Have a Hot Time, Hades!

It hit me then. Zeus had no intention of telling the others that I should be in charge. I had to speak up for myself! But as I opened my mouth, Zeus slapped a deck of cards onto the table.

"We'll play for it," he said. "Poker. The winner will be Ruler of the Universe. Second place will have charge of the seas. Third, fourth, fifth, and sixth places can pick whatever they want to rule on earth." He began shuffling. "I'll deal. Jokers are wild."

Zeus dealt. When I picked up my cards, I couldn't believe it. Not a single face card! Nothing but a smattering of threes, fives, and eights. I looked around the table. Hestia and

Hera didn't look happy with their cards. Po and Demeter were scowling. Only Zeus eyed his cards with a satisfied smirk.

We anted up and started playing. The game didn't last long. When it came time to show our hands, the only one with any cards to speak of was — guess who?

Zeus spread out his hand. "Four aces!" he cried. "Yesss! I'm CEO, Ruler of the Universe!"

"I have four queens," said Hera. "I get the seas!"

"That is *so* not fair!" cried Po. "You don't have a clue about how to rule an ocean. Or a river. You don't even know how to swim."

Hera folded her arms across her chest. "I'll take lessons."

"Give me the seas, Hera!" Po begged. "Please! Pretty please with seaweed on top?"

"Yech," said Hera. "I hate seaweed."

"See?" cried Po. "I rest my case!"

"I have a full house," said Hestia, showing two jacks and three nines. "That makes me third. I want to be Goddess of the Hearth."

Hera narrowed her eyes. "What's a hearth?" she asked. "Is it better than the seas?"

"Much better," said Hestia. "A hearth is a fireplace. It's the center of every household in Greece." A dreamy look came into her eyes. "Just think of the burnt offerings and sacrifices I'll get every single night!"

"You take the seas, Po," said Hera.

"All right!" shouted Po.

"I'll be goddess of the Hearth," said Hera.

"But that was *my* idea!" cried Hestia.

"So? I have a better hand than you do," said Hera. "I want the hearth!"

"I have clovers!" said Demeter, showing a hand full of clubs. "I shall be goddess of all things that grow from the earth!"

"Wait," said Hera. "Agriculture. That's big. Maybe I want that."

Demeter burst into tears then, and everyone started yelling and shouting at once. Hestia dumped a goblet of nectar onto Hera's head. Enraged, Hera started hurling ambrosia salsa at everyone, and Po started chanting, "Food fight!

Food fight!" At that moment I was so sick of my brothers and sisters that my only wish was to get as far away from them as possible. And that's when it hit me. The perfect place for me to rule.

I stood up. I waited until the shouting died down.

"I have decided what realm I shall rule," I announced calmly.

"You can't have the seas!" said Po, and he, too, burst into tears.

"I don't want to rule the seas," I said. "I don't want to rule any part of the earth, either. I, Hades, shall rule the Underworld."

Everyone gasped.

"The Underworld?" Zeus's mouth dropped open in surprise. Obviously, he'd been afraid that I'd challenge him for Ruler of the Universe. Then he pulled himself together. "Wow, yeah, you do that, Hades. It's *perfect* for you!"

"It's settled then," I said. "I'm out of here."

"So long!" said Zeus. "Have a hot time, Hades!"

He was so eager that when he jumped up to

hug me goodbye, three more aces fell out of his sleeve.

"Zeus! You cheated!" cried Hera. "We're playing again! I'm dealing!"

I closed my eyes and did what Granny Gaia recommended for when a god wants to take a superfast trip from one place to another. But I went nowhere. And that's how I discovered that the Underworld is the only place in the universe that even a god can't *ZIP!* to.

So I took off walking, and nine days later, I found myself standing beside the River Styx. I took a deep breath. Ah! The air smelled sweet to me.

"Taxi!" I called to Charon.

As I waited for Charon to pole over, it occurred to me that living in the Underworld would be a little bit like living down in Dad's big, dark belly. It would feel like my first home. And I'd have my weird uncles, the Cyclopes and the Hundred-Handed Ones, to keep me company. Campe, too. I smiled. I knew I'd be happy here.

Once again, I heard dogs barking. I turned,

and there was that little three-headed pup racing toward me.

"Hey, Cerberus!" I said, giving him the old triple pat.

A rolled-up piece of parchment was stuck under one of his collars. I pulled it out and opened it.

Here's what it said:

Dear Hades,

Cerberus has taken a mighty big liking to you and wants to be your dog. He'll make a first-rate guard dog of the Gates of the Underworld, don't you think? I know you'll take good care of my pup.

Best wishes,
Echidna

The little tri-headed pooch looked up at me with all six eyes. His whole rear end was happily wagging with his tail. I grinned. I had a kingdom. I had family waiting for me down here. And now I had my very own underdog. As Charon's river taxi nosed up to the shore, I felt like the luckiest god in the universe.

"Ahoy there!" called Charon. "One way or round-trip?"

"One way," I told him as Cerberus and I stepped on board. "I'll be staying down here for a while."

EPILOGUE

That's the real story of how Zeus became Ruler of the Universe. And of how I became King of the Underworld.

Not bad for a first book, was it?

After I finished it, I gave my ghost writers a couple weeks off. I spent that time thumbing through *The Big Fat Book of Greek Myths,* trying to decide which story to work on next. It was hard to decide. Zeus had mangled all the myths. There were so many choices!

One evening as I sat in the den reading, the door cracked open, and Hyperion stuck his head in.

"Hey, ol' buddy," the Titan said. "Anybody home?"

"Come in, come in," I said.

Hyperion had retired, handing over his duties as Ruler of Light to Apollo and Artemis. He lived in the Underworld now, where the sun never shone. But he still wore his old blue sunglasses on top of his head. He grabbed a nectar brewski from the fridge, then plopped down opposite me in the big Titan-sized chair I'd had made for him.

"Looks like I caught you with your nose in a book," Hyperion said.

"You did." I held up my copy of *The Big Fat Book of Greek Myths*. "Take a look, read it for yourself. You won't believe it."

Hyperion whistled. "You did *that*?"

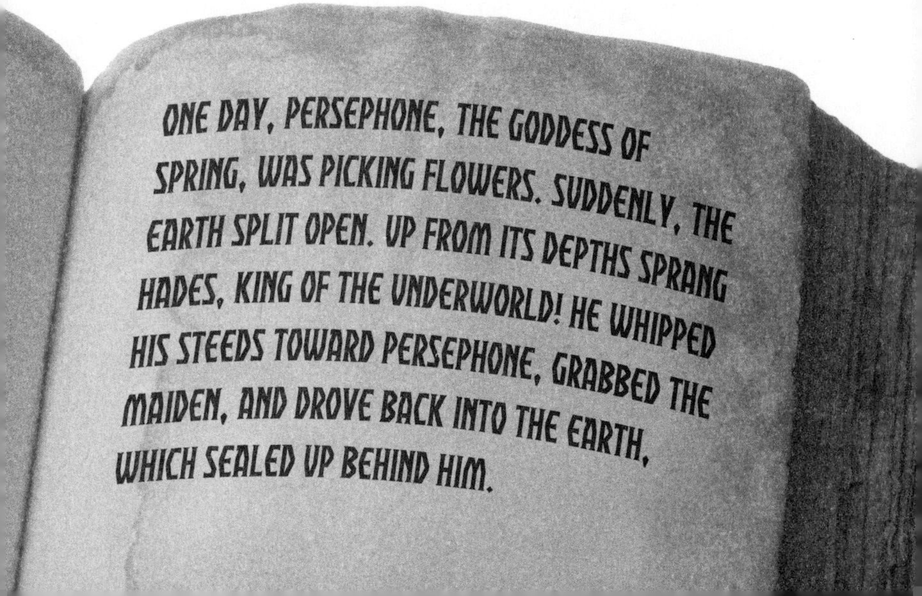

ONE DAY, PERSEPHONE, THE GODDESS OF SPRING, WAS PICKING FLOWERS. SUDDENLY, THE EARTH SPLIT OPEN. UP FROM ITS DEPTHS SPRANG HADES, KING OF THE UNDERWORLD! HE WHIPPED HIS STEEDS TOWARD PERSEPHONE, GRABBED THE MAIDEN, AND DROVE BACK INTO THE EARTH, WHICH SEALED UP BEHIND HIM.

"No!" I said. "It never happened! That myth-o-maniac Zeus made it up just to make me look bad!"

Hyperion shook his head. "That ol' boy can really tell a whopper," he said. "But what really happened, Hades? How *did* you and Persephone come to get hitched?"

"It's a crazy story," I said, remembering. "You know, I've been trying to figure out which myth to rewrite for my next book, and I think that might be the one."

I smiled. "I think I'll call it *Phone Home, Persephone!*"

"Boy, howdy!" said Hyperion. "I can't wait to read it."

King Hades's Quick-and-Easy Guide to the Myths

Let's face it, mortals. When you read the Greek myths, you sometimes run into long, unpronounceable names like *Aphrodite* and *Echidna* — names so long that just looking at them can give you a great big headache. Not only that, but sometimes you mortals call us by our Greek names and other times by our Roman names. It can get pretty confusing. But never fear! I'm here to set you straight with my quick-and-easy guide to who's who and what's what in the myths.

aegis (EE-jis) — a magical shield or breastplate that no weapon can pierce; chicken-hearted Zeus never leaves home without his.

ambrosia (am-BRO-zha) — food that we gods must eat to stay young and good-looking for eternity.

Aphrodite (af-ruh-DIE-tee) — the goddess of love and beauty. The Romans call her *Venus*.

Apollo (uh-POL-oh) — the god of light, music, and poety; Artemis's twin brother. The Romans couldn't come up with anything better, so they call him *Apollo*, too.

Artemis (AR-tuh-miss) — goddess of the hunt and the moon; Apollo's twin sister. The Romans call her *Diana*.

Athena (uh-THEE-nuh) — goddess of the three w's: wisdom, weaving, and war. The Romans call her *Minerva*.

Atlas (AT-liss) — the biggest of the giant Titans; known for holding the sky on his shoulders.

Campe (CAM-pee) — giantess and Underworld Jail Keep.

Cerberus (SIR-buh-rus) — my fine, III-headed pooch; guard dog of the Underworld.

Charon (CARE-un) — river-taxi driver; ferries the living and the dead across the River Styx.

Cronus (CROW-nus) — my dad, a truly sneaky Titan, who once ruled the universe. The Romans call him *Saturn*.

Cyclops (SIGH-klops) — any of three one-eyed giants. Lightninger, Shiner, and Thunderer, children of Gaia and Uranus, and uncles to us gods, are three *Cyclopes* (SIGH-klo-peez).

Demeter (duh-MEE-ter) — my sister, goddess of agriculture and total gardening nut. The Romans call her *Ceres*.

Dionysus (die-uh-NIE-sus) — god of wine and good-time party guy. The Romans call him *Bacchus*.

drosis (DRO-sis) — short for *theoexidrosis* (thee-oh-ex-ih-DRO-sis); old Greek speak for "violent god sweat."

Echidna (eh-KID-nuh) — half lovely young woman and half spotted serpent; mate to Typhon; mom to a strange brood of monsters, including my own underdog, Cerberus.

Gaia (GUY-uh) — Mother Earth; married to Uranus, Father Sky; mom to the Titans, Cyclopes, Hundred-Handed Ones, Typhon, and other giant monsters, and granny to us Olympian gods.

Hades (HEY-deez) — Ruler of the Underworld, Lord of the Dead, King Hades, that's me. I'm also god of wealth, owner of all the gold, silver, and precious jewels in the earth. The Romans call me *Pluto*.

Hera (HERE-uh) — my sister, Queen of the Olympians, goddess of marriage. The Romans call her *Juno*. I call her "The Boss."

Hermes (HER-meez) — god of shepherds, travelers, inventors, merchants, business executives, gamblers, and thieves; messenger of the gods; escorts the ghosts of dead mortals to the Underworld. Romans call him *Mercury*.

Hestia (HESS-tee-uh) — my sister, goddess of the hearth; the Romans call her *Vesta*.

Hundred-Handed Ones (HUHN-druhd HAN-did WUNZ) — three oddball brothers (Fingers, Highfive, and Lefty), who each have fifty heads and one hundred hands; brothers of the Cyclopes and Titans.

Hyperion (hi-PEER-ee-un) — a way-cool Titan dude, once in charge of the sun and all the universe. Now retired, he owns a cattle ranch in the Underworld.

ichor (EYE-ker) — god blood

immortal (i-MOR-tuhl) — a being, such as a god or a monster, who will never die, like me.

mortal (MOR-tuhl) — a being that will die. I hate to break it to you, but *you* are a mortal.

Mount Etna (ET-nuh) — the highest active volcano in Europe, located in Sicily; beneath it lurks the fire-breathing monster, Typhon.

Mount Olympus (oh-LIM-pess) — highest mountain in Greece; its peak is home to all major gods, except for my brother Po and me.

nectar (NECK-ter) — what we gods like to drink; has properties that invigorate us and make us look good and feel godly.

Pan (PAN) — god of woods, fields, and mountains; has goat's horns, ears, legs, tail, and a goatee. His earsplitting yell can create a wild fear known as "panic."

Poseidon (po-SIGH-den) — my bro Po; god of the seas, rivers, lakes, and earthquakes; claims to have invented horses as well as the doggie paddle. The Romans call him *Neptune*.

Rhea (REE-uh) — Titaness, wife of Cronus; mom to Po, Hestia, Demeter, Hera, Zeus, and me, Hades.

Roman numerals (ROH-muhn NOO-mur-uhlz) — what the ancients used instead of counting on their fingers. Makes you glad you live in the age of Arabic numerals and calculators, doesn't it?

I	1	XI	11	XXX	30
II	2	XII	12	XL	40
III	3	XIII	13	L	50
IV	4	XIV	14	LX	60
V	5	XV	15	LXX	70
VI	6	XVI	16	LXXX	80
VII	7	XVII	17	XC	90
VIII	8	XVIII	18	C	100
IX	9	XIX	19	D	500
X	10	XX	20	M	1000

Tartarus (TAR-tar-us) — the deepest pit in the Underworld and home of the Punishment Fields, where burning flames and red-hot lava eternally torment the ghosts of the wicked.

Themis (THAY-miss) — a Titaness, also called Justice, even when she's being unjust to us Olympian gods.

trident (TRY-dent) — a long-handled, three-pronged weapon made by the Cyclopes for Poseidon.

Typhon (TAHY-fon) — an enormous, donkey-headed, fire-breathing monster with serpent fingers; now spends all of his time in Sicily.

Underworld (UHN-dur-wurld) — my very own kingdom, where the ghosts of dead mortals come to spend eternity.

Uranus (YOOR-uh-ness) — my grandpa, also known as Sky Daddy, first Ruler of the Universe; Gaia's husband, and father to the Titans, the Cyclopes, and the Hundred-Handed Ones.

Zeus (ZOOSE) — rhymes with goose, which pretty much says it all; last, and definitely least, my little brother, a major myth-o-maniac and a cheater, who managed to set himself up as Ruler of the Universe. The Romans call him *Jupiter*.

AN EXCERPT FROM

THE BIG FAT BOOK OF GREEK MYTHS

At first, there was only darkness. Then Mother Earth and Father Sky appeared. They had twelve giant Titan children. The youngest, Cronus, became the father of the greatest god of all time, the brave and mighty Zeus.

Cronus was married to Rhea, another Titan. Their children, Demeter, Hera, Hades, Hestia, Poseidon, and the almighty Zeus, became the first Olympians. After being told that his son would overthrow him, Cronus swallowed his children as they were born to prevent the prophecy from coming true.

Rhea saved the great and powerful Zeus by tricking Cronus into swallowing a stone. Rhea secretly gave birth to Zeus on the island of Crete. Zeus was kept hidden in a cave on Mount Ida and grew up there until he could return to save his siblings.

Zeus gave Cronus a potion that made him throw up the children he'd swallowed. They were so grateful that they asked Zeus to be the leader of the Olympians. Cronus was furious. A war broke out between the Titans and the Olympians called the Titanomachy, or War of the Titans.

The battle raged for ten years. Zeus bravely freed the Cyclopes and the Hecatoncheires, hundred-handed giants, from Tartarus. In return for their freedom, they joined the Olympians' side. The Cyclopes gave Zeus the power over thunder and lightning. They also gave Poseidon a trident and Hades the cap of invisibility.

With these tools, Zeus was able to defeat Cronus and the rest of the Titans. He imprisoned the Titans in Tartarus, a prison in the deepest part of the Underworld. Atlas, one of the Titans that fought against mighty Zeus, was punished by having to hold up the sky.

After the battle, Zeus generously shared the world with his brothers by drawing lots. Zeus, king of the gods, got the sky and air; Poseidon got the waters; Hades got the Underworld.

KATE MCMULLAN is the author of the chapter book series Dragon Slayers' Academy, as well as easy readers featuring Fluffy, the Classroom Guinea Pig. She and her illustrator husband, Jim McMullan, have created several award-winning picture books, including *I STINK!*, *I'M DIRTY!*, and *I'M BIG!* Her latest work is *SCHOOL! Adventures at Harvey N. Trouble Elementary* in collaboration with the famed *New Yorker* cartoonist George Booth. Kate and Jim live in Sag Harbor, NY, with two bulldogs and a mews named George.

GLOSSARY

chariot (CHA-ree-uht) — a small vehicle pulled by a horse, used in ancient times for battle or races

commute (kuh-MYOOT) — to travel back and forth regularly between two places

dominion (duh-MIN-yuhn) — power to rule over something

eternal (i-TUR-nuhl) — lasting forever

laurel (LOR-uhl) — an evergreen bush or tree with smooth, shiny leaves

modest (MOD-ist) — not boastful about abilities, possessions, or achievements

prophecy (PROF-uh-see) — a prediction

realm (RELM) — a kingdom

reunion (ree-YOON-yuhn) — a meeting between people who haven't seen each other in a long time

spawn (SPAWN) — offspring or children

territory (TER-uh-tor-ee) — an area of land

tunic (TOO-nik) — a loose, sleeveless garment

I. All of the Olympic gods played different sports in the very first Olympic Games. Discuss what sport you would you have played if you'd been in the games.

II. Talk about other Greek myths that you know. Do you know any myths from other cultures? Talk about how they are similar or different from other myths.

III. Who is your favorite character in this story? Talk about why you chose that character. (Don't worry, I won't be offended if you don't pick me.)

I. After the Olympic Games, my brothers and sisters and I divided up the universe. Zeus, of course, chose the biggest part. If you got to be in charge of something, what would it be? Write about it.

II. My big brother Zeus and I usually have totally different versions of how the myths actually happened. Try writing chapter XV from Zeus's perspective. How do you think he saw things?

III. I come from a BIG family. Write about your family.

MYTH-O-MANIA

MYTH-O-MANIA
HAVE A HOT TIME,
HADES!
KATE McMULLAN

I

MYTH-O-MANIA
PHONE HOME,
PERSEPHONE!
KATE McMULLAN

II

MYTH-O-MANIA
STOP THAT BULL,
THESEUS!
KATE McMULLAN

V

MYTH-O-MANIA
KEEP A LID ON IT,
PANDORA!
DO NOT OPEN
KATE McMULLAN

VI

READ THE WHOLE SERIES AND LEARN THE REAL STORIES!

III

IV

VII

VIII

Casey Westmoreland Was A Woman Who, Without Very Much Effort, Could Bring Out Strong Desires In Any Man.

And to make matters worse, she was Corey's daughter and Durango's cousin. That meant she was doubly off-limits.

"Regardless of what she thinks, I did the right thing," McKinnon muttered, trying to place his concentration back on grooming his horse, and not how Casey had looked when she walked out of the barn. All he wanted from a woman was a short, hot, satisfying affair with no ties. Casey Westmoreland had the words *home, hearth* and *motherhood* all but stamped on her forehead. And that was the type of woman he avoided at all cost.

He refused to let any female become an emotional threat to his well-being ever again.

Dear Reader,

When I first introduced the Westmoreland family, I decided to write about a family of five brothers, six male cousins with only one sister in the group—Delaney Westmoreland. Her story became the first one in the Westmoreland family series.

But after writing about all those sexy Westmoreland men, I got the urge to write about another female Westmoreland. That's when I decided to introduce Uncle Corey's triplets, Clint, Cole and *Casey*. So now I will finally get to write about another female Westmoreland, Casey Westmoreland.

And from the moment I introduced McKinnon Quinn in *Stone Cold Surrender*, I knew he would become Casey's love interest. Their fathers were best friends, and I wanted Casey to eventually make Montana—where McKinnon lives—her home.

So now I am pleased to present Casey and McKinnon's story. Their road to finding love is complicated. They are both very stubborn individuals; he is tortured by a personal secret and she has a troubled past. But there are things between them that won't be ignored—sexual chemistry, physical attraction and a blazing hot love affair....

Enjoy,

Brenda Jackson

SEDUCTION, WESTMORELAND STYLE

BRENDA JACKSON

Silhouette™
Desire
Published by Silhouette Books
America's Publisher of Contemporary Romance

ISBN-13: 978-0-373-76778-6
ISBN 10: 0-373-76778-1

SEDUCTION, WESTMORELAND STYLE

This edition published by arrangement with Harlequin Books S.A.

Visit Silhouette Books at www.eHarlequin.com

Printed in U.S.A.

Books by Brenda Jackson

Silhouette Desire

Delaney's Desert Sheikh #1473
**A Little Dare* #1533
**Thorn's Challenge* #1552
Scandal between the Sheets #1573
**Stone Cold Surrender* #1601
**Riding the Storm* #1625
**Jared's Counterfeit Fiancée* #1654
Strictly Confidential Attraction #1677
Taking Care of Business #1705
**The Chase Is On* #1690
**The Durango Affair* #1727
**Ian's Ultimate Gamble* #1756
**Seduction, Westmoreland Style* #1778

*Westmoreland family titles

Kimani Romance

Solid Soul
Night Heat

BRENDA JACKSON

is a die "heart" romantic who married her childhood sweetheart and still proudly wears the "going steady" ring he gave her when she was fifteen. Because she's always believed in the power of love, Brenda's stories always have happy endings. In her real-life love story, Brenda and her husband live in Jacksonville, Florida, and have two sons.

A *USA TODAY* bestselling author, Brenda divides her time between family, writing and working in management at a major insurance company. You may write Brenda at P.O. Box 28267, Jacksonville, Florida 32226, by e-mail at WriterBJackson@aol.com or visit her Web site at www.brendajackson.net.

To Gerald Jackson, Sr., my husband and my hero.

To my readers who will be cruising with me
to Mexico in April with the Madaris/Westmoreland
Family Reunion Cruise. This one is for you.

To my heavenly Father, who gave me the gift to write.

There is surely a future hope for you,
and your hope will not be cut off.
—*Proverbs* 23:18

One

Casey Westmoreland entered the barn and paused, mesmerized by the sound of the warm, seductive masculine voice speaking gently to the huge black stallion being given a brush down. She was mesmerized even more by the man himself.

McKinnon Quinn.

In her opinion, he was as gorgeous as any one male had a right to be. Mixed with Blackfoot Indian and African-American Creole, she couldn't help but wish for more time to just stand there and admire what she saw.

Tall and ruggedly built with thick wavy black hair that fell to his shoulder blades, his blue shirt swathed a massive chest, and the well-worn jeans that covered a well-structured butt almost took her breath away when he leaned over to replace the brush with a comb. She didn't need for him to turn around to know what his features looked like. They were ingrained deep in her brain. He had an angular face with eyes as dark as a raven's wing, high cheekbones, medium-brown skin that almost appeared golden, a straight nose, stubborn jaw and full lips. She took a trembling breath and felt the warmth of a blush stain her cheeks just thinking about those lips and her secret fantasy of having her way with them.

Another thing she knew about McKinnon Quinn was, that at thirty-four, he was considered by many—especially now that his best friend and her cousin, Durango Westmoreland, had recently gotten married—to be the most eligible bachelor in Bozeman, Montana and its surrounding areas. She'd also heard his bachelor status was something he valued with no plans to relinquish.

It was her opinion from their first meeting a little over two years ago that there was a quiet and innately controlled nature about him. Although he shared a rather close relationship with her cousins, there was still something about him that gave the impression that not too many others got close to him. He picked those he wanted to be associated with and any others he kept at a distance. Whenever she was around him she always felt he was watching her, and she could always feel his gaze on her like it was some sort of a physical caress.

"Are you going to state your business or just stand there?"

His words, spoken in a deep, cutting voice, caught her off guard and made her wonder if he had eyes in the back of his head. She was certain she hadn't made a sound, yet he had sensed her presence anyway.

"I know how important grooming time is and didn't want to intrude," Casey heard herself saying after a moment, deciding to finally speak up.

It was only then that he turned around and she forced herself to continue breathing—especially when a surprised glint shone in the dark eyes that connected with hers. "Casey Westmoreland. Durango mentioned you were here visiting your dad," he said in a voice as intense as the eyes looking at her.

Your dad. That term in itself was something Casey was still getting used to since discovering she had a father who was very much alive after being told he had died before she was born.

"I'm not visiting, exactly. I've decided to move to Bozeman permanently," she said, wishing he wasn't staring at her so intently.

She watched as he hooked his thumbs in the pockets of his jeans—a stance that immediately placed emphasis to his entire muscular physique. Surprise once again lit his eyes. "You're moving to Bozeman? Permanently?"

"Yes."

"Why?"

He all but snapped the question and she wondered why he would care one way or the other. "Corey…I mean, my dad, is hoping that moving to Bozeman will give us a chance to get to know each other better." Even after two and a half years it was still somewhat difficult to call Corey Westmoreland "Dad" as her two brothers had begun doing.

McKinnon nodded and she noted that the eyes studying her were more intense than before. He had a close connection to her father since Corey was the best friend of McKinnon's father. In fact, to her way of thinking, it was a deeper connection than the one she herself shared with Corey if for no other reason than because McKinnon had known her father a lot longer than she had.

"That's what Corey thinks, but is that what you think as well?" he asked, his voice breaking into her thoughts.

What I really think is that it would help matters tremendously if you'd stop looking at me like that, she wanted to say suddenly feeling like she was under a microscope. Whether he intended it or not, his gaze was provocatively sensual and was sending a heated rush all through her. "I think it wouldn't hurt. I've lived in Beaumont, Texas all my life and when the lease expired on the building holding my clothing store—and I wasn't given the option of renewing it—I considered the possibility of relocating elsewhere. I've fallen in love with Montana the few times I've been here and agree that moving here will give me the chance to develop a relationship with Corey."

"I see."

Casey doubted that he did. Not even her brothers fully understood the turmoil existing within her after finding out the truth. From the time she was a little girl her mother had painted this fairy-tale image of the man who'd fathered her and her brothers—the man who'd supposedly died in a rodeo accident while performing, leaving her mother pregnant with triplets.

Carolyn Roberts Westmoreland had made it seem as if she and Corey Westmoreland had shared the perfect love, the perfect marriage and had been so dedicated to each other that she'd found it hard to go on when he'd died. According to her mother, the only thing that had kept her going was the fact that Corey had left her with not *one,* not *two,* but *three* babies growing inside her womb. Triplets who would grow up smothered in their mother's love and their father's loving memory.

It hurt to know her mother had weaved a bunch of lies.

Corey Westmoreland had never married Carolyn Roberts. Nor had he known she was pregnant with triplets. Legally, her mother had never been a Westmoreland. And to make matters worse, Corey had never loved her mother. For years he had been in love with Abby, a woman he had met years before meeting Casey's mom, and Abby was the woman he'd been reunited with and eventually married just a couple of years ago.

"And there's another reason I wanted to move here," she decided to add, getting to the reason for paying McKinnon a visit. "I felt a career change would do me good, and by moving I can do something I've always loved doing."

"Which is?"

"Working with horses—which is why I'm here. I understand you're looking for a horse trainer and I want to apply for the job."

Casey tried ignoring the sensations that flooded her insides when McKinnon's gaze moved up and down her five-foot-three petite physique. His gaze glittered when it returned to her face, as if he was amused by something. "You're kidding, right?"

She lifted a brow. "No, I'm not kidding," she said, crossing the floor to where he stood. "I'm dead serious."

She watched as his jaw tightened and his eyes narrowed and immediately resented herself for thinking he looked infuriatingly sexy.

"There's no way I can hire you as a horse trainer," he said in a rough voice.

"Why not?" she asked with as much calmness as she could muster. "I think if you were to take a look at my résumé, you'd be impressed with my qualifications." She offered the folder she was holding in her hand to him.

He glanced at the folder but made no attempt to take it from her. "Maybe I will and maybe I won't, but it doesn't matter," he said, giving her an intimidating stare. "I'm not hiring you."

His words, spoken so calmly, so matter-of-factly, sent anger coursing through her veins, but she was determined to keep her cool. "Is there a reason?" she asked, still gripping the folder in her hand, although she no longer offered it to him since he'd made it blatantly clear he wasn't interested.

After several tense moments he said, "There're a number of reasons but I don't have time to go into them."

Casey steeled herself against the anger that swept through her body but it was no use. His words had assaulted her sensibilities. "Now wait just a minute," she said, her eyes clashing with his.

He crossed his arms over his chest and to Casey, his height suddenly seem taller than six-three. "Don't have time to wait either," he said smugly, glaring down at her. "This is a working ranch and I have too much to do. If you're interested in a job then I suggest you look someplace else."

Casey, known to be stubborn by nature, refused to back down. McKinnon had effectively pushed her anger to the boiling point. And when she saw he had gone back to grooming the horse, as if totally dismissing her, her anger escalated that much more.

"Why?" she asked, struggling to speak over the rage that had worked its way up to her throat. "I think you owe me an explanation as to why you won't consider hiring me." For a long while McKinnon remained stubbornly silent and Casey waited furiously, patiently, for him to respond, refusing to move an inch until he did.

Finally, after several tense moments, McKinnon sighed deeply and turned back to face her, feeling that he didn't owe her anything. He saw the angry lines curving her lips and thought that from the first time he'd seen her, he had found her mouth as tempting as the shiny red apple Eve had offered to Adam. And he bet her lips were just as delicious and probably even more sinful.

For crying out loud, couldn't she feel the sexual chemistry flowing between them even amidst all that anger radiating from her? And from him? The moment he had turned around and seen Casey standing in the middle of the barn, he'd felt a zap of emotions shoot to every part of his body as well as his testosterone spike up a few notches. The woman was so striking that even the bright sunlight, which rarely showed its face in these parts, didn't have a thing on her.

She exuded an air of sexiness without much effort and although she was frowning quite nicely now, the few occasions he had seen her smile, her mouth had a way of curving enticingly that made you want to kiss the smile right off her lips. Even now her angry pout was a total turn on.

Then there were her physical attributes. Dark brown hair that was cut in a short and sassy style complimented her mahogany-colored features, eyes the color of the darkest chocolate that could probably make you melt if you gazed into them long enough, and a petite frame that was clad in a pair of jeans that appeared made just for her body.

He had just seen her last month at her cousin Delaney's surprise birthday party. He was of the opinion that each and every time he saw her she just kept getting prettier and prettier, and his attraction to her that more extreme. She even had the ability to smell good while standing in a barn filled with a bunch of livestock. Whatever perfume she was wearing was doing a number on him and besides that, although he couldn't see her legs right now, he had them plastered to his memory. They were long, shapely and—"

"Well, McKinnon?"

He met her gaze as he tossed the brush in a pail and shoved his hands in the back pockets of his jeans. "Okay, I'll give you a reason. This is a horse ranch and I'm looking for someone who can train horses and not ponies. Corey would never forgive me if something were to happen to you."

He inwardly shuddered as if imagining such a thing, then added, "For Pete's sake, you're no bigger than a mite. The horse that needs to be trained is meaner than hell and I need to get him ready for the races in six weeks. As far as I'm concerned, you're not the person for the job. Prince Charming is too much animal for you to handle."

Anger flared in Casey's eyes and she drew herself up to her full five-foot-three. "And you're making that decision without giving me a chance to show you what I can do?"

"Yes, evidently I am," he drawled.

"Then you're nothing but a male chauvinistic—"

"Think whatever you like, but the bottom line is that I'm not hiring you. I'm sure there're other jobs in Bozeman that might interest you. And since you're familiar with running a clothing store, you might want to check in town to see if there're any employment opportunities available in that area."

Casey stared at him as she struggled to control the fury that threatened to suffocate her. He was right. She was wasting her time here. "In that case, there's nothing left for me to say," she said tightly, staring at his impassive features.

"No, there really isn't." And to prove his point he picked

up the brush and began grooming the horse again, totally dismissing her once more.

Without saying anything else, an angry Casey strode toward the exit of the barn.

McKinnon watched Casey leave and released a deep sigh of frustration.

He knew she was pretty pissed with him but there was no way he would hire her to work on his ranch. Most Arabians by nature were mild-mannered and people-oriented, but the horse sent here for training lacked a friendly disposition by leaps and bounds. The only explanation McKinnon could come up with was that someone had treated the horse badly in the past, and it would take a skilled trainer to turn things around. He knew Casey had been born and raised in Texas, so chances were strong she was used to horses. But still, if things worked out and he expanded his business to train more horses, she would be dealing with studs that were known to be mean-spirited. He refused to be responsible if something were to happen to her.

Besides that, there was another reason he wouldn't hire Casey. He had decided six years ago after Lynette Franklin had walked out on him that a woman had no place on his ranch.

Just thinking of Lynette sent resentment through all parts of his body. But then to be fair, he couldn't rightly fault her for wanting something he couldn't give her. And when she had left, she had made him realize that a serious relationship with any female was something he would not involve himself in again.

His thoughts grudgingly shifted back to Casey. His attraction to her was more lethal than what he'd had for

Lynette. Casey was a woman who, without very much effort, could bring out strong desires in any man. And to make matters worse, she was Corey's daughter and Durango's cousin. That meant she was definitely off-limits.

"Regardless of what she thinks, I did the right thing," he muttered, trying to place his concentration back on grooming Thunder, and not on how Casey's curvy backside swayed when she walked out of the barn. All he wanted from a woman was a short, hot, satisfying affair with no ties. Casey Westmoreland had the words *home, hearth* and *motherhood* all but stamped on her forehead. And that was the type of woman he avoided at all cost.

He refused to let any female become an emotional threat to his well-being ever again.

The moment the sunshine hit Casey's face she inhaled, trying to get her teenager under control. She doubted there were any words to describe how she felt toward McKinnon Quinn at that moment. The man was impossible!

She glanced around and grudgingly admitted his sprawling ranch was simply beautiful. The house wasn't as huge as her father's but she thought it had a lot of class and exuded an appeal as strong as the man who owned it. He had adroitly erected the structure on a beautiful piece of land that had a picturesque view of the mountains in the background.

It was a sunny day in early May and the weather reminded her of a day in Texas. McKinnon's men were busy at work and as she walked toward her car to leave, she noted several beautiful horses were being led into a corral. She turned suddenly when one of the men's shouting caught her attention in time to see this huge monstrosity of a horse break free from the man's hold and start charging after him.

When the horse reared up on hind legs with full intent to stomp the man to death, she held her breath and watched as the man made a smart move and fell to the ground, immediately rolling out of harm's way. It seemed the animal was in rare form, and when several of the men ran forward to grab hold of his reins, he tried attacking them and sent them running for cover. One of them wasn't quick enough and the horse took off, charging after him.

Without any thought of what she was doing or that she was putting her life in danger, Casey raced toward the charging animal trying to get his attention. She frantically waved her hands in the air and whistled. Pretty soon the animal turned huge dark, flaming eyes in her direction and with a tilt of its head, a flare of its nostrils and a turn of its body, she then became his target. She felt the hairs on the back of her neck rise, putting her on full alert, however, instead of running for cover, she stood still.

McKinnon rushed out of the barn at that very moment. He had heard all the commotion and when he saw Prince Charming turned toward Casey, and she just standing there as if frozen in place, his heart slammed in his chest.

"Casey, run, dammit!"

When he saw she didn't move, he decided to run toward her, knowing that with Prince Charming's speed there was no way he was going to reach her in time, but he would die trying. Suddenly a rifle was shoved into his hands by one of his men and he knew he had to destroy the animal before it took Casey's life. At that moment it didn't matter one iota that the animal he was about to take down had cost Sheikh Jamal Ari

Yasir over a million dollars. McKinnon's only concern was doing whatever it took to protect Casey Westmoreland.

He raised the gun to take aim and fire when one of his men shouted, "Wait! Take a look at that."

McKinnon blinked, amazed at what he was seeing. Fear hadn't frozen Casey in place—she had been talking to the blasted animal and somehow she had gotten through to it. Prince Charming had come to a screeching halt within ten feet of Casey and was now trotting over to her with his tail wagging like they were the best of friends. She was holding her hand out to him and the horse cautiously came up to her and began nuzzling her hand.

McKinnon lowered the rifle. He knew that, like him, everyone was holding their breaths watching, waiting, and staring in pure astonishment. Then, once she felt confident that she had gained the animal's trust, Casey grabbed hold of the reins and begin walking him slowly back toward a hitching post.

"Well, I'll be. If I wasn't seeing it with my own eyes, I wouldn't believe it," McKinnon heard one of his men whisper behind him.

"Take a look at that," another man said as if awe struck. "That woman has Prince Charming practically eating out of her hands instead of him eating her hands off. Who the hell is she?"

McKinnon handed the rifle back to his foreman, Norris Lane, and shook his head. He'd heard the men's stunned comments. He would not have believed it without seeing it either. "That's Corey Westmoreland's daughter," he said gruffly.

"Corey's daughter?"

"Yeah," McKinnon said as he watched Casey tie the

animal to the hitching post and then lean over to whisper something in his ear before turning to walk away.

Whatever conversation, were taking place between his men was lost on McKinnon as he began walking toward Casey. His heart was still pounding wildly in his chest since he wasn't even close to recovering from the impact of seeing the horse charge toward her. Damn! He felt as if he'd lost a good ten years off his life.

When they reached each other, instead of stopping Casey glanced at him with unconcealed irritation glaring in her eyes and walked right past.

McKinnon stopped and turned in time to see her walk over to her car, open the door and get in. He cursed silently as he watched a furious Casey Westmoreland drive away.

Two

Early the next morning, McKinnon was sitting at his kitchen table drinking a cup of coffee before the start of his work day when Norris walked in. He took one look at his foreman's expression and knew that whatever news he came to deliver, McKinnon wasn't going to like it.

"Good morning, Norris."

"Morning, McKinnon. Beckman's quit. He hauled ass sometime during the night and left a note on his bunk stating yesterday was the last straw. I guess that little episode with Prince Charming made him rethink staying on until you found a replacement."

McKinnon cursed under his breath as he sat his coffee cup down. This wasn't news he wanted to hear. Gale Beckman had come highly recommended from an outfit in Wyoming. He had taken the man on, convinced he could do the job, and offered him one hell of a salary to train

Prince Charming, one of Sheikh Yasir's prized possessions. Evidently Beckman had felt he'd met his match with the horse. Granted, Prince Charming had been in rare form yesterday, but still, in the world of horse-breeding you couldn't expect every horse to be meek and biddable. Far from it. Most were unfriendly and aggressive at best, hot-tempered and volatile at worse.

"Where are we going to find another horse trainer this late in the game?"

Norris' question reeled McKinnon's thoughts back in. He and his best friend Durango Westmoreland had started their horse breeding business a few years ago because of their love for the animals. McKinnon handled the day-to-day running of the operation while Durango, who was still employed as a park ranger for Yellowstone, managed the books.

When Sheikh Jamal Ari Yasir, a prince from the Middle East who was married to Durango's cousin Delaney, had approached them a couple of months ago about taking on the training of Prince Charming to ready him for the races this fall, they had readily accepted, not foreseeing any problems and thinking it would be a way to expand their business from horse breeding into horse training as well.

Successfully getting Prince Charming trained was their first major test in that particular area, and their success with that endeavor would assure the sheikh sent more business their way and provided good recommendations to his friends and business associates. But the while situation looked bleak since they really hadn't made any real progress and valuable time was being wasted.

McKinnon leaned back in his chair. "I guess the first thing I need to do is place a call to my contacts again," he said finally answering, although he was quick to think that his contacts' reliability was on shaky ground since they had been the reason he'd hired Beckman in the first place.

"What about Corey Westmoreland's daughter?"

McKinnon stiffened, pushed away from the table and stood. "What about her?"

"Well, you saw how she handled Prince Charming yesterday. She had that blasted animal eating out of her hands, literally. Do you think she might be interested in the job?"

McKinnon decided now was not the time to mention to Norris that Casey *had* been interested in the job—in fact, that had been her reason for showing up yesterday. Instead he said, "Doesn't matter if she would be. You know my policy about a woman working on this ranch."

Norris stared at him for a long moment before shaking his head and saying, "It's been over four years now, McKinnon. How long will it take you to get what Lynette did out of your mind…and heart?"

McKinnon sucked in a deep breath before saying, "I've done both."

Norris was one of the few who knew the full story about Lynette. He had been with McKinnon the night they'd arrive back at the ranch from rounding up wild horses in the north prairie to find that Lynette had packed up and left, leaving a scribbled note as to the reason why.

McKinnon's brisque words should have warned the sixty-year-old Norris that this was a touchy subject—one McKinnon had no desire to engage in; but Norris, who'd known McKinnon since the day he was born, paid no mind. "Then act like it, son. Act like you've put it behind you."

McKinnon cursed under his breath. "You actually expect me to ask Corey Westmoreland's daughter to come work for me and live on his ranch? You saw her yesterday.

She's no bigger than a mite. Granted she handled Prince Charming okay, but what about the others to come after that? Some twice as mean. Besides, I need a trainer that I can invest in long-term."

"I heard she's moving to town to be close to her father. To me that speaks of long term."

McKinnon's gaze narrowed. Evidently Norris had asked questions of the right people after Casey's impressive performance yesterday. Abruptly, McKinnon walked over to the window and looked out. He had barely slept last night for remembering the sight of Casey standing frozen in place while that blasted animal charged toward her. He hadn't felt so helpless before in his entire life. The thought of what that horse could have done to her sent chills through his body even now.

"The decision is yours, of course, but I think it will be to your advantage, considering everything, to hire her," Norris said behind him. "The sheikh expects that blasted horse trained and ready to race in less than two months. And the way I see it, Corey's daughter is our best bet."

McKinnon turned and shot a hard glare at Norris. "There has to be another way," he said, his features severe and unyielding.

""Then I hope you find it," Norris replied before moving to walk out the door.

He hadn't found another way.

And that was the reason McKinnon found himself arriving by horseback on Corey's Mountain later that same day. Seeing the spacious and sprawling ranch house, set among a stand of pine trees and beneath the beauty of a Montana sky, had bittersweet memories flooding his mind.

He could recall the many summers he'd spent here as a young boy with Corey's nephews—all eleven of them. Just how Corey managed all of them was anyone's guess, but those summers had been some of the best of McKinnon's life. He'd been foot loose and fancy-free, and the only thing he'd worried about was staying away from the black berries he was allergic to.

These days things were different. He had a lot to worry about. He had both a ranch and a business to run, and now it seemed the woman he'd always intended to keep at a distance would be living on his land, within a stone's throw away…. If she accepted his job offer.

And that was the big question. After the way they'd clashed yesterday, would she even consider coming to work for him now? His contacts in the horse industry hadn't been any help and now it came down to eating crow and doing the one thing he hadn't wanted to do—offer Casey Westmoreland a job.

When he reached the ranch house he got off his horse and tied him to a post before glancing around, his gaze searching the wide stretch of land, scanning the fields and pastures. Corey's land. Corey's Mountain. McKinnon shook his head thinking it was rather sad that during those times he and Corey's eleven nephews were spending time on this mountain, somewhere in Texas Corey had three kids he'd known nothing about—a daughter and two sons. Triplets. Being the good man that he was, Corey was trying like hell to make up for lost time.

A sound coming from somewhere in back where the stables and corral were located caught McKinnon's ears, and before moving up the steps to the front door, he decided to check things out back. As soon as he rounded the corner a swift surge of intense desire flooded him. He recognized Casey sitting on the back of a horse, surrounded by a group of men—one he recognized as her father.

He stopped walking and stood there, leaned against the house and stared at her, remembering the first time he'd laid eyes on her. It had been here, on this very land, standing pretty close to this same spot, while attending her cousin and his good friend, Stone Westmoreland's wedding. It just so happened that Corey, who she had met for the first time that day, was also getting married.

It had been just minutes before the wedding was to begin and he had been talking with Durango and his brothers, Jared and Spencer. He had glanced around the exact moment a group of people had parted, giving him a spacious view of what he thought had to be the most beautiful woman he'd ever seen. He'd heard about Corey's triplets and had already met her two brothers, but that day had been the first time he had set his eyes on Casey Westmoreland.

Every male hormone within his body had gone on full alert and his libido hadn't been the same since. He had stood there, the conversations between him and the men long-forgotten as he watched her moved around the yard talking with her cousin Delaney. There had been such sensuality in her movement, such refined grace, that he found it hard to believe she was the same woman sitting on a horse now. But all it took was a glance of her face to know that she was one and the same. The same woman determined to stay etched inside his brain.

And then, as if she knew he was standing there staring at her, she glanced over in his direction and their gazes locked and held. He watched her stiffen, felt her anger and knew he had his work cut out for him. Chances were strong that after yesterday he was the last person she wanted to see.

But still he kept staring at her, liking the way the sun was shining on her hair, giving it a lustrous glow against the light blue blouse she was wearing. She had on jeans—that much he could see although his total view was hampered by the men standing around her.

As if wondering what had captured his daughter's attention, Corey glanced in his direction and smiled. He then said something to Casey and a brief moment later the older man was walking toward him. McKinnon shoved off from the wall and moved forward to meet the man he considered a second father. Corey and McKinnon's father had been best friends for years, long before McKinnon was born.

Towering over six-five with a muscular build, Corey Westmoreland was a giant of a man with a big heart, a love for the land and his family and friends.

"McKinnon," Corey Westmoreland said, smiling as he embraced him in a bear hug. "What brings you up here?"

"Casey," McKinnon said simply. He couldn't help noticing the older man's expression didn't show any surprise. "She came to see me yesterday about a job."

Corey chuckled. "Yes, she told me about that."

McKinnon could imagine. "I'm here to offer her the job if she still wants it."

Corey shrugged. "You're going to have to discuss that with her. I guess I don't have to tell you that you did a pretty good job of pissing her off."

McKinnon nodded. He'd always appreciated Corey's honesty, even now. "No, you don't have to tell me." He glanced over to the area where Casey had been earlier when he heard several loud shouts. He lifted a brow. "What's going on?"

"Casey's about to try her hand at riding Vicious Glance."

McKinnon jerked his head around and practically glared Corey in the face. "You can't let her ride that horse."

Corey shook his head grinning. "I'd like to see you try talking her out of it. She's been here enough times to know what a mean son a bitch that animal is, but she's determined to break him in."

"And you're letting her?" McKinnon had both outrage and astonishment on his face. Everyone who had visited Corey's Mountain knew that Vicious Glance—named for the look the mean-spirited animal would give anyone who came close—was a damn good stud horse, but when it came to having anyone sitting on his back, he wasn't having it. More than one of Corey's ranch hands had gotten injured trying to be the one to change that bit of history.

"I'm not *letting* her do anything, McKinnon. Casey's a grown woman who's past the age of being told what she can or cannot do," he said. "I did ask her nicely to back down but she feels Vicious Glance isn't too much horse for her to handle, so we're about to see if that's true. You might as well follow me and watch the show like the rest of us."

McKinnon sucked in a deep breath and for the first time wondered if Corey had lost his mind. This was the man's *daughter*—the same one who could end up breaking her damn neck if that horse threw her. But before he could open his mouth and say anything else, Corey reached out and touched his shoulder. "Calm down. She'll be fine."

McKinnon frowned wondering who Corey was trying to convince—especially after seeing the expression of worry that quickly crossed the older man's face. "I hope you're right," McKinnon said, pulling off his Stetson and wiping his forehead with the back of his hand. Already he was perspiring from worrying. Dammit, what was the woman trying to prove?

Without saying anything else, he placed the Stetson back on his head and walked with Corey over to where the other men were standing. Casey glanced at him, glared and looked way. Corey shook his head and somberly whispered to McKinnon, "Seems she's still pissed at you."

"Yep, seems that way doesn't it," McKinnon replied. But at that moment, how Casey felt about him was the least of his worries. Like the other men standing around, he watched, almost holding his breath, as she entered the shoot to get on a blind folded Vicious Glance's back. She swung her petite body into the saddle and he grabbed hold of the reins one of the ranch hands handed to her.

McKinnon's pulse leaped when she gave the man a nod and the action began when the blind fold was removed from the horse's eyes. Vicious Glance seemed to have gone stark raving mad, bucking around the corral, trying get rid of the unwanted occupant on his back. A few times McKinnon's breath got caught in his throat when it seemed Casey was a goner for sure, but she hung on and pretty soon he found himself hollering out words of encouragement to her like the other men.

She was given time to prove her point before several of the men raced over and quickly whisked her off the horse's back. Loud cheers went up and McKinnon couldn't help but smile. "Who in the hell taught her how to handle a horse like that?" he asked, both incredulously and relieved as he glanced over at Corey.

The older man grinned. "Ever heard of Sid Roberts?"

"What wannabe cowboy hasn't," McKinnon replied, thinking of the man who had grown up to be a legend, first as an African-American rodeo star and then as a horse trainer. "Why?"

"He was Casey's mother's brother; the man Carolyn went to live with in Texas, and who eventually helped her raise my kids. It's my understanding that when it came to horses, he basically passed everything he knew down to Casey. Clint and Cole had already dreamed about one day becoming Texas rangers, but I'm told that Casey wanted to follow in her uncle's footsteps and become a horse trainer."

McKinnon was listening to everything Corey was saying, though his gaze was glued to Casey. They had calmed Vicious Glance down and she was standing beside the animal whispering something in his ear, and as crazy as it seemed, it appeared the horse understood whatever it was she was saying. "So what happened?" he asked Corey. "Owning a dress store is a long way from being a horse trainer."

"Her mother talked her out of it, saying she needed to go to college and get a degree doing something safe and productive."

McKinnon nodded. "So she gave up her dream."

"Yeah, for a little while, but she's determined to get it back." Corey glanced up at McKinnon. "Just so you know, Cal Hooper dropped by last night and offered her a job over at his place working with his horses."

McKinnon frowned and looked at Corey. "Did she take it?"

"No, she told him she would think about it." Corey chuckled. "I think he kind of gave her the creeps."

And with good reason, McKinnon thought. Everybody around those parts knew that even in his late forties, Cal Hooper, a local rancher, still considered himself a ladies' man and had a reputation for playing fast and loose with women. If the rumors one heard were true, he was also the father of a number of illegitimate children around Bozeman. McKinnon's gaze shifted to Casey once again. She was walking toward them and he could tell from the pout on her lush mouth that she wasn't glad he was there. In fact, she looked downright annoyed.

"McKinnon," she acknowledged when she reached them.

"Casey. That was a good show of horsemanship," he said.

"Thank you." Although she'd said the words he could tell from her expression that she couldn't care less what he thought.

"I agree with McKinnon. You did a fantastic job out there, Casey."

The smile she gave her father was genuine. "Thanks, Corey. Vicious Glance will be fine now. He just needed to know that someone else, namely whoever is riding him, is always in control."

"Well, I need to talk to Jack about how we'll be handling him from now on. Excuse me for a moment," Corey said before walking off, leaving them alone.

A few brief moments after Corey left, McKinnon tilted his hat back and looked down at Casey. His eyes narrowed. Before offering her the job there was something he needed to get straight with her, here and now. "Don't you ever set foot on Quinn land and pull a stunt like you did yesterday. You had no way of knowing what that blasted horse was going to do. You could have been killed."

"But I'm very much alive, aren't I?" she said snippily,

deciding the last thing she needed was for this man to dictate what she could or could not do." "You're not my father, McKinnon."

"Thank God for that."

Casey drew in a deep, irritated breath. "I think we've said enough to each other, don't you think?" She moved to walk away.

"Aren't you curious as to why I'm here?" he asked.

She frowned up at him. "Not really. I assumed you came to see Corey."

He shoved his hands into his pockets. "I came to see you."

She placed her hands on her hips and narrowed her eyes. "And why would you come to see me?"

"To offer you that job you were interested in yesterday."

She glared at him. "That was yesterday. I have no desire to work for a male chauvinist tyrant."

McKinnon frowned. "A male chauvinist tyrant?"

"Yes, that about describes you to a tee. Now if you will excuse me, I—"

"The pay is good and you'll need to stay at the ranch, in the guesthouse."

Casey threw her head back and squared her shoulders. "Don't let me tell you where you can take the pay and guesthouse and shove it, McKinnon. Like I said, I'm no longer interested. Now if you'll excuse me, I have things to do."

He watched as she walked off, swaying her hips with each and every step she took. He couldn't help but admire her spunk, but he refused to let her have the upper hand. "Casey?" he said, calling after her.

She stopped walking and slowly turned around. "What?"

"Think about my offer and let me know within a week."

Her glare was priceless. "There's nothing to think about

it, McKinnon. The last thing I want is to work for you." She then turned back around and continued walking.

Her words irritated the hell out of him because deep down he didn't want her to come work for him either. But dammit, he needed her…rather he needed her skill with horses. And more than anything he had to remember there was a difference in the two.

Three

The nerve of the man, Casey thought as she slipped into the soapy water in the huge claw-foot bathtub. He was an American, so why didn't he understand English? How many times did she have to say she didn't want to work for him to make herself clear?

She settled back against the tub and closed her eyes. The man was simply infuriating and like she'd told him, he would be the last person she worked for. She would consider going to work for Cal Hooper first, even though that man made her skin crawl each and every time he looked at her. At least she could defend herself against the likes of the Cal Hoopers out there, thanks to all those self-defense classes her brothers had made her take over the years.

But when it came to McKinnon Quinn she was as defenseless as a fish out of water. There was just something outright, mind-blowingly hot about a tall man in a pair of tight jeans, especially when he had a nice-looking rear end. Add to that an honest-to-goodness handsome face and any woman in her right mind would be a goner. Holy cow, she was only human!

She eased down further in the water, wishing for the umpteenth time that she could get the man out of her mind. He had made her madder than a pan of hot fish grease yesterday with his how-great-thou-art attitude. But today he'd shown up offering her the job that he'd told her he wouldn't hire her for. Well, that was too friggin' bad. Like she told him, he could take the job and shove it for all she cared.

Deciding to rid her mind of McKinnon Quinn once and for all, she opened her eyes and glanced around. The room Abby had given her to use was simply beautiful. With all the silk draperies, cream-colored walls and extensive decorating, it was obvious the decor of the room had had a woman's touch, as had the rest of the house. Corey's ranch at one time may have been a man's domain, but now it was evident that a woman was in residence, and that woman was Abby.

Abby.

From the first time she found out about her, Casey had figured she wouldn't like the woman who held her father's heart to the point where he hadn't been able to love another woman—not even her own mother who had loved Corey Westmoreland until her dying day. But all it took was a few moments around Corey and Abby to know just how in love they were and probably always had been, even through his fifty-something years as a bachelor, and Abby's fifteen-year marriage to a man she didn't love.

Casey smiled. She had to admit that she had grown fond of the very proper Bostonian her father had married, who happened to be the mother of Madison, her cousin Stone's wife. Since finding out the truth about her father, Casey had come to realize that she'd had a slew of relatives—more Westmorelands, cousins from just about every walk of life—and they had been genuine in opening both their friendship and their hearts to her and her brothers.

She glanced at the clock. Abby would be serving dinner in half an hour and dinner time, Casey discovered, was a big ordeal for Abby since she had a way of making things somewhat formal. So instead of wearing jeans like she usually did, it was during the evening meal that she would put on a skirt and blouse or a dress.

She eased out of the tub to dry off and her thoughts shifted back to McKinnon. She hoped she'd seen the last of him for awhile. Although she wouldn't work for him, she was determined to work for somebody. She could only accept her father and Abby's hospitality for so long. Although she knew they wanted her to stay there with them, Casey only planned to live here for so long. She needed and wanted her own place.

She smiled thinking that in a way her father and Abby were still newlyweds—or at least they acted like they were. More than once she had almost walked up on them sharing a very heated kiss. A part of her was happy for what they shared, but then those times had been a blunt reminder of what she didn't have in her own life.

Although she had dated while living in Texas, most men hadn't wanted what she'd been determined to one day be—a virgin bride. Most wanted to try out the goodies before committing and she refused to do that; especially after being fed from knee-high her mother's story book rendition of how romantic things had been for her and Corey.

Casey had been determined to find that same kind of

special love for herself, and as a result, had decided the only man she slept with would be her husband. But since finding out the truth about her own parents, keeping her virginity intact hadn't meant as much to her anymore. She just hadn't met a man who'd drawn her interest enough to share his bed.

Her thoughts went back to McKinnon and she gritted her teeth, refusing to consider such a thing. The man was as exasperating as he was enticing. And at the moment, she had much more important things to think about—like finding a job.

She sighed and decided that after dinner she would return to her room. She had picked up a newspaper in town yesterday and intended to cover the Want Ads section. It was time she took control of her future. Making the decision to move to Montana to be close to Corey had been the first step. Now finding employment and a place to stay would be her second.

"I'm glad you took me up on my offer to stay the night, McKinnon," Corey said, handing the young man a glass of some of his finest scotch. "Although you're a skilled horseman, it's too dangerous for you to attempt going back down that mountain this late. It would have been dark before you got to the bottom." He then chuckled before tacking on, "And Morning Star and Martin would have my hide if anything were to happen to their oldest son."

McKinnon grinned knowing that was true. He had a very special relationship with his mother and father, as well as his three younger brothers. Matthew was twenty-seven, Jason was twenty-five and Daniel was twenty-three, and all three were unattached with no thoughts of settling down any time soon.

It was hard for McKinnon to believe at times that Martin Quinn was actually his stepfather and not his biological father. He was in his teens when he'd been told that his natural father, a Creole of African-American descent, had died in a car accident before he was born, and that a pregnant Morning Star—a member of the Blackfoot Indian tribe, had gone to work for the esteemed Judge Martin Quinn as a bookkeeper, only to end up falling in love and marrying him before the child was born.

"So, how are things with the horse business?"

Corey's question pulled McKinnon's thoughts back. "They would be a lot better if I can get Casey to come work for me. I know I blew things yesterday but I had a reason for it. You know how I feel about another woman living at my ranch."

Corey nodded. Yes, he did know but then they weren't talking about just any other woman—they were talking about his daughter. He wasn't born yesterday. He knew about the heated sparks that always went off when McKinnon and Casey were within a few feet of each other. In the past they had pretty much kept their distance but things wouldn't be quite that easy here in Montana, especially since Corey and McKinnon's parents were the best of friends.

"So how are you going to talk her into it?" He asked, knowing that McKinnon would make an attempt. When it came to the art of persuasion, biological or not, he was Martin Quinn's son and Martin hadn't moved up the ranks of powerhouse attorney to circuit judge in these parts without his persuasive nature.

Corey smiled. Poor Morning Star hadn't known what had hit her all those years ago when she'd been talked into a marriage of convenience that had ended up being anything but that.

"Don't know yet, but I won't give up," McKinnon said. "I promised Jamal that I would have that horse ready for him this fall, and I intend to do just that."

"I hate to interrupt such important male conversation, but dinner is ready," said a beautiful Abby Winters Westmoreland as stuck her head in the door and smiled. "And Casey will be down in a minute."

"We'll be there in a second, sweetheart," Corey said, smiling back at the woman he loved to distraction—had always loved.

McKinnon watched the loving exchange between Corey and Abby, which was similar to what he always saw between his parents. Some people were lucky to find their soul mate and spend the rest of their lives together in wedded bliss. He had long ago accepted that he wouldn't be one of the lucky ones. His future was set without any permanent woman in it.

Casey hurried down the stairs knowing she was already a few minutes late for dinner. One of her brothers had phoned to see how she was doing. Even all the way from Texas, Clint and Cole were trying to keep tabs on her. She smiled thinking she was used to it and although she would never admit it to them, it felt good knowing they still cared about her well-being. Born triplets, the three of them had a rather close relationship, and by her being the youngest, Clint and Cole made it their business to try and be her keepers.

She moved quickly to the dining room and stopped dead in her tracks when she saw McKinnon sitting at the table. She tried to mask her displeasure at seeing him when he and her father stood when she entered the room.

"McKinnon, I'm surprised you're still here," she said, trying to keep the cutting edge out of her voice.

She knew the smile that he gave her was only meant to infuriate her, but before he could respond her father offered an explanation. "It would have been too dangerous for him to try going back down the mountain this late, so I invited him to spend the night," Corey said, once both men sat back down after she took a seat.

"Oh." Casey tried not to show the cringe that passed through her body in knowing that McKinnon would be there all night. Just the thought that they would be sleeping under the same roof was nothing she wanted to think about. So she didn't. As soon as grace was said and the food passed around, she tried concentrating on something else. "Everything looks delicious, Abby."

Abby smiled over at her. "Thanks, Casey." The older woman then turned her attention to everyone at the table. "I got a call from Stone and Madison today. They're in Canada on a book signing tour and said to tell everyone hello. They hope to be able to swing by here in a few weeks."

"That would be wonderful," Casey said, meaning it. She'd discovered that there had been only two females born in the Westmoreland family in her generation—her and Delaney. Delaney lived out of the country with her desert sheikh, but whenever she came to the States she made a point of contacting Casey, and had even traveled once to Beaumont to visit with her last year But now that Delaney was pregnant her traveling had been curtailed somewhat.

Then there were the wives of her cousins she'd gotten to know. Shelly, Tara, Jayla, Dana, Jessica, and Savannah were as friendly as friendly could be. And Madison claimed her as a stepsister instead of a cousin-in-law.

Deciding to completely ignore McKinnon as much as she could, she turned and struck up a conversation with Abby, who was sitting beside her. They got caught up in a discussion about the latest fashions, and who had broken up with whom in Hollywood.

As much as she tried not to overhear her father and McKinnon's conversation, Casey couldn't help but eavesdrop on their discussion regarding the best way to train a horse. She couldn't believe some of the suggestions McKinnon was making. He would be a complete failure in this latest business venture of his if he were to follow through with any of them.

"It might be best if you stuck to horse breeding instead of horse training, McKinnon," she couldn't resist tossing in. "Anyone with any real knowledge of horse training who's keeping abreast on the up-to-date methods would know that using a strap on a horse is no longer acceptable."

McKinnon lifted a brow like he was taking what she said with a grain of salt. "Is that so?"

"Yes, it is so. Although pain and intimidation may have been the way years ago, things have progressed a lot since then. Trainers are using a kinder and gentler approach to communicate with horses," she stated unequivocally. "And it's sad that some horse owners are still under the impression that such techniques as snubbing a horse to the post or running horses in mindless circles until they're exhausted are the way to go and still being used. "

McKinnon leaned back in his chair. "And what if you had a not-so-docile animal like Prince Charming? Or a bunch of wild horses? What would you do then?"

"Same thing since it would make no difference. However, in the case of Prince Charming, I'd say someone, and rather recently I assume, mistreated him. But luckily at one time or another, he had a nice trainer and when I began talking to him to calm him down, he remembered those kinder days. That's the reason he didn't hurt me. I'm against using strong-arm tactics of any kind when working with horses."

"And I appreciate your opinion, Casey, but I have to disagree. Although I'm against anyone being outright mean and brutal to a horse, I still find the traditional way of doing things much better. And you're right—you were lucky yesterday with Prince Charming, however, I doubt that the kinder approach is for every horse. It will be almost impossible to get Prince Charming ready for the races in the fall without using some kind of strict disciplinary method."

"And *I* disagree."

He locked eyes with her. "You have that right to disagree, Casey. But this is Montana and not Texas. We tend to do things differently here."

"But a horse is a horse and why should you do things differently if the results could be the same?" she asked, taking a sip of her lemonade.

She was trying hard to remain nice but McKinnon was making it plum difficult. Why did the man have to be so bull headed? "It bothers me that some horse trainers are only interested in rushing a horse's training in that quest to seek immediate gratification when all it takes is gentle, loving care. If those methods are used over a period of time, a horse will be anxious, willing and eager to give back to its owner."

"You make it sound like a horse is almost human, Casey."

"No, I'm not saying that but what I am saying is that when it comes to horses, there has to be a foundation of trust established upon which all further development and training must be built. Without it, training a horse like Prince Charming to do anything, especially to win a race, will be hopeless as well as impossible."

McKinnon basically agreed with everything she'd said but he wouldn't let her know that. He would continue playing devil's advocate until he had her just where he wanted her.

"I think you're wrong on that account, Casey."

"And I think you're too close-minded to see that I'm right."

He lifted a brow, not taking his eyes off hers. "I dare you to prove me wrong."

"Consider it done," she said, without thinking.

He leaned forward in his chair. "Good. And since you're so keen on the idea of the new way of doing things, I'll pay you fifty thousand dollars for your efforts. You have eight weeks and you'll have to stay on my ranch in the guest house."

Casey blinked. What was he talking about? So she asked him.

He smiled. "You just accepted the challenge to prove me wrong with Prince Charming. But if you're not sure of your capabilities I'll most certainly understand and let you back out of it."

She glared at him. "I know what I'm capable of doing, McKinnon."

"So you say but I don't want to put you on the spot. I'll fully understand if you decide you can't handle things."

Casey's glare intensified. "When it comes to a horse, McKinnon, I can handle just about anything."

He shrugged. "You have eight weeks to prove it."

Casey glanced around the table at her father and Abby. They had been quiet during her and McKinnon's entire conversation and were now staring at her. There was no way she could back out now, although a part of her felt that McKinnon had somehow deliberately set her up.

She then turned her attention back to McKinnon, glaring at him. "Fine, I'll show you just what I can do, McKinnon Quinn. I just hope you're ready for me."

McKinnon leaned back in his chair. He decided not to tell Casey that if he lived to be the ripe old age of one hundred, he would never, ever be ready for her.

Four

The dark blue car caught McKinnon's eyes the moment it pulled into the yard. He'd been walking out of the barn and stopped a moment to look at the woman sitting behind the wheel. Casey had said that she would arrive within two days and she had kept her word.

He still had mixed feelings about her being there, but he had a business to run and hiring her on had made business sense. He would just have to call on his common sense and keep as much distance between them as possible. At least she would be living in the guest cottage out back and not under the same roof, he thought, as he watched her swing those shapely, gorgeous legs of hers out of the car. He sucked in a deep breath.

He glanced around and saw that he wasn't the only one who'd noticed her arrival…or her legs. His men had stopped what they were doing to stare, especially when

Casey grabbed a duffel bag out of the back seat. She was wearing a mint-green blouse that showed off firm, perfect breasts and a waist-cinching skirt whose hem swished around those gorgeous legs.

When she went to the back of her car and lifted the trunk, her luggage made it apparent to anyone looking that she was moving in. Most of McKinnon's men knew of his long-standing rule that a female had no place living on his ranch. He also knew they were staring at her for another reason—other than the obvious male one. The last time she had been there she had earned their respect with the way she had handled Prince Charming. The way they saw it, she had saved Edward Price from getting stomped to death while placing her own life in danger to do so.

When it seemed that every ranch hand who worked for him was now racing toward the car to help Casey with her luggage, almost tripping over each other in their haste, he shook his head. He knew then and there that he would have a very serious talk with his men and make sure they understood that just like them, Casey had been hired to do a job and that was the only reason she was there.

When it became apparent that Jed Wilson and Evan Duvall were about to knock each other over to offer Casey their assistance, McKinnon decided to intervene. "Okay, you guys can get back to work. I'll help Casey with her things."

He saw the disappointed look on the men's faces as they turned and followed his orders, leaving him and Casey alone. He met her gaze. "Casey." He could tell from her expression that she didn't want to be there.

"McKinnon. If you'd be so kind to show me where I'll be staying over the next weeks, I'd appreciate it."

She had managed to temper some of her anger but not

all of it. She was still somewhat ticked off. "Just follow me. I'll come back for your luggage later. The guesthouse is out back."

They walked around the ranch house together and not for the first time, Casey thought that McKinnon's ranch was erected on a beautiful piece of land under the warm of the Montana sky. It was another nice day and again the weather reminded her of a day in Texas. She sighed deeply. She was already missing home.

"Are you okay?"

She glanced up at him. She wished his eyes weren't so dark, so intense, so downright seductive. "Yes, I'm fine. I've been in Montana a little over a week and I'm missing Texas already."

"It's warmer here than usual for this time of the year," he said, his voice dry as he looked ahead and not at her. "That means a colder than usual winter."

She shuddered. "I don't do cold weather very well."

"If you're planning on hanging around in these parts, my best advice to you is to get used to it," he said curtly. "Otherwise, you'll be shivering all over the place. Montana is known for its beauty as well as its freezing cold winters."

Speaking of shivering…one passed through her body at that moment when their arms brushed. Geez. No man had ever given her the shivers before. She couldn't help but take in the beautifully muscled body walking beside her, making it downright difficult for her to breathe.

When they reached what she assumed was the guesthouse, Casey stood aside for him to open the door. He motioned her in and then followed behind her. She relaxed a bit when he moved to the other side of the room and took that time to glance around. The place was beautiful. For a guest-house, it was massive and the living room was neatly decorated in earth-tone colors. The furniture had been handcrafted of a beautiful dark wood and the huge window that showcased the mountains gave the room a comforting effect.

"There's a bedroom and bath down the hall that you can check out while I bring in your luggage."

She turned toward the sound of McKinnon's voice. "Okay."

"There's not a kitchen since most meals are eaten at the big house, but it won't be a problem if you prefer taking your meals here. Just let Henrietta know."

Casey lifted a brow. "Henrietta?"

"Yes, she's my cook and housekeeper."

Casey nodded. "She lives here on the ranch?"

"No," McKinnon said rather quickly, as if such a thing was not possible. "Henrietta and her husband Lewis live a few miles from here, not far from my parents' place. She gets here every morning around six and leaves every evening around that same time." He pushed away from the wall. "I'll be back in a second with your luggage."

He left the room and Casey was relieved to be out of his presence for a little while. Everything about McKinnon exuded sensuality, and as a woman, she was fully aware of him as a man. But more than anything, she was determined to tamp down whatever hot and racy feelings he brought out in her—and fight the sizzling desire that had a tendency to slam into her body whenever he came within a few feet of her.

Deciding to shake those feelings now, she crossed the room to look out the window at the mountains looming in the background. She was here to do a job and nothing more. So how difficult could that be?

* * *

As McKinnon had suggested, Casey looked around while he brought in her luggage. When he returned moments later and found her standing beside the massive oak bed, his pulse began racing. There was just something about a beautiful woman sanding next to a bed that would do it to a man each and every time.

Casey turned around when she heard him enter the room and could actually feel the sexual tension that surrounded them. That wasn't good. Angry at his inability to control his emotions like he usually did around a woman, he placed her luggage on the bed. "I'll leave you to unpack," he said gruffly. "Since you don't have to officially start work until tomorrow, you can use today to get settled in."

"I will, and thanks for bringing in my things."

"Don't mention it," he said, glancing at the time on his watch. He then glanced back at her. "And knowing Henrietta she'll be dropping by sometime today to introduce herself."

"I'll look forward to her visit."

McKinnon wished he could keep his concentration on what Casey was saying rather than her features which appeared more striking than ever. It was her eyes, her mouth, her hair that was styled perfectly for her face.

"Will there be anything else, McKinnon?"

He gave himself a mental shake and frowned at her question. She had caught him staring. "No, there's nothing else. I'll see you at dinner."

"No, you won't."

"Excuse me?"

"I said you won't see me at dinner. I've been invited out."

Her announcement only added to his irritation. He tried not to wonder who she would be sharing dinner with. Cal Hooper? Someone she'd met since arriving here? Why the hell did he care and more importantly, why did the thought bother him? "Okay, fine. Enjoy your meal." He turned to leave.

"McKinnon?"

He turned back around. For some reason he was feeling annoyed, aggravated, impulsive; like hitting something, breaking somebody's bones, namely whoever she was meeting up with later. "What?" he responded gruffly.

He could tell from her expression that she hadn't liked the tone of his response. "For some reason I get the impression that you really don't want me here but that you're willing to put those feelings aside to utilize my talents," she said, putting her hands on her hips and glaring at him. "That's all well and good because frankly, I don't want to be here either."

He crossed his arms over his chest and glared back. "Then why are you?"

"To prove a point that all women aren't incompetent when it comes to horses."

His frown deepened. "I never said they were."

"You didn't have to. You made your thoughts known when you didn't hire me that first day."

A part of McKinnon struggled with what she was saying because she was so far from the truth it was pathetic. The reason he hadn't hired her that first day had had nothing to do with what he thought of her abilities as a horse trainer, but what he'd thought of her abilities as a woman. A very desirable woman. He couldn't tell her that though.

"You're wrong, Casey. I have a high degree of respect for women who handle horses. In fact, the greatest horseman I know happens to be a female and she can outride, outrope and probably outshoot any man I know. And I hold her in the highest regard."

Casey lifted a brow, wondering who this paragon of a woman was. "And who is she?" she asked.

"My mother, Morning Star Long-Lance McKinnon Martin," he said before turning and leaving the room.

"Now, aren't you a pretty little thing!"

Casey turned and met the older woman's smiling face. Her smile was so bright and cheery, she couldn't do anything but smile back. "Thanks. You must be Henrietta."

The woman's laughter echoed through the room. "Yes, that's me. And you are definitely Corey Westmoreland's child. You look just like him, just a whole lot prettier."

"Thank you."

"McKinnon gave me strict orders not to bother you until you'd gotten settled in. I thought these might pretty up the place for you even more," she said, handing Casey what looked to be a bouquet of hand-picked fresh flowers.

Casey beamed. "Thanks, they're beautiful."

"You're welcome. I grew them myself. I have a flower garden on the other side of the ranch house." She chuckled. "That's McKinnon's way of making me tow the line by threatening to have my garden mowed down, but he doesn't scare me any."

"He doesn't?"

"Heck no. I've been with that boy since the day he was born. I was his first and only nanny, so I know how to deal with him."

A part of Casey wondered how McKinnon had been as a child but decided not to ask. "And you're still with him now?" she asked while finding the perfect spot on a table in the living room for the flowers.

"Yes, only because he needs me. If I didn't make sure he got a home-cooked meal every so often he would probably starve to death. And speaking of cooked meals, I understand you're passing up the chance for me to fix a special one for you tonight."

Casey grinned, thinking she liked this large, robust woman already. "Sorry about that but I was invited over to my cousin's house for dinner."

Henrietta nodded. "I imagine you're talking about Durango. In that case I understand. I'm still grinning over the fact that boy's married with a baby on the way. That just goes to show that miracles can happen to a devout bachelor when the right woman comes along."

Casey hoped she wasn't throwing out any hints about the possibility of her and McKinnon ever getting together because that wouldn't happen. Ever. The man was too reserved, rigid and resigned for her taste. "Yes, I'm happy for Durango and Savannah. They are very happy together," she said, leaving it at that and hoping Henrietta would, too.

"Well, I guess your decision to eat elsewhere is the reason McKinnon told me I didn't have to cook. Now he has plans for himself. I guess he'll be going into town tonight."

A part of Casey didn't want to think what he would do when he got there and who he would see. "I guess that means you'll have a night off," she said.

"Yes. I'll be leaving in a few hours unless there's something you need me to do. I tried to get this place ready for you as best I could."

"And you did a wonderful job, Henrietta. It's beautiful

and I know I'm going to feel right at home for the short time I'll be here."

"And that's what McKinnon wants."

Casey doubted it, but decided not to tell the older woman that. However, there were a couple of things the woman could possibly tell *her,* things she preferred not asking McKinnon about. The less she saw of him the better. But it would help to know how early things got moving at the ranch in the mornings. The last thing she wanted was to be sleeping in while everyone else was up and working. The men employed by her father started their day as early as four in the morning. "How would you like to join me for a cup of coffee? There are some questions I have about the workings of this ranch and I'd rather not bother McKinnon with them."

Henrietta smiled. "I'll be glad to tell you whatever you want to know. You got a coffee pot here?"

"Yes, although there isn't a kitchen to set it in. Since all I needed was an electrical plug, I'm using that table in the hallway. We can sit in the living room on the sofa. I simply love the view from there."

"Isn't it just magnificent?" Henrietta said glancing over at the window. "The only thing wrong with this house is that it doesn't have a kitchen. I told McKinnon that while he was building it, but he said it didn't need one since he intended for it to be a guest-house and not a guest lodge. It's only a few feet from the big house, so anyone getting hungry can come in there to eat."

Casey nodded, not surprised he looked at things that way given his stubborn and uncompromising nature. "Well, you just get settled on the sofa over there and I'll bring the coffee to you."

As she turned to leave she had a feeling that Henrietta would be one of the reasons she would find the time she spent on McKinnon's ranch rather pleasant after all.

McKinnon stopped his truck the moment he pulled into Durango's yard, recognizing the dark blue car immediately. It appeared that Savannah had invited Casey to dinner tonight as well. So much for the mystery of who she was having dinner with. He then frowned wondering if the newly-wedded couple were trying their hand at match making?

A part of McKinnon refused to believe Durango would do something like that. After all, his best friend knew the reason he could never entertain the idea of settling down and marrying. However, chances were Durango hadn't shared anything about McKinnon's medical history with Savannah. Savannah Claiborne Westmoreland, who he thought of as a sister since she'd married Durango, probably thought he needed an exclusive woman in his life. Once married, some people had a tendency to think everyone around them should be married, too.

He got out of the truck knowing it would be difficult as hell to be around Casey tonight. He should have declined Savannah's offer to dinner when she called, and stuck with his plans to go into town, eat at one of the restaurants and then seek out a little female companionship. He wasn't counting but it had been a while since he'd been with a woman, more than six months. The ranch had kept him too busy to seek out a willing bed partner.

He shook his head, convinced that was the reason he was finding Cascy so dcsirable, but quickly knew that wasn't true. He'd always found her desirable.

The moment his best friend opened the door to his

home, McKinnon said, "Your wife hasn't talked you into playing matchmaker, has she, Rango?"

Durango shook his head grinning. "You know me better than that. In fact, I didn't know you were coming until a couple hours ago. But I shouldn't be surprised. Savannah's decided that you need someone special."

McKinnon frowned. "I have someone special. His name is Thunder," he said of his horse.

Durango chuckled. "I care to differ. A horse wouldn't do well in your bed every night."

"I don't need a woman in my bed every night." A serious expression then covered McKinnon's features. "I take it that you haven't told Savannah that I can't have a special woman in my life even if I wanted one."

Durango met McKinnon's gaze. "No. That's your secret to share, not mine."

"Thanks."

"Hey, you don't have to thank me and you know it," Durango said.

McKinnon nodded. Yes, he did know it. He and Durango had been the best of friends since that botched up job of becoming blood brothers when they were ten. It was an incident that had nearly sent McKinnon to the emergency room for stitches when the knife they'd used had sliced into his hand too deep.

"But you already know my feelings on the matter, McKinnon. You can always consider—"

"No, Rango. It doesn't matter. I made my decision about things a long time ago."

"Hey, I thought I heard someone at the door," Savannah Westmoreland said, breezing as much as she could into the room as a woman who would be giving birth to one large baby in four months. For awhile the doctors had thought she would be having twins but a recent sonogram had shown one big whopping baby—a girl.

She quickly crossed the floor and gave McKinnon a peck on the cheek. "You're looking handsome as ever," she said smiling up at him.

McKinnon lifted a dark brow. In a way he was grateful for Savannah's interruption of his and Durango's conversation. The issue of his medical history was something they couldn't agree on. "Sounds like you're trying to butter me up for something," he said, studying her features for traces of guilt.

Savannah laughed. "Now why would I do that?"

McKinnon crossed his arms over his chest. "That's what I'd like to know—and don't you dare flash those hazel eyes at me."

Savannah shook her head grinning, and then with a wave of her hand she pushed her shoulder-length curly brown hair out of her face. "I'm not flashing my eyes, so stop being suspicious of me." Then she quickly said with a smile, "I forgot to mention that I also invited Casey to dinner tonight. She's in Durango's office talking on the phone. Tara just called. She's having her first sonogram in a few weeks and she and Thorn are excited about it."

McKinnon shook his head. "What will your family do with all these babies being born, Rango?"

Durango chuckled. "Nothing but make room for more. I talked to Stone last night and he and Madison are coming through on their way from Canada. I have a feeling there's a reason for their visit."

McKinnon was about to open his mouth to say something when Casey walked into the room. He could tell from her expression that she was surprised to see him, which meant she had known nothing about his invitation to dinner. She had changed clothes and was wearing another skirt and blouse. This outfit just as alluring as the one she'd had on earlier.

"McKinnon."

"Casey," he said stiffly, returning her greeting.

"Okay guys," a smiling Savannah said, looking at McKinnon and then back at Casey and ignoring the deep frown coming from her husband. "I hope everyone is hungry because I prepared a feast."

Five

After dinner was over, McKinnon quickly left. Spending too much time around Casey wasn't good. All through dinner he had found himself looking over at her, feeling his flesh prickle each and every time their gazes connected. And even when she wasn't looking his way, he was looking hers; studying her mouth and thinking of over a thousand plus things he could do with it. And he kept admiring her well-toned body every time she got up from the table while his mind worked overtime imagining that same beautiful body bare.

He had declined desert, thanked Savannah for preparing such a wonderful meal and told Durango he would touch base with him sometime during the week. Then he nodded at Casey and left, trying to make it home in record time. There was something about having a sexual ache for a woman you couldn't have that made a man want to burn the rubber off his tires. Damn, he was lucky that one of Sheriff Richard's deputies hadn't been parked along one the back roads with a speed trap.

Once McKinnon opened the door to his home, he headed straight to the kitchen for a beer. A half hour later, after enjoying his beer and taking a cold shower, he slipped between the crisp white sheets intent on getting a good night's sleep. But before he could close his eyes his mind went to the past and the reason he was sleeping in this bed alone.

He had purchased this land when he'd turned twenty-five knowing when he had bought the ranch house that he would live in it alone. He'd also known he would be one of those men who died a bachelor—refusing to take the risk of ever having a wife and children—once he'd found out about the rare bone disease his biological father had passed on to him.

When he'd met Lynette, he had fallen for her and thought she had loved him just as much—so much that he had felt comfortable for the first time to ask a woman to move in with him, as well as to reveal the full extent of his medical history to her. He had all intentions of asking her to marry him if she was willing to accept him the way he was. But no sooner had he told her, less than forty-eight hours, later she was gone. She left a letter that merely said she couldn't marry a man who would deny her the chance to be a mother.

He received another letter from her almost a year later, apologizing for her actions and letting him know that she had met someone, had gotten married and was expecting his child.

He cursed as he threw the covers back, got out of bed and slipped into his jeans. It was nights like this when he needed to escape and become part of the wild. He knew when he walked into the barn and Thunder saw him, his friend would understand. That horse was smarter than any animal had any right to be. Whenever they rode, it was man and beast together, flying in the wind in a way his Ford Explorer couldn't touch. At least not within the confines of the law, anyway.

Tonight he needed speed which was faster than lightning and in his mind, swifter than any speed boat. Tonight he needed to put out of his mind the one woman he needed to keep at a distance, and stop imagining how she would feel in his arms, how that ultra fine body of hers would feel molded tight against his. But what was really driving him insane was fantasizing about her taste and how delicious it would be on his tongue.

Damn. Casey Westmoreland was getting under his skin—and that was something he'd sworn not to let another woman do again.

Casey stood at her bedroom window and looked out, clearly seeing the mountains beneath a moon-kissed sky. Shivers ran all through her body at the memory of being in McKinnon's presence tonight, sitting across from him at the dinner table trying to concentrate more on her food than on him.

And then there was the part of the night when she'd helped Savannah clear the table and he'd handed her his plate. The moment their hands had touched she felt a heated sensation shoot from the bottom of her feet all the way to the top of her head. There were also moments she had caught him staring at her like she was the dessert he would get after the meal. Just thinking about that deep look of desire she'd seen in his eyes had heat flaring up inside her and no matter what she did, there was nothing she could do to smother it.

She'd tried sleeping but her thoughts wouldn't let her be. Heat would start in her stomach and move lower down her body while visions of McKinnon Quinn danced in her head. How could she concentrate on getting Prince Charming trained when something else dominated her thoughts?

Knowing going back to sleep was out of the question, she slipped into a robe after deciding to take a walk outside. There was a courtyard connecting the cottage to the main house that was surrounded by the flowers Henrietta had planted. It was a beautiful night and she wanted to stand underneath the Montana sky and smell the flowers.

She had been standing outside in the courtyard for well over fifteen minutes and was about to go back inside when she heard a sound. Her heart jammed in her ribs and her breath caught. She blinked, not sure if she was seeing things or if McKinnon was actually there within ten feet of her, sitting bareback on his huge black horse and staring at her.

She blinked again and watched as he slowly slid off Thunder's back and she realized it wasn't a hallucination.

She shook her head to clear it before her gaze latched onto his. She felt her breathing grow shallow as he slowly moved closer.

The moon overhead cast enough light on him and his devastatingly good looks to make her appreciate that she was born a woman. His hair hung loose and wildly around his shoulders, and he was bare chested and wearing jeans. His body was solid, muscular and for a moment her breath caught because he reminded her of a savage beast. But she knew that the man coming toward her—although private and reserved—was no threat to her. At least not physically. Emotionally was another matter.

"What are you doing out here?" he asked in a deep, husky drawl that sent goose bumps spreading all over her body. He came to stand directly in front of her.

From the moon's glow she could see the intensity in the depths of his dark eyes. "I couldn't sleep and decided to come out here for a spell," she said as her hands automatically went to the belt around her robe to tighten it, fully aware that her meager clothing offered no protection nothing against the heat she saw in his eyes.

"You should go back inside," he said in a gruff voice.

"I was about to," she said, taking a gathered breath. Then she asked, "What are you still doing up?"

At first she thought he wasn't going to respond, but then he said, "I couldn't sleep either and decided to ride Thunder."

"Oh." She inhaled deeply. "Well, I'd better go back in. Good—"

"I know the reason why neither of us can get any sleep," he said, taking a step closer to her.

She stared up into his dark eyes. "Do you?"

"Yes. We need this." And then he wrapped his arms around her and lowered his mouth as his lips captured hers. Then he placed his hands on her hips, molding her body firmly to the fit of him. Without wasting any time, his tongue found hers and he heard her gasp at the contact and immediately knew…at thirty years of age, Casey Westmoreland had never been properly kissed before. And damn it all to hell, he planned on doing the honors, here and now.

His fingers tightened at her waist the moment he deepened the kiss, taking what appeared no man had before, an in-depth taste of her. Being inside her mouth felt soothingly warm and downright delicious. A wave of sexual need entrapped him when she parlayed each stroke of his tongue and his brain cells started to overload. At that moment nothing else mattered except having Casey in his arms, kissing her, devouring her this way.

One part of his mind said he needed to stop, but another part said to continue what he'd started since this would be the last opportunity he would have to do so. Tomorrow she officially began working for him and he would have to be sensible. He would not become romantically involved with one of his employees—especially this one. She was a Westmoreland for heaven's sake! But tonight he wanted as much insensibility as he could get.

A sigh escaped from her mouth into his and he continued on and on, mating their mouths, exchanging their breaths, sharing their taste. His tongue moved all over her mouth, in every direction, sucked, licked, nibbled, dabbed, all while performing some of the most inherently erotic things he'd ever done to a woman's mouth.

With no thoughts of ending it. Instead he wanted to take things further. He wanted to move his mouth from her lips and trace a path past her neck and open her robe, push her night shirt out of the way and capture the nipples he'd seen pressed against her tops.

He reached up, slipped his hand inside her robe and touched her breast and let out a satisfied sigh. Even through the lace of her night shirt he could tell that she was perfectly shaped. Then he loosened the front of her robe, needing to touch her if not kiss her there. The moment his hand came into contact with her breast, every part of him got harder and he felt like he was going to explode right then and there.

He pulled back from the kiss and before she could utter a single word, he leaned down and latched onto a nipple, sucked on it, licked it like a hungry man. He heard moan after moan gurgle up in her throat and she arched her back, giving him greater access to her breasts. He was greedy for her and could tell from the sounds of her moans she was in another world, enjoying his mouth on her. He wondered how she would feel if his mouth moved lower and invade another area of her body.

He shifted their positions, ready to lift his mouth to find out, when somewhere in the distance a coyote howled and McKinnon pulled back, but only so far. He still lingered over her nipple, took his tongue and traced the outlines of it again before raising his head and going for her lips again, testing her softness, savoring her taste.

"Casey," he said quietly, as if the sound would break the spell they had gotten caught up in.

"Yes," she responded, and he heard several tremors in her voice and inwardly smiled knowing he had placed them there.

"I definitely like the way you taste," he said, pulling back and looking down at her, while putting her lacy tank top back in place and pulling her robe closed. He saw her bemused expression and he wanted to kiss it right off her face. He smiled. "You don't kiss often, do you?"

She leaned forward and pressed her face against his chest as if in embarrassment. When she muttered a few words he couldn't make out, he lifted her chin and tilted her head back so their gazes could meet. "When was the last time a man has thoroughly and completely kissed you?" he asked quietly.

"Never. I've never been kissed like that before. You're the only man who's done something like that to me."

Her words made him tighten his arms around her waist and he lowered his mouth to hers again, needing another taste, one to retain in his memories forever. He deepened the kiss, more than before and actually heard her purr. The sound sent blood racing to all parts of his body.

When they parted moments later they were both pulling in shallow and choppy breaths. Casey took a couple of steps back. "I think I really do need to go inside now."

And before McKinnon could stop her, she took off in the darkness, hurriedly walking back toward the cottage.

High up on a mountain, another individual was finding it hard to sleep. Corey Westmoreland stood at the window gazing out, wondering if all was well with his daughter. She had called earlier to say she had unpacked and liked the cottage she would be living in for the next few weeks. But what she hadn't said and what he couldn't help wondering was how she and McKinnon were getting along.

He turned when he heard the sound of feet touching the floor and smiled as he watched his wife—the woman he loved more than anything—softly walk over to him and right into his outstretched arms. "Sorry, honey, I didn't mean to wake you," he whispered softly against her ear, giving her a peck there.

"You're worried about Casey, aren't you?"

He nodded, knowing he couldn't and wouldn't keep anything from Abby, especially his feelings. "Yes. Clint and Cole are concerned as well."

"Is it because she's taken the job with McKinnon?"

Corey shook his head. "No, McKinnon and Casey are going to have to work out their own problems in that area.

What her brothers and I are concerned about is whether she's come to terms with what Carolyn told her all those years ago. Casey's been going through a lot emotionally since finding out the truth."

Abby nodded as she cuddled closer into her husband's arms. "What I think Casey needs to help pull her life together is the love of a good man—and I believe McKinnon is that man."

Corey shrugged. "He could very well be but he won't let that happen. I told you about his medical history. Ever since he discovered that he's a carrier of that rare blood disease, he made up his mind that he would never marry and father children. It was a hard decision for him. Then, a few years ago he met someone he thought would be the perfect mate, but once he told her the truth about his medical condition and his decision not to ever father any children, she left him high and dry. McKinnon has had a lot of hurt and pain in his life, Abby."

"And so has Casey. That's why they need each other."

Corey shook his head. "McKinnon won't see it that way."

"I want to think that eventually he will. Everything happens for a reason. I think you and I are living proof of that. If it's meant for them to be together then they will. All they need is time and opportunity, and with her living right there on his ranch, right under his nose, they will have that. McKinnon needs Casey as much as Casey needs him." She lifted her head, looked into Corey's face and smiled. "I have a feeling that before long, you'll become the father of the bride."

Corey returned her smile and pulled Abby closer into his arms. McKinnon was an outstanding young man but right now he was hurt and angry. He just hoped his daughter would be able to handle him. But then if anyone could, it would be a Westmoreland.

McKinnon slipped beneath the sheets after taking his second cold shower that night. He had gotten sweaty riding Thunder and hot after kissing Casey. If he thought he hadn't been able to get to sleep before, he sure as hell wouldn't get any now—not with memories of devouring Casey's mouth and breasts so blatantly vivid in his mind.

She had tasted just likc hc'd known she would, and with a particular flavor that was all hers. And just the thought that she was a novice sent sensuous chills down his body. He wondered if the over-protectiveness of her two brothers as the reason for her lack of experience. He shook his head, dismissing that assumption. He had gotten to know Casey well enough to know that although Clint and Cole may have looked out for her over the years, it had been her decision regarding the level of her involvement with any man. Most women he knew at her age had been kissed hundreds of times—on every part of their body—and he couldn't help wondering the extent of her knowledge. A part of him would love to find out, but another part—the one that knew maintaining distance between him and Casey was the best thing—fought the idea with a passion.

Passion.

And that was what he was trying not to think about, especially when it came to Casey. He definitely had to toe the line. There was no way he could treat her like he treated other woman he wanted in his bed. First of all, he needed to get that idea out of his mind because it wouldn't. And to be sure of that, he would start keeping his distance beginning tomorrow. The only time he would seek her out was when he needed to know the progress she was making with Prince Charming.

Satisfied that he had at least gotten that much cleared up and settled in his mind, McKinnon sought a comfortable position in bed and hoped like hell he got some semblance of a fairly decent amount of sleep.

Six

"Casey is doing a downright fine job with Prince Charming," Norris said, glancing over at McKinnon.

"Is she?" McKinnon asked, trying to sound nonchalant but at the same time angry that his pulse rate always seemed to increase with the mere mention of her name. It had been a week since he'd seen her—at least up close. The day following the night they'd kissed, he'd made himself scarce, leaving it up to Norris to give her his expectations regarding Prince Charming.

He knew from Henrietta that she preferred taking her meals alone at the guest cottage, however, it seemed the two women had gotten rather chummy and shared lunch together at the big house every day. Once he'd known Casey's schedule, he had adjusted his to make sure he wasn't around when she was. But that didn't really help matters because there were plenty of things to remind him of her presence. He caught the scent of her each and every time he walked into his home.

She had made things a little easy for him this past weekend by leaving on Friday evening to spend time on her father's mountain, not returning until late Sunday. He had kept himself pretty busy going over breeding records but had found that every so often he would get up and look out the window as if anxiously awaiting her return.

And then at night whenever he went to bed, all he had to do was close his eyes to remember the feel of his mouth on hers, his tongue in that mouth and the flavor of her that seemed to be embedded in his taste buds. The bottom line was that he wanted to be with her the way a man needed to be with a woman.

Hell, he'd even gone into town a couple of nights ago to his and Durango's old hangout, Haley's Bar and Grill, but hadn't seen a single woman he wanted to sleep with. The only woman he wanted was the one living in his guest cottage—the one who was definitely off limits to him. But still, that didn't mean he couldn't dream about her at night, wishing she was in bed with him while he stripped her naked and…

"Damn." McKinnon cursed when he saw the cut on his hand, thanks to the barbwire fence he was trying to repair on a section of his property. He should have been concentrating on what he was doing instead of fantasizing about Casey.

Luckily for him the cut wasn't deep, which meant it shouldn't require stitches. But it would require him putting something on it. He had taken off his gloves to get a better grip on the pliers when the thing had slipped.

"You okay, McKinnon?"

He glanced over at Norris. "I got a cut from this

barbwire and need to go up to the house to put something on it. I'll be back in a minute."

Norris looked at the cut, saw the amount of blood and lifted his brow in concern. "Maybe you need me to take you into town so Dr. Mason can take a look at it."

"No, I'm up on my tetanus shots and it doesn't need stitches. I'll be fine."

"You sure?"

"Yes, I'm sure."

"Okay. I don't want Morning Star and the Judge to have my ass if something happens to you. Why don't you stay at the house and let me and the boys finish things up here."

McKinnon lifted his brow, wondering if Norris was about to accuse him of being more of a hindrance than a help again. He would be the first to admit that his mind hadn't been focused lately for thinking about Casey but still… "And you sure you and the guys will have the fence repaired by morning?"

Norris chuckled. "Look McKinnon, I was repairing barbwire fences before the day you were born." And for good measure the older man then added, "And I'm yet to get a cut on any of my fingers. Now go."

"All right, I'm going," McKinnon said, moving toward Thunder.

"I don't know where your mind has been lately, but it's been wandering quite a bit," he heard Norris say, but refused to acknowledge the man's comment by turning around.

A half hour after cleaning his wound, applying antiseptic and putting on a bandage, McKinnon walked out of the bathroom, glad Henrietta had gone into town to do her weekly grocery shopping. If she'd seen the cut on his hand, no matter how minor the injury, she would have harassed him until he went into town for Doc Mason to stitch him up.

He turned when he heard a knock at the door. Remembering that Henrietta wasn't in, he moved through the living room to open it. Immediately his breath caught at the same time his pulse escalated and he felt a tightness in his jeans. Casey was standing there and the sight of her, the scent of her, suddenly made his skin feel overheated.

He cleared his throat, forced the lump down. "Casey, is there anything I can do for you?" he said as normal as he could while trying to force from his mind all the things he would love doing for and to her.

She seemed just as surprised to see him as he was to see her. "No. I was about to leave to go into town and wanted to know if Henrietta wanted me to pick up anything."

It was then that he took in what she was wearing—a dress that that he bet would ruffle around her legs when she walked. It was light pink and the color made her look totally feminine, alluring and desirable. And she had light makeup on, and even added a dash of color to her lips. Lips he remembered kissing once and would love kissing again.

He cleared his throat for a second time before saying, "Henrietta isn't here. She went into town to pick up the weekly supplies and groceries." Then he checked his watch. "You're through for the day all ready?"

He regretted asking the question before it left his mouth—especially when he could tell from her expression it got her dander up. "Yes," she replied, rather stiffly. "I put in a couple of extra hours this week and asked Norris yesterday if I could finish up early today. I have an appointment in town."

He frowned. "An appointment?"

"Yes. A real estate agent has a couple of places to show me."

His frown deepened. "You're moving? Our deal called for you to stay here in the guesthouse."

"I know what our deal called for, McKinnon," she said, locking gazes and tempers with him, "and I plan to honor it," she snapped. "I'm looking for a place to stay once my job here is finished."

"What about Corey's place?"

"What about it?"

"I assumed that's where you'd be staying since the reason you decided to move here was to get to know him better."

"But that doesn't mean I have to be underfoot. Besides, he and Abby need their privacy," she said, like that should explain everything.

In a way it did. McKinnon knew exactly what she wasn't saying. The couple was openly affectionate, but he was used to such behavior because his own parents were the same way.

"I can't live there permanently," Casey added. "I need my own place. If I were to get a job I can't be coming back and forth off Corey's Mountain everyday."

McKinnon nodded. To get on or off the mountain you could only drive so far and then had to travel the rest of the way by horseback. At least that's how things had been before Serena Preston had moved to town and started a helicopter business. In addition to doing private tours, she provided air transportation to and from those ranches higher up in the mountains twice a week. But using air transportation on a frequent basis could get rather expensive.

"What happened to your hand!" Casey's words cut into his thoughts and he glanced down to notice it had started bleeding again through the bandage.

"I cut it on barb-wire earlier."

"Aren't you going to the doctor?" she asked, her voice sounding somewhat panicky.

"Hadn't planned on it," he said, leaning in the doorway. "I've put something on it."

"But it's bleeding."

"I noticed."

She looked at him with total exasperation on her face. "Your need to see a doctor for your hand, McKinnon. If you want I can take you there since I'm going to town."

He lifted a brow. "What about your appointment?"

"It's not for a couple of hours. The reason I was leaving so early was to do some shopping, but I can do that anytime. Getting your hand taken care of is more important."

McKinnon gazed at her for a moment, saw the concern etched on her face. This was the woman he had avoided for a week. The woman he went to bed dreaming about each night. The woman whose kiss still lingered in his mouth. The woman he wanted with a passion.

The woman he could not have.

But he wanted to spend time with her this afternoon. Find out how things had been going with her. He didn't want to hear it second-hand from Henrietta or Norris. He wanted to hear her voice, smell her scent, invade her space…

"McKinnon, do you want me to drive you to the doctor's office in town or not?"

Her words interrupted his thoughts and as he gazed into her eyes he made a decision. He would spend a couple of hours with her today but then tomorrow it was back to business at usual. He would put distance between them again. "You sure it won't mess up your appointment time?"

"Yes, I'm sure."

He nodded. "Then hold on, let me grab my hat."

Casey drove while McKinnon sat in the seat next to her not saying anything, just absently staring out the window at the endless miles of scenic meadows, pastures and mountains they passed.

He was frowning—as usual. She wondered how often he smiled. She'd seen him do so once when he had been standing in a group talking to her cousins. Spencer had shared some joke and all the men, including McKinnon, had laughed. But other than that one time, she was yet to see the corners of his lips crinkle up. She couldn't help but wonder about both the sadness and anger she often saw in his gaze. She had asked Durango about it once but he'd shrugged saying he didn't know what she was talking about.

And it was obvious McKinnon had avoided her this week. Even now she could tell that he was tense and angry about something, but she didn't know how to go about breaking through his defenses. She was used to dealing with moody males, thanks to Clint and Cole. The moodiness she could deal with, but not the anger because she didn't understand the reason for it.

A part of her knew it had something to do with the kiss they'd shared that night a week ago. Why had he gotten upset about it? They were both adults and he was the one who'd suggested doing it in the first place, saying a kiss was what they needed to sleep, and of course she'd gone along with it since kissing him was something she'd wanted to do for a long time. And he'd been right about the kiss. She had slept like a baby and had awakened the next day with a longing to see him, but he'd evidently regretted what they'd share and had other ideas and began putting distance between them…until now.

"So, how are things going with Prince Charming?"

The sound of his voice jerked her back to the present. She glanced over at him. He wasn't looking at her but his muscular body was reclined back against the seat staring straight ahead and the Stetson he wore low on his head shielded his eyes. Tight jeans were stretched across his thighs and the blue shirt accentuated a strong, sturdy chest. His hair was pulled back in a ponytail and his profile was just as sexy as the rest of him.

Unwanted images were forming in her mind—especially of how wild and untamed he'd look that night in the courtyard. She wished the kiss they'd shared could have gone on and on since she had enjoyed it so much. No man had ever kissed her that way before and…

"Casey?"

Abruptly she was snapped back to reality. He was looking at her with those dark eyes of his and suddenly she was filled with this urgent, compelling hunger to kiss him again.

"Yes?"

"I asked how things were going with Prince Charming."

And naturally when you asked I was thinking about something that I shouldn't be. "We're in the getting-to-know-you-better stage," she said, forcing the words from her mouth through thick abated breath. "I'm walking him a lot to get a feel of his balance and taking note of those things that might distract him, make him not alert as he should be. I'm trying to develop a good impression with him—one that will last. He's still somewhat tense and I'm trying to rid him of that. Once that happens then the bonding can begin."

"What about working on his speed?"

Casey could see from out the corner of her eye that McKinnon was still looking at her but she refused to look back when she responded. "He has speed, McKinnon, otherwise Jamal would not have purchased him to use in the races. Once I get rid of the tension and the bonding starts, then he'll do some amazing things, including increasing his speed. You'll see."

McKinnon got quiet again for awhile. He thought about the reason she was going into town, frowned and then said, "have you considered moving in with Durango and Savannah instead of getting your own place somewhere?" For some reason he was bothered by the thought of her living in the city alone. "I bet they'd be glad to have you as a guest for awhile."

Casey's hands tightened on the steering wheel. "For goodness sakes. They're still newlyweds. I would feel like I'm imposing on them."

He nodded. "Yeah, I can see your point. Even with Savannah being pregnant, it seems every time I drop by they're either getting out of the bed or getting into it."

Lucky them, she wanted to say but changed her mind.

"You could stay with my folks," he suggested.

Casey glanced over at him and met his gaze. Once again she felt the sizzle and tried to ignore the heat swirling around in her stomach and between her legs. She quickly placed her eyes back on the road, tightening her hands on the steering wheel and squeezing her thighs together. She didn't fully understand these sensations that always swamped her when he looked at her a certain way.

She tried to get a grip and think about what he'd just said about her moving in with his parents. How she could tell him in a nice way that his folks were just as bad as her father and Abby? She hadn't known that older couples could be so openly affectionate.

She cleared her throat and glanced back over at him. "I would feel like I'd be imposing on them as well."

McKinnon smiled. "Yeah. Like Corey and Abby, they do take being touchy and feely to a whole other level, don't they."

"And it doesn't bother you?" she asked.

"No, my brothers and I are used to it. My parents love each other very much and have no problem openly displaying that love. I think it's kind of special."

She'd been led over the years to believe what her parents had shared had been special, too. Boy, was that wrong. wanting to change the subject, she decided to ask him about what was still bothering her. "Why wouldn't you entertain the thought of me working on your ranch that first day, McKinnon?"

He glanced over at her, grateful her eyes were still on the road and not on him. He didn't want to look into her face when he lied. He couldn't be completely honest when he told her the reason behind his decision not to hire her. That he'd figured his constantly being around her, having her live on his ranch was a temptation he couldn't to deal with.

So instead he said, "Like I told you, if anything happened to you I would have Corey to deal with, not to mention all those other damn Westmorelands."

She shook her head smiling. "There *are* a bunch of them, aren't there?"

He lifted a brow. "Bunch of *them?* Need I remind you that you are one of them."

The smile on her face suddenly vanished. "Yes, and it took me all of twenty-eight years to find that out."

McKinnon heard the bitterness in her voice. It was his understanding that she still had issues regarding the lies her mother told her about her father. For some reason, she couldn't let go and move on.

"There might have been a reason your mother did what she did," he said quietly, recalling the reason his mother had never told him that Martin wasn't his biological father until she'd been left with no choice. "There are some things we aren't meant to understand, and what happened between your mother and Corey is probably one of them."

Casey sighed deeply. She wasn't surprised that he knew the whole story—their fathers were best friends and had been for years. But then, given Corey Westmoreland's popularity, she was certain that everyone in these parts had heard about his long-lost triplets.

"Don't try and make excuses for what she did to me and my brothers, McKinnon. All those years we thought our father was dead but he wasn't. Just think of all that wasted time when we could have known him."

"But you're getting to know him now. I hate to say that old cliché but better late than never, fits in this case."

Casey frowned. "No, it doesn't fit, and I prefer that we change the subject." A few minutes later she said, "We'll go see the doctor first to get you all fixed up."

McKinnon shook his head. In addition to being feisty, she was stubborn. "Whatever."

A couple of hours later, as they walked out of the doctor's office, Casey glanced over at McKinnon. "Are you sure you don't want me to take you back to the ranch now?"

He frowned. "I only got two stitches, Casey, not twenty, and I still don't think I needed them. And that damn tetanus shot wasn't necessary, but then Dr. Mason has always been heavy-handed when it came to needles."

After he opened the car door, slid onto the seat and buckled the seat belt, he glanced over at her. "Will you still have time to make your appointment?"

"Yes, the area isn't far from here. The first place is an apartment that's over an empty building."

He turned and looked at her like she'd lost her mind. "Why would you want to live in a place like that?"

After snapping her own seat belt in place, she glared over at him, not liking his tone. "It's not that I *want* to live in such a place, McKinnon, but when it comes to available housing, Bozeman isn't overflowing with it."

He sat back and stared out the window saying nothing. Why did he care where she decided to live? It was her business and not his.

She was right—it didn't take long for her to get to where they were going. The real estate agent, an older, stout lady with a huge smile on her face, was waiting for them and once they were out of the car and introductions were made, she ushered them up the stairs to the apartment.

McKinnon glanced around, immediately not liking the place already. He knew the area. It wasn't bad but then it wasn't good either. It was close to a business district with a bar on the corner. The place could get pretty rowdy, especially on certain nights of the week, not to mention on the weekends. She would never be able to get any rest.

When they reached the top of the stairs, the Realtor, who had introduced herself as Joanne Mills, moved aside to let them enter. "Nice place," Casey said, placing her hands on her hips while she glanced around the huge room. "I can see potential."

McKinnon couldn't, and while Casey continued talking he tried concentrating on what she was saying and not on what she was doing. Having her hands on her hips had drawn his gaze to her small waistline, curvy hips and thighs. A waist he had touched the night they'd kissed, and thighs and hips that he'd molded against his own.

"McKinnon?"

He quirked an eyebrow at hcr. "What?"

"What do you think?"

"I don't like it," he said in a gruff voice. "There's too much work to be done before it can be occupied."

Casey frowned. "It wouldn't hurt for you to be a little positive."

"Just speaking the truth." He turned to Ms. Mills. "You don't have anything in a more settled residential area? I don't like the fact that there's a bar on the corner."

Before the woman could answer, Casey said in an irritated voice, "You don't have to live here, McKinnon. That bar won't bother me." She then turned to Joanne. "But the size of the kitchen does. It's too small. I like cooking on occasion and there's not enough cabinet space. What's next on the list?"

McKinnon didn't like the next couple of places either and Casey had to admit that neither did she. It was late afternoon when they'd seen the last apartment and Ms. Mills promised to call when other listings came up.

"You might do better just to buy a piece of land and build on it," McKinnon said as they headed to the car.

"I might have to do that," she said, but knew that building a place would take even longer. She glanced up at the man walking beside her, thinking that although he had gotten on her last nerve a few times today by being overly critical of the places they'd seen, she had enjoyed spending time with him. "How's your hand holding up?"

He glanced over at her. "I told you my hand is fine. To prove that point, I'll drive back to the ranch."

Casey didn't have a problem with that since she'd found concentrating on the road and not him rather difficult. She'd been too distracted by his mere presence, and now that he had removed the rubber band from his hair, the curly mane flowed freely down his back, making him look more savage than tame. And then there were his smoky, dark eyes that would lock with hers. More than once while sitting in the doctor's reception room she'd glanced up from the magazine she'd been flipping through to find him watching her with an unreadable expression on his face. Each time their gazes connected her desire for him intensified that much more, and although she tried looking in another direction, it seemed her eyes kept inexplicably returning to his, only to find him still staring.

She handed him the keys. "If you want to drive, that's fine with me."

"Thanks." McKinnon opened the car door for Casey and stood back to let her get inside, trying to ignore the way her dress raised a little when she sat, showing a nice amount of thigh. He was attracted to her something awful and spending time with her had only intensified that attraction. Sitting and watching her at the doctor's office had been her thrilling. He was sure he had made her nervous but he hadn't been able to help it. She was take-your-breath-away beautiful and while staring at her he wondered about a number of things. How she would look naked?

What sounds she would make when she came? Visions of them wrapped up together in tangled sheets had immediately materialized in his mind.

He composed himself as he moved around the car to get in on the driver's side. He was used to seeing what he wanted and going after it, but had to constantly remind himself that with Casey came limitations. Hell, forget limitations—with Casey Westmoreland there was a no-fly, total hands-off zone, which he'd already breeched with that kiss. But he was determined to try and adhere to it from now on, no matter what.

"Hey, McKinnon, wait up!"

McKinnon gritted his teeth as he turned around. Rick Summers, who'd always been a pain in McKinnon and Durango's side, was approaching at a rapid pace. Rick wasn't someone they considered a friend. In fact, from the time he'd moved into the area a few years ago, he'd practically made it his business to try and compete against them where the ladies were concerned. He really thought a lot of himself, and when it came to the treatment of women he could be a total jerk.

"Rick, what can I do for you?" McKinnon asked, annoyed when the man reached the car.

Rick gave him a smooth smile. "I was on my way to visit a friend and thought I recognized you coming out of the house that's for sale. Thinking about moving into town, McKinnon?"

"No."

The man then peered through the open window to where Casey was sitting and all but licked his lips. "I also saw your lady friend. Aren't you going to introduce us?"

McKinnon stopped short of saying "no" but knew he

really had no choice. "Casey, I'd like you to meet Rick Summers, and Rick, this is Casey Westmoreland."

A surprised look appeared on Rick's face. "Westmoreland?"

"Yes. She's Durango's cousin and Corey Westmoreland's daughter."

A smile touched Rick's lips and McKinnon knew the man was giving Casey what he thought was his most flirtatious smile. "Nice meeting you, Casey," he said, opening the car door to shake her hand.

Casey returned the man's smile. "Nice meeting you, too, Rick."

"Are you just visiting a spell?" Rick asked curiously.

"No, I'm moving to Bozeman."

McKinnon knew by the darkening of Rick's eyes he had definitely latched on to that response. "To live with your father up on his mountain?"

Casey chuckled. "No, somewhere here in town."

McKinnon watched as Rick's smiled widened into a look McKinnon compared to a wolf on a hunt. "In that case, I hope we run into each other again…real soon." He tipped his hat and walked off smiling.

McKinnon shook his head, and when he slid into the driver's seat, he slammed the door shut as his protective instincts kicked in. If Rick Summers thought for one minute he would be adding Casey's name to his little black book, he could think again. Although who she dated was none of his business, the thought of her getting mixed up with the likes of Summers didn't sit well with him.

"He seems like a nice guy."

McKinnon glanced over at Casey. "In this case looks are deceiving because Rick's not a nice guy. He's an ass and

I suggest you stay away from him." He could tell by her expression that she didn't appreciate his suggestion.

And as he drove toward the highway that would take them back to the ranch, he decided that whether she liked it or not, he intended to keep Summers away from her.

Seven

"What are you doing for dinner?"

Casey stiffened as she got out of the car. Now that they were back at the ranch, surely he wasn't going to invite her to eat with him. "The usual," she heard herself say. "Henrietta usually fixes me something, and I eat it at the guesthouse while doing journal entries of Prince Charming's daily progress on the computer. Why?"

"Just asking. Thanks again for the ride into town."

"Don't mention it."

Common sense told McKinnon that this is where they would part ways. She would go to the guest house and he would go to the ranch house, and if he was real smart he would avoid her again this week. He'd spent some time with her today. He'd heard her voice and inhaled her scent and now he had gotten her out of his system for a while. Hell, not by a long shot. But as he forced himself to keep walking toward his front door, something made him turn around.

"Casey, how about if—"

Whatever words he was about to say died on his lips. She was gone, having made a swift exit to the guest house. His disappointment quickly turned into annoyance. Evidently she'd taken as much as she could of him for one day. He wished he could say the same but couldn't. He could have taken more of her…a lot more. He had been constantly aware of her as a woman—a woman who probably didn't know the extent of her own sensuality or sexuality. And he was a man who would love tapping into what she didn't know; expose her to a few things. Hell, more than a few.

Thirty minutes later, after taking a shower and being careful to keep his stitches dry, he made his way to the kitchen to warm up his food. He'd been following this same routine for years, ever since Lynette had left. He was used to it and preferred things this way. He was about to stick his plate into the microwave when the phone rang.

He reached over and picked it up. "Yes?"

"How are you, McKinnon?"

He smiled upon hearing his mother's voice. "I'm fine. How are you and Dad?"

"We're both doing well. We just got back today. We've been up on Corey's Mountain visiting, which is why I'm calling. Abby and I decided it would be nice to give a party for Casey."

He tensed. "A party? Why?"

"To welcome her to the area. A lot of our neighbors know about Corey's triplets and some have even met Clint and Cole. But very few have had a chance to meet Casey, and we think a party will be a wonderful way to arrange that, to welcome her to the community."

Sounded like his mother and Abby had their minds made up. "So what do you need me to do?" Nothing he hoped.

"In addition to not working her too hard where she's too tired to attend her own party and enjoy herself, how about making sure she gets here."

McKinnon stiffened. He had endured one car ride with Casey and wasn't sure he would be able to do another anytime soon. It seemed the scent of her was still all over him. "When is this party?"

"Next Friday night, here at our ranch at eight. Can I depend on you to help?"

He sighed. There wasn't too much Morning Star Quinn couldn't get out of him and she knew it very well. "Yes, I won't over work her that day and I'll make sure she gets there."

"Thanks, McKinnon. I appreciate it. By the way, it's not a surprise or anything like that. I just finished telling Casey about it and she's fine with it."

"That's good," he said with grim resolve before hanging up the phone.

Another night and Casey couldn't sleep. Nor could she get McKinnon off her mind. He had invaded her dreams and she didn't like it.

Actually, that wasn't true.

She *had* liked it. So much to the point where she had awoke filled with desire so intense she felt it deep in her belly. She'd heard of belly aches before but nothing like this one.

She slipped into her robe and, as was the norm whenever she found she couldn't sleep, decided she'd take a stroll around the courtyard and enjoy the beauty of the night.

A few moments later she went out the front door and onto the brick paved walkway. A flood light off the front of the ranch house glowed, but just enough to illuminate some of the new flowers Henrietta had boasted of planting this week.

"Couldn't sleep again tonight?"

Casey placed her hand over her chest. Just like the last time, she hadn't heard McKinnon's approach. She slowly turned, thinking what she really needed was to find a reason to go back inside the guesthouse. It didn't take much to remember what had happened the last time they'd been out in the courtyard together.

However, instead of taking off, she answered, "No. I have a lot on my mind."

The eyes staring at her were dark, intense…sexy. "You're thinking about the party?"

She raised a brow. "The party?"

"Yes. Mom called and told me about it."

"Oh." It was on the tip of her tongue to tell him that the party his mother and Abby had planned for her was the last thing on her mind. She'd been thinking about a party all right, a party of two. There were no party hats—just a big bed, silken sheets, and plenty of heat between two naked bodies. "No, I wasn't thinking about the party," she said. And that was all she intended to tell him.

He came closer into the moonlight, into her line of vision. His hair was flowing around his shoulders and she wanted to hook her finger around a few strands and pull his mouth down to hers, to take possession of his tongue the same way he had taken hers that night. She wanted to—

"The stars are really out tonight."

McKinnon's comment brought her back to the present which was just as well, since her thoughts were going places they had no business venturing. Following his gaze, she tilted her head back and glanced up into the sky. "Yes, they are, but in my book if you've seen them once, you've seen them all."

"Hey, you better not let Ian hear you say that. He's the astronomer in the Westmoreland family."

Casey smiled. "Oops, I forgot. And speaking of Ian, I guess everyone is getting prepared for his wedding next month. I hear it's supposed to be one grand affair at the Rolling Cascade Casino."

McKinnon nodded. "Yeah, and I bet Lake Tahoe won't be the same when Brooke becomes a permanent part of his security team." A few moments later he added, "And speaking of Lake Tahoe, you looked good that night at Delaney's birthday party."

A tiny tremor passed through her. She doubted he gave many compliments. "Thank you. You looked rather dashing yourself." And he had. They hadn't said more than a few words to each other that night, but she had noticed him and it seemed from his compliment that he had noticed her as well.

"I talked to Norris when we got back from town. He said that our fathers dropped by to check on Spitfire while we were gone."

"Spitfire?"

"Yes, she's the mare that Thunder impregnated. Corey's the one who gave her to me a couple of years ago. We agreed then that he would get her first foal."

Casey glanced up at him. "You like Corey a lot, don't you?"

He glanced over at her wondering why she'd asked the question. "Yes. He and my dad were friends before I was born. I can't remember a time when he wasn't a part of my life."

He smiled and Casey blinked thinking that was the first smile she'd ever seen on McKinnon Quinn's lips. "Do you know what one of the things I admired most about him while growing up is?"

"What?"

"His love for his family. He was a young single man, yet every summer he would invite all of his nephews and his one lone niece to spend the summer months with him, and he would always include me."

"Sounds like all of you had a rowdy good time every year."

McKinnon chuckled and Casey found the sound rich and sincere. "Trust me, we did. Especially those times Delaney got left back in Atlanta and we could get into all kinds of trouble without anyone telling on us."

Casey smiled. "Sounds like Corey would let all of you get away with murder."

"Oh, we knew how far to take things with him. But he would make everything we did fun for us. How he kept all of us over those summers months without going insane is beyond me."

Casey paused a moment to digest his statement. Had her father known about her and her brothers, they would have been included in those summers as well. But he hadn't known.

When a few moments passed and she didn't say anything, McKinnon said softly, "Sorry. Maybe I shouldn't have mentioned those summers."

Casey glanced up at him. It was as if he'd read her thoughts. "No, it's okay. Besides, you can't rewrite history,

McKinnon. I don't begrudge any of you for the times you spent with my father when Clint, Cole and I didn't. It's not anyone's fault." But my mother's, she wanted to scream.

McKinnon brushed a lock of hair back from her forehead, thinking the short, sassy style looked cute on her. The glow from the moon highlighted her features in a way he found incredibly sexy.

"McKinnon?"

"Yes?" He heard that little tremor in her voice; the same one that had been there right before he'd kissed her.

"I think I should go back inside now."

"Why? I kind of like it out here, don't you?"

"Yes, but…"

He heard the apprehension in her voice at the exact moment his gaze was drawn to her mouth. "But what?"

She sighed, and he watched the sound escape through her lips. In fact, he actually felt the warm breath against his own lips, which meant he had subconsciously lowered his head closer to hers.

"The last time we were out here together," she finally said, "something happened to make you avoid me for a week." She decided not to spell it out to him since she was sure he knew what she was talking about. "If you're going to have any regrets about anything we do, then I'd rather we didn't do it."

"Anything like what?" he asked, inching his lips even closer to hers.

"Whatever," she said, nervously chewing her bottom lip.

As quick as she'd ever encountered, he darted his tongue out and slowly began licking around her lips, trailing a path from corner to corner. "By anything, do you mean something like this?" he asked as his tongue continued to toy with her lips.

"Yes," she whispered, barely able to get the word out. "Something like that."

"And what about this?" he asked, reaching up, drawing her face closer with his hands, so close she could see the dark intensity in his eyes. He began nibbling on her lips, gently, thoroughly, seemingly partial to the plumpness of her bottom lip. After hovering there for a few seconds, he then moved to her top lip, giving it equal play.

She felt her stomach clench, felt the heat forming between her legs and wished he would stop torturing her and just go in for the kill—she was dying a slow, sensuous death with every teasing stroke of his tongue.

"I like kissing you," he whispered against her moist lips.

She could tell and wondered if he realized he wasn't exactly kissing her, just tormenting her. Then, without warning, she had a fantasy flashback of him doing this very thing in her dream, almost making her beg before finally giving her what she wanted. She had never experience lust before now. Didn't have an inkling of how profound and potent it was. Had never known how it felt to want a person to an extent that was mind blowing.

But what was making her feel heady was the fact that she knew he wanted her, too. The tightness in his jeans, the large bulge she felt pressed against her was evidence of that fact. And the more he tortured her mouth, the more he was working the both of them into a state of extreme arousal.

Deciding she'd had enough, she gripped a section of his hair. He stopped, looked at her, their eyes just as close as their lips. She saw the desire, the need, the outright hunger in his gaze, and then none too gently tugged on his hair and pulled his mouth down to hers.

She opened hers over his, not knowing exactly what she

was doing but having a good idea of what it was she wanted. And when he parted his lips, she inserted her tongue, determined to find that pleasure she'd found before.

She didn't have long to wait.

He launched into the kiss full speed, demonstrating his ability and flexibility; an impact she felt all the way to her toes. The fact that all the blood in her body had rushed south would explain her recklessness, her desire, this ingrained need to have her way with him she decided. Sensations ratcheted through her and she was driven to satisfy this hunger she had never felt before, this need to—

"Sorry to interrupt."

Casey and McKinnon quickly ended their kiss but he held onto her tight, refusing to allow her to put distance between them. "What is it, Norris?" he asked in an irritated tone, ignoring the curious look on his foreman's face. It wasn't the first time he'd been caught kissing a woman and it probably wouldn't be the last.

"Spitfire's in trouble."

"Damn." McKinnon muttered under his breath, easing Casey out of his arms. "What's wrong with her," he asked in a rough but worried voice.

"She's in labor and having problems. I called Paul but Beth said he's over at the Monroe's spread taking care of their sick cattle. She's not sure when he'll be able to get here."

Casey had regained her senses enough to absorb most of the conversation between McKinnon and Norris. She knew that Beth Manning was a park ranger who worked with Durango and that her husband Paul was the vet in the area. Before she could think of anything else beyond that, McKinnon, ignoring Norris' presence, brushed his lips with hers and then whispered against her moist lips, "I have to go." And then he was gone, rushing beside Norris to the stables.

"Is she all right, McKinnon?"

McKinnon glanced up as Casey walked into the barn. She had changed from her night gown and robe into a pair of jeans and a top. The outfit was more practical and, in his book, just as sexy.

He swallowed deeply and glanced back at the mare in the birthing stall. "I hope so, but it seems her first foal is giving her one hell of a time."

"Oh, poor baby."

"Yeah, and the daddy over there isn't handling things too much better," McKinnon said as he glanced over at Thunder who was anxiously prancing back and forth in his stall. "If you'll take care of Spitfire and try keeping her calm, I'm going to move Thunder to one of those empty stalls in the back. The less he knows about what's going on, the better."

"Sure," Casey said, moving closer to the mare. McKinnon had talked like Thunder was a person rather than a horse, and she knew her brothers felt the same way about their horses.

Alone with Spitfire, she spoke gently to the mare, trying to keep her calm. She had been around pregnant horses enough to know when the time came for them to deliver, they had a tendency to increase their anxiety levels, just like humans. Having a baby, no matter who was doing the having, was no picnic.

"She's okay?" McKinnon asked, stepping back into the stall sometime later.

Casey glanced up at him. "Yes, she's doing fine. Have you heard anything from Paul?"

"He called my cell phone while I was moving Thunder. He's left the Monroe's and is on his way, so hopefully he'll have something to calm Spitfire down."

McKinnon came to stand closer to Casey. "You're probably tired after all you've done today. I have a feeling it's going to be a long night. Why don't you go back up to the guest house and go on to bed."

Casey stared up at him. He was trying to get rid of her, to put back into prospective what he thought their relationship should be yet again. "I'm fine, McKinnon and since tomorrow is Saturday, I can sleep late if I want."

He met her gaze for a long moment and said nothing, but she felt him putting his guard back up. She couldn't help wondering why he refused to let her get close. A part of her said let it go, that if that's the way he wanted to be then so be it. Another part, the part that felt there was more to it than what she was seeing, decided not to let it go. There was a reason for McKinnon's behavior and she intended to find out what it was.

"Isn't he a beautiful colt?" Casey said excitedly about the foal Spitfire had given birth to a couple of hours earlier. Both mother and baby were doing fine, and proud Poppa Thunder had whined proudly.

"Yes, he most certainly is," McKinnon said as the two of them walked back toward the house. "And I know your dad is going to be pleased."

"I'm sure he will be." After Paul arrived, everyone got busy and there was no time to concentrate on anything but the business at hand. But now they were back to square one.

"You mentioned something about sleeping late in the morning. Does that mean you plan to stay on the ranch all weekend?" McKinnon asked, his voice neutral as if he didn't care one way or the other.

"My parents are off the mountain visiting with yours for the weekend. In fact, I'm going with both parents to a play in town tomorrow night. You're welcome to join us if—"

"No, thanks. I'll have work to do."

She nodded, knowing this was his way of putting distance between them again. "All right. Then I'll see you later."

Before he could comment, and whether he intended to do so was doubtful, she turned and walked quickly toward the guest house.

Savannah called and invited Casey over for Sunday dinner. Durango would be working that day and she hated eating alone. Casey appreciated the invitation to get off McKinnon's ranch for a while since once again he had made himself scarce where she was concerned. Besides, Casey appreciated the company of a female close to her age, and since meeting Savannah at Chase's wedding the two had developed a close friendship.

They talked about a lot of stuff but Casey would be the first one to admit their current topic was one she wouldn't mind changing. She glanced over at Savannah as she finished her meal. "Why do you think something is going on between me and McKinnon?"

Savannah tilted her head and smiled. "Because there is," she said simply. "You can deny it all you want but it's there. But honestly, I think you really don't recognize it for what it is."

The Silhouette Reader Service™ — Here's how it works:

Accepting your 2 free books and 2 free gifts places you under no obligation to buy anything. You may keep the books and gifts and return the shipping statement marked "cancel." If you do not cancel, about a month later we'll send you 6 additional books and bill you just $3.80 each in the U.S. or $4.47 each in Canada, plus 25¢ shipping & handling per book and applicable taxes if any.* That's the complete price and — compared to cover prices of $4.50 each in the U.S. and $5.25 each in Canada — it's quite a bargain! You may cancel at any time, but if you choose to continue, every month we'll send you 6 more books, which you may either purchase at the discount price or return to us and cancel your subscription.

*Terms and prices subject to change without notice. Sales tax applicable in N.Y. Canadian residents will be charged applicable provincial taxes and GST. All orders subject to approval. Credit or debit balances in a customer's account(s) may be offset by any other outstanding balance owed by or to the customer. Please allow 4 to 6 weeks for delivery.

Casey knew that was definitely a possibility since she had little experience with men. "And how do you know it's there?"

Savannah's smile widened. "Because I've seen the two of you at several functions. I've watched how you look at each other when the other's not noticing. I know first-hand how that is because that's how things started with me and Durango. Things got so intense between us that we were in bed together the day after we met."

She then rubbed her stomach and grinned. "And as you know, the rest is history."

Casey chuckled. "But the two of you are so much in love, which means the marriage didn't happen because you got pregnant."

"That was supposed to be the reason but that's the clincher," Savannah said, smiling broadly. "We didn't know we were in love. Or maybe deep down somewhere we knew it but were afraid to acknowledge it. I'm just glad we came to our senses. I can't imagine my life without Durango and I want the same thing for you and McKinnon."

Casey shook her head. "Whoa, back up, hold on. I think your eyes are so full of love for Durango that you think everyone else's eyes should have that same glow. But to set the record straight, there's nothing going on between me and McKinnon."

"If you think so, but I believe otherwise. Whenever the two of you are together, it's like spontaneous combustion just waiting to happen. And I don't think you fully understand just how explosive that can be."

Umm, after two kisses, which she had no desire to discuss at the moment, she did know how explosive passion could be. "Okay, I'll be the first to admit I'm extremely attracted to McKinnon. What woman wouldn't be? But an attraction is as far as things go. He has chosen the life of a bachelor and right now I'm trying to figure out what I want to do with my own life. So much of it has been filled with nothing but lies."

She chuckled harshly. "Do you know I was so wrapped up in all that fairy-tale stuff my mother used to feed me about her and my father that I wanted that same type of love for myself to the point that I'm still a virgin?"

Casey sighed deeply. There was no turning back now—she'd revealed her secret. In a way she was glad to get it out. She'd never had a sister and her brothers were the last people she could talk about something like that.

"I think it's wonderful that you're still a virgin," Savannah said, shifting to more comfortable position in her chair. "I wished I had saved myself for Durango. My one and only guy before him was a selfish bastard and I regret the day I ever met him, let alone sleep with him."

She glanced over at Casey before she continued. "But then I had no reason to believe in tales of romance and love. My father was the biggest bastard of them all. Trust me when I say he didn't set a good example."

"Yes, but at least you hadn't been fed lies your whole life," Casey said softly.

"No, but I still think you have a lot to be thankful for. Your mother took very good care of you and your brothers. That couldn't have been easy for a single woman, and it seems you were all raised with good values. Not all kids can claim that, Casey. And before she died, your mom wanted all of you to know the truth when she could have carried the information to the grave. Although you missed not having a father around while growing up, you did finally get to meet him and look what a wonderful man he is. I'll trade Jeff Claiborne for Corey Westmoreland any day."

Silence engulfed the room for several seconds before

Savannah spoke. "There might be something else you're overlooking."

"What?"

"Why your mother fabricated the story that she did. That could have been her way of coping with life, of dealing with the realization that the one man she loved more than life itself had a heart that belonged to another. That had to have been hard on her."

Casey gazed at Savannah, thinking she'd never thought of it that way. For the past two years she had been so angry at what her mother had done that she never given thought to the pain her mother must have endured knowing that no matter how much she loved Corey, he hadn't loved her back.

"I want you to promise me something, Casey."

Casey lifted a brow. "What?"

"If you ever do come to realize you care for McKinnon, don't give up on him and walk away, no matter what. I'm not a psychic by any means, but I feel something. Even when he appears happy I can detect his sadness and I don't know why. It's like there's something private eating at him but I have no idea what it could be. I've caught him looking at me and Durango during some of our play times with a pensive look in his eyes. And although he claims he doesn't ever want to marry and have children, I think that deep down he really does. I've tried talking to Durango about it but he refuses to discuss certain things about McKinnon with me. But then I have to respect that the two of them share this special bond."

Casey nodded. She knew of the bond the two men shared.

"Well, I've said enough," Savannah said, getting up from the table. "Just promise me that if the time comes, you'll remember what I said."

Casey sighed and met Savannah's gaze. "I promise."

Eight

In the comfort of his office McKinnon tossed a report on his desk. The white stallion he had imported all the way from the Blue Mountains of Australia had arrived earlier that day. Crown Royal was a magnificent animal with stunning looks, exceptional athletic ability and temperament. After his capture, he had spent time with renowned horse trainer Marcello Keaston and was more than ready for the task intended for him to do, and the brood mare selected was of the highest quality and value. McKinnon had no doubt that Crown Royal's first crop of foals would bring in a pretty penny at any auction.

He stood and stretched, and automatically his gaze drifted across the room to the calendar on the wall. It had been four days since he'd interacted with Casey. He had made it a point to keep his distance and it seemed she was doing likewise. The woman had a way of pulling his emotions in a way he couldn't afford to indulge.

He glanced toward his office door when he heard a knock. "Come in."

He smiled when Durango walked in. "How are things going, Rango?"

"Fine. I dropped Savannah off at a hair salon in town and thought I'd come here to kill some time. I just saw Crown Royal. Man, he's a beauty."

McKinnon chuckled proudly as he sat back down. "Yes, he is and I intend for him to make us plenty of money over the next few years. I've gotten a call from Mike Farmer already."

Durango's smile widened. "News travel fast."

McKinnon nodded. "Which is fine with me as long as it's in our favor, and you know Mike. He wants to be the first in everything and has the money to make it happen. He's hinted at acquiring the entire crop of Crown's first foals, now that we've selected Courtship as the mare." Courtship, a product of Thunder and a valuable Australian mare name Destiny, had already proven her worth as a fine magnificent piece of horseflesh and was known for her speed.

"And I got a call from Jamal today as well," McKinnon said, smiling.

"Did he want to know how Prince Charming was coming along?" Durango asked, leaning against the closed door.

"Yes, and he wants me to meet with a couple of his associates who'll be in D.C. this week. They're interested in our breeding program."

Durango nodded. "Will Jamal be attending this meeting?"

"No. Delaney's condition is keeping him in Tehran for a while. They'll attend Ian's wedding next month but other than that, Delaney's doctors don't want her jet setting all over the world."

Durango chuckled. "I can understand that since we have a lot of pregnant Westmorelands. So, will you be traveling to D.C.?"

"Yes, I leave first thing in the morning and probably won't be back until Saturday."

Durango nodded again. "Sounds like you'll miss Casey's party."

"There's a pretty good chance that I will." McKinnon didn't want to add that perhaps that was a good thing. "Would you like something to drink?"

Durango shook his head. "No, thanks. Savannah's cooking tonight and I don't want to spoil my appetite. You're invited, by the way."

McKinnon thought on Durango's invitation. If he was invited then chances were Casey had been invited as well. He quickly decided to pass on the invitation. The last thing he wanted was to torture himself by looking across the table at her, knowing he couldn't touch her. "Thanks for the invite but I have a lot of paper work to do before taking off in the morning."

Before Durango could comment that his reason was a lame excuse, McKinnon quickly added, "While you're here, Rango, can you look over the books? I'm sure you'll find everything in order."

"Don't I always?" Crossing the room, Durango took a seat at the extra desk.

When they'd decided to enter the partnership they had known that horse breeding was a risky business, but the risks were now paying off. In just a few years, not only had M&D earned the respect of their colleagues in the horse breeding world, but it was showing more of a profit than either Durango or McKinnon had imagined.

"So how is Casey working out?" Durango asked a few minutes later.

"Good. She's using a different approach that takes longer, but I have no doubt it will work. She knows what she's doing, that's for sure." McKinnon decided not to mention how, on numerous occasions, he would often stand at the window in this office and watch her interact with the horses. But mainly he watched *her.* And each time he saw her he thought about the heated kisses they had shared.

Damn it to hell, the need to feel her mouth beneath his again was almost overwhelming, although he'd been fighting the craving for days. Even now he could distinctively remember the warmth of her lips and how they would automatically part under his, the swift breath she'd take just seconds before his tongue mingled with hers and—

"And how are you handling her being here on the ranch?"

McKinnon gave Durango a look that grimly said he wasn't handling it very well. "Your cousin is a beautiful woman who can be a distraction if I let her be one, Rango."

Durango nodded. "And for you that's a bad thing, isn't it?"

McKinnon let out a deep sigh. "You of all people know that it could be if I were to let anything get out of hand. As long as we maintain an employer-employee relationship, we're fine," he said, knowing he hadn't even been able to really do that. "I made a decision a few years ago that I knew would affect any future relationship I had with a woman. At the time I felt it was the right one to make. I still do."

"Yes," Durango said, closing the accounting books. "I understand and like I told you then, I support your decision.

But having that procedure done wasn't the end of the world. Why don't you want to consider your other options?"

McKinnon didn't answer. At least not immediately. When he did his voice was filled with the anguish he sometimes felt. "I *have* considered those options but I can't expect every woman I meet to want to consider them as well, Rango. Lynette didn't. Trust me, it's easier this way."

Durango leaned forward in his chair, his gaze fixed on his best friend's features. "Choosing a life where you'll spend the rest of your days alone isn't the way, McKinnon. At one time we both thought living like that would work for us, but since having Savannah in my life, I'm glad things happened the way they did. I probably would have died a very lonely and miserable man. Besides, it can't be as easy as you claim if I read correctly what I saw in your eyes whenever you looked at Casey that night at dinner. You want her in a bad way—that much was obvious, at least to me. But I think it might be a little deeper than that. I think you might be falling for her, McKinnon."

"No," McKinnon growled, denying Durango's allegations as he narrowed his gaze at him. "You're dead wrong on that one."

Durango was silent for a moment and then he leaned back in his chair. "We'll see."

"Damn it, there's nothing to see." Exasperated and angry that he'd allowed Durango's false assumption to needle him, he pushed out of his chair. "I'm going out," he said tersely.

Durango lifted a brow. "Where?"

"To ride Thunder."

He spun around on booted heels and before Durango could blink, an angry McKinnon had walked out of the room.

* * *

Casey squinted against the brightness of the May sun when she saw the horse and rider slowly approach. She held her breath when she recognized it was McKinnon. Beneath the Montana sky, his hair was loose and hung around his shoulders, touching his chambray shirt. His jeans were worn and as far as she was concerned he looked perfect, all the way down to his boots, as he sat atop the huge horse with the rugged mountains as a backdrop. She swallowed and tried to downplay the fluttering that was going on in her chest. Seeing him reminded her of the heated kisses they'd shared, each one seemed to get bolder and more daring.

"Hello, McKinnon," she said when he stopped close to where she was standing with her horse beside the stream. She had finished with Prince Charming early and decided to do a little riding. At least today she wouldn't be eating alone since Savannah had invited her to dinner.

"Casey. You decided to go out riding I see," he said, eyeing her. His tone was cautiously polite.

"Yes, and before you insinuate otherwise, I did give Prince Charming a good workout today."

"I wasn't going to insinuate otherwise. From what I hear his speed yesterday was even better than what Jamal assumed, which means your way of doing things is working."

"I told you it would," she said pointedly, crossing her arms over her chest.

He nodded. "Yes, you did." A few minutes later, after dragging in a deep breath, he said, "I'm leaving in the morning for D.C. and I probably won't be back until sometime Saturday. If you need anything while I'm away see Henrietta or Norris."

The thought of him leaving, knowing he wouldn't be around—although she knew he had been avoiding her again—made a part of her stomach dip, but she inhaled in swift denial. Why should it bother her if he was leaving town? He meant nothing to her and she meant nothing to him. "Thanks for letting me know," she said, trying to keep her voice steady. "Have a safe trip."

Tightening his hand on the reins, he turned Thunder to leave and as he did Durango's words slammed into his ears. Even before his best friend had spoken them, McKinnon had come to suspect the allegations were true. His feelings for Casey had been growing since the day she set foot on the ranch, and that wasn't good because nothing could ever come of it…of them. But still, there was no way he could get on a plane tomorrow without taking the memory of another kiss with him.

He trotted a couple of feet before bringing Thunder to a stop and turning the horse around. The reason he had left to go riding was to escape the memory of her. But here she was. She stood there, meeting his gaze as an electrified silence stretched between them. With a will he couldn't resist, he climbed off Thunder and slowly began walking toward her, eliminating the distance separating them.

Casey watched McKinnon. His handsome features were hard as granite in one sense, but filled with a sensuous longing in another. She had sworn after the last time they'd kissed and he'd made himself invisible afterwards that he wouldn't get near her again. But the closer he got, the more she suspected what she had begun feeling for McKinnon was too bone-deep to deny him anything.

Casey's gaze flicked to his features when he came to a

stop directly in front of her. She could tell by the way his hands were balled into fists at his side that he was fighting the urge to take her in his arms. So she decided to make it easy on him and take him into hers.

She reached up, cupped his face with her hands and on tip-toe, leaned forward, intent on giving him something to think about while he was away. First she readied his lips with a couple of quick swipes of her tongue, ignoring his sharp intake of breath with each stroke.

She decided this was her kiss and she would go slow, be gentle and savor every moment. Working more on instinct than experience, she brushed her fingertips against his jaw and on a deep sigh, his mouth opened and she inserted her tongue and began lapping him up like he was the tastiest morsel she'd ever devoured. And when his tongue joined hers, something that mirrored a quake caused her insides to rumble with a need she felt only while in his arms. She felt herself drowning and quickly grabbed hold of his shoulders to keep from falling.

She released his mouth when she heard one of the horses, either his or hers, make a sound. She rested her forehead against McKinnon's as they both tried to regain their breath.

Moments later, McKinnon stepped back and she watched as he rubbed a hand across his eyes and down his face. Then he muttered something that sounded a lot like "damn" before waking away. She watched as he remounted Thunder and then rode off like the sheriff's posse was after him.

"You okay, Casey?" Savannah asked later that afternoon while the two of them were sitting outside on the porch, enjoying the view of the mountains. Durango was inside watching a basketball game on television.

Casey glanced over at Savannah who had cooked chicken and dumplings, a Westmoreland recipe she had weaseled from Chase Westmoreland, the cook in the family. Chase and his wife owned a soul-food restaurant in Atlanta. And it just so happened that Chase's wife, Jessica, was Savannah's sister. To say the least, the meal had been delicious.

And speaking of delicious…her thoughts shifted to McKinnon. He was probably back at the ranch packing to leave in the morning. She wondered if he was still thinking about the kiss they'd shared earlier that day as she was.

"Casey?"

Casey sighed. "Yes, I'm okay. I was thinking about something."

Savannah glanced over at her and smiled. "Some*thing* or some*one*?"

Casey smiled. It was definitely someone. McKinnon Quinn had a knack for kissing her crazy one minute, then putting distance between them the next. "I just don't get it," she said softly.

"Get what?"

Casey's gaze flicked to Savannah. "Why would a man who acts like he enjoys kissing me one minute put distance between us the next? As if he regretted what he's done?"

Savannah chuckled. "Sounds like he's afraid of getting in too deep. Do you have a problem with him kissing you?"

"Yes. No. I—I don't know," Casey muttered, clearly frustrated. "But our kisses don't mean anything."

"And what makes you think that?"

Casey rolled her eyes. "Trust me, they're just kisses. If they meant something, he wouldn't regret doing it the next day."

Savannah nodded. "McKinnon evidently wants you but

is working hard to apply the brakes. I'm wondering how long he can hold out on not having you."

Casey shrugged. "I can't be worried about something like that."

Savannah gave a ladylike snort. "Casey Westmoreland, aren't you the least bit interested to know why he's afraid to get into a serious relationship?"

"I'm not as naive as you might think, Savannah. I have two brothers, remember, so I know why some men prefer not getting into serious relationships. It's called commitment phobia. McKinnon is full of testosterone with a capital T. And like Clint and Cole, I'm sure he accepts the concepts of sex and intimacy as a way of life. I used to watch how my brothers would operate, changing women as often as they changed their shirts. I was the one whose head was filled with romantic illusions of forever love and till death do you part."

"But still, if a man showed interest in me one day then tried acting like I didn't exist the next, I'd like to know why," Savannah said. "That way I'd know how to handle him."

While driving home from Durango and Savannah's home Casey inwardly admitted that Savannah had raised a pretty good question. Why was McKinnon putting brakes on anything developing between them?

There was only so much kissing a couple could do before kissing turned into cuddling, stroking, getting naked … and then what? Did he think they could continue to kiss without ever wanting to take things further? Already whenever he took her into his arms she felt emotions she hadn't experienced before. Her body would get hot and bothered like it had recognized it's mate—as if that in itself wasn't the craziest thing.

Or was it?

Her chest heaved at the possibility and heat was spreading to all parts of her body. Could McKinnon be her true mate? Her mother always claimed that a woman would know the man that was meant for her. And although her mother had filled her mind with lies about her and Corey, all Casey had to do was look around to know true love did exist for some people—like Durango and Savannah, her father and Abby, and McKinnon's parents, to name a few. Then there were all those Westmorelands who were happily married.

She was determined when she saw McKinnon again that she would get some answers. If he was playing a game with her then he would find that she was a worthy opponent. She wasn't all that experienced when it came to man-woman stuff, but she was not a woman to take lightly.

McKinnon glanced out his bedroom window the moment he heard Casey returning. He took advantage of his position near the window to study her unobserved. It was dark, but the flood lights around his home provided enough lightning to clearly see her.

She was wearing a pair of jeans with a V-neck green blouse. She had on what appeared to be a pair of sturdy boots and her short hair seemed tousled or windblown, giving one the impression she had just gotten out some man's bed or had driven home with the car window down. He wanted to lay blame on the latter and not the former. The thought of her in any man's bed beside his was a very disturbing one.

When she went inside the cottage and closed the door, he moved away from the window, wondering how he could feel so possessive toward a woman that wasn't even his and could never be. Any man who knew his situation would have the common sense and the decency to leave her alone. In fact, any man with a lick of sense would not have kissed her in the first place, let alone kiss her a few more times after that. He knew the score.

He also knew he wanted her.

There was no rhyme or reason as to why he felt the way he did considering everything. But he would give anything to take her into his arms one last time and brand her his, even if it was only for a minute, an hour...a night. He had found out the hard way that when it came to Casey, kissing her would not be enough. She was able to arouse a desire in him so strong and potent that it didn't take much to make his body hard with one hell of a relentless throb.

Like it was doing now.

He inwardly swore as he slammed his luggage shut. He wanted to feel the hardness of her nipples pressed against his chest. He wanted to fit her body to his, position her as close as she could get to relieve his ache, stop the throbbing. He wanted to kiss her again, slide his tongue into her mouth, devour her, savor every stroke as he feasted on her taste...or let her control things the way she'd done earlier that day by the stream. As inexperienced as she was, her technique had been flawless and had his loins blazing to the point the fire was still burning now. He had this connection to Casey that he just couldn't shake. A man with a whole lot of sense wouldn't act on it but around her he seemed to be senseless.

Even now he could picture her getting ready for bed, taking a shower, letting the water stream over her naked body. More than anything he wanted to be in that shower with her, take her against the tile wall, hear her call his name the moment he made her come.

Warning bells went off in his head, reminding him of the reason there could never be anything serious between them, but he dismissed the reason with a low, husky growl as he made his way out of his bedroom toward the back door. At the moment he was too far gone to even think straight.

Casey heard the loud knock on her door the moment she stepped out of the bedroom. She tightened the sash of her robe as she crossed the room, wondering if anything had happened to Prince Charming.

She glanced out the peephole and saw it was McKinnon and quickly unlocked the door and opened it. "What happened?"

"Nothing happened."

Casey met his gaze, saw the unmistakable intensity of an aroused man in his eyes—a man who fully intended to get stimulated even further. She couldn't decide if she should snatch him inside and have her way with him, or run for cover. She quickly recalled her talk with Savannah, and even more recent, the talk she'd had with herself while driving home. She swallowed hard, fighting the desire and the urge to give this man any and everything he wanted. She had to stand her ground and not make things easy for him. Well, not too easy.

She tilted her head back and tried not to focus on that look in his eyes. "Then, why are you here, McKinnon?" She couldn't be more direct than that, she thought.

McKinnon stared at her. She was as he'd thought, still damp in some places from her shower and ready for bed. He reached out and caught her hand in his before she realized what he was about to do. He felt the shiver that passed through her, heard her sharp intake of breath. "I'm here because I'm leaving in the morning and I wanted to kiss you goodbye before I left."

"Why? So you can have a reason to ignore me when you get back on Saturday?"

Her words were sharp and sliced right through him. She had taken his behavior after every kiss as a rejection of her, but he'd only been trying to preserve his sanity by not starting something with her that he'd known he couldn't finish. He had seen putting distance between them as the only answer. Where he saw it as a positive, she'd taken it as a negative. But now he was past the point of trying to be noble. There was an air of intimacy surrounding them and they were both breathing it, being consumed by it, nearly drowning in it.

"No, that's not the reason why. I want to kiss you so I can carry the taste of you with me."

She inhaled sharply, thinking he knew exactly what to say to make her come unglued. When the warmth of his fingers closed around hers, she knew she was loosing the battle. But she refused to give in until she had the answers she sought. "Why? Why did you stay away after each time we kissed, McKinnon?" she asked softly.

He stared at her for a second and knew he had to be honest with her, as much as he could. "I didn't see it as staying away from you, Casey. I saw it as distancing myself from temptation. It was either that or make an attempt to take you to bed every time I was around you. I wanted you just that much."

"And you saw that as a bad thing?" she asked, needing to understand.

"I damn sure don't see it as a good thing. You're Corey's daughter, Durango's cousin. To me the Westmorelands are like family. I can't see starting something with you that would lead nowhere. I doubt any of them would appreciate it if I did."

"And you're sure it would have led nowhere?" she asked quietly.

"Yes. I don't intend to ever get serious about a woman. Marriage is not in my future."

"May I ask why?"

"No. That's one topic that's not up for discussion. Just take my word that it's not and let's leave it at that."

His words were a sure sign that some woman had hurt him. Was that the reason he was still bitter and hell bent on not giving his love to someone else? "So, why are you here, McKinnon? I'm still Corey's daughter and Durango's cousin, and you're still not looking for anything permanent in your life."

He released her hand to lean in the doorway and took a moment to let his gaze rake over her from the top of her head to the toes of her bare feet. She looked sexy in her short silk black robe. "Because," he said softly, meeting her gaze again. "In addition to being Corey's daughter and Durango's cousin, I can no longer deny that you're also a very desirable woman."

He reached out and placed a knuckle beneath her chin, forcing their eyes to meet when he added, "And a woman I want in my bed."

The huskily spoken words sent more shivers through her body, made the nipples of her breasts press tight against her robe and made heat stream down her stomach to settle between her legs. "And you made that decision, just like that?"

"No," he said easily. "It took me almost three weeks and only after you took the initiative and kissed me earlier today, making me realize and accept that you're a woman with needs as well."

Casey wondered what he would think if he knew that he was the one defining those needs, because the "needs" he was referring to had never been awaken until now. Not only had they been awaken, they were stirring to life and seemed to have a mind of their own. She nervously nibbled her lips.

"Wouldn't you rather nibble my lips?"

Casey swallowed against a massive lump in her throat. His question had her imagining such a thing taking place. She was suddenly aware that she was losing ground with him. He had a way of stirring up her emotions and her passion. She drew in a shaky breath and took a step back He followed, closing the door behind him.

He stood tall, broad-shouldered. His muscular chest was covered in a tan shirt that seemed to highlight his golden-brown skin. His mane of hair flowed around his shoulders and the dark eyes staring at her had an intensity that nearly took her breath away. McKinnon Quinn was definitely any woman's fantasy.

Before she could take another step he reached out and snagged her arm, bringing her closer to him. "When I said I wanted to take your taste with me, I meant it."

Then McKinnon leaned down and captured her mouth with his, swallowing her sigh of pleasure in the process. With the sound, a fission of heated desire flowed through his veins and he intensified the mating of their mouths, erasing the physical distance they had endured the past weeks, as well as the one they would encounter over the next three days. He devoured her mouth like a hungry man who needed the taste of her as much as he needed to breathe, and when he wrapped his arms around her, bringing her luscious curves closer to the fit of him, he pressed against her, wanting her to feel just how much he needed her, wanted her.

She reciprocated, as if wanting him to know the same by slipping her arms around his waist as he continued to feast on her mouth. The taste of him always amazed her. He had the scent of man but the taste of sweet chocolate.

She felt herself being lifted into his arms but instead of taking her into the bedroom as she assumed he would do, he carried her over to the sofa and gently placed her there. He stood back and looked down at her. She looked back at him, seeing the thick bulge behind the zipper of his jeans as well as the dark look in his eyes.

He slowly eased down on his knees in front of her and leaned over and opened her robe to discover she wasn't wearing anything except her panties. His gaze met hers just seconds before he lowered his head to capture a nipple into his mouth, feasting on it with as much intensity as he had with her mouth earlier. Each pull on her nipples sent a sensuous tug through her abdomen and heat escalating in her center. He braced his hands on both sides of her as he continued a hungry path down her body with his mouth. When he reached her stomach, he kissed her navel, drew circles around it with the tip of his tongue, before moving lower.

She assumed her panties would stop him but she soon discovered he didn't intend for them to be a deterrent. She stiffened when he used his hands to ease the flimsy material down her legs, exposing the area of her that he sought. Then he touched her there and the moment he did, she shuddered as intense heat consumed her.

His fingers moved through the dark curls, teasing the sensitive nub, testing the wetness between her legs before he slid a finger inside and began stroking her.

"McKinnon."

She said his name on a sensuous purr as he continued to stroke, sending shock waves of pleasure straight through her, making her incredibly aroused and filled with a need that was mind consuming.

He lowered his head and she made a move to get up until she felt the sharp tip of his tongue invade the area where his fingers had been. The sensations that single swipe of his tongue made were so potent she thought she would pass out. And when he gently lifted her hips to position her closer to his mouth, she moaned out his name from deep within her throat.

He relentlessly stroked her with his tongue, stimulating every sensory nerve within her, making her tremble all over. He had started a fire within her that she doubted could ever be extinguished. And just when she thought she was about to burn to a crisp, sensations overtook her, making her cry out before she could stop from doing so.

She closed her eyes, thinking that would soften the impact, but it made it that much more forceful, turning her entire body inside out. A heartbeat of a second later, something inside of her exploded and her body shattered into a million sensuous pieces.

When he finally removed his mouth from her, she opened her eyes and met his gaze. Before she could say anything, he kissed her, letting her taste herself on his lips.

Moments later when McKinnon pulled his mouth free, he stood as he gazed down at her. His body was throbbing and ached to be inside of her but knew tonight was not the time. She had to accept him on his terms before that could happen.

"McKinnon?"

He leaned down and gently pulled her up to hold her in his arms. When he released her, he met her gaze. "Before we can go beyond this, Casey, I need to be sure that you understand that this is all we can ever share. I have to know that you can be satisfied with that. Think about it while I'm gone." His mouth then came down on hers as if he was branding her; kissing her with a desperation that had her moaning all over again.

He pulled back and not saying a single word he turned and headed for the door. And without looking back he left.

Nine

"McKinnon, you're back," Morning Star Quinn said, surprised and smiling up at her oldest son. "We weren't expecting you until tomorrow and thought you'd miss the party altogether."

"I was able to wrap everything up a day earlier," he said, glancing around. This wasn't a small party. His mother and Abby had definitely done things up on a larger scale than he'd expected. But then he really shouldn't have been surprised.

As he scanned the room he was looking for one person in particular—the honoree, the woman who'd been on his mind every day since he'd been gone. He smiled when his gaze was snagged by Stone Westmoreland. Evidently Stone had arrived in Montana while McKinnon had been away.

He nodded at Stone, then moved his gaze on. A group of invitees standing in a crowd parted briefly, allowing a better view and McKinnon's body stiffened when he saw Casey hemmed in a corner by Rick Summers. She looked simply beautiful in a latté-colored skirt and matching blouse.

"McKinnon, would you like something to drink?"

His mother's question momentarily pulled away his attention and he glanced down at her and forced a smile. "No, I'm fine. I think I'll mingle." Mingle hell, he thought, moving straight to the area where Casey and Summers were standing. Neither of them had noticed his arrival.

"McKinnon. I thought you weren't returning until tomorrow," Durango said, appearing out of nowhere and blocking his path.

"Not now, Rango," McKinnon all but snarled. "The only thing I want to do is put my fist in Summers' face."

Durango lifted a brow. "Why would you want to do something like that?" he asked in a low tone.

"Because Rick Summers is a—"

"Bastard," Durango said, finishing the sentence for him. "That's nothing new. Come on, let's grab a couple of beers and go somewhere and chill."

McKinnon narrowed his gaze at Durango. "I don't want to chill. I want to—"

"Smash Summers' face in, I know, but you need to cool down and tell me why seeing Casey with him has gotten you all worked up. She's my cousin so I have a valid reason to be interested in the proceedings—especially knowing the ass Summers is—but whether you've noticed or not, I'm not the only Westmoreland here tonight. Stone's here. So are Corey, Clint and Cole."

McKinnon glanced around. "Clint and Cole are here?"

"Yeah, but maybe they're keeping an eye on the wrong man. Maybe they should be keeping an eye on you. The last time we talked you claimed you weren't falling for Casey. If this isn't falling, I'd like to know what it is when a man wants to smash another's face just for talking to a woman who means nothing to him? Maybe instead of smashing up Summers' face, you need to give what I just said some serious thought."

Then Durango walked off.

Casey quickly concluded that she wouldn't be able to hide her annoyance much longer if Rick Summers continued to deliberately hog her time. In less than twenty minutes she'd discovered the man was so full of himself it was a shame. He had an ego a mile long and at some point during his lifetime, some woman had convinced him he was every female's ideal man.

She glanced around. Where were Clint and Cole when she needed them? She'd been hoping one of them would come and find some excuse to take her away, but so far that hadn't happened.

She continued to glance around the room when her breath suddenly caught as her gaze locked with McKinnon's. Adrenaline was mixing with surprise and making all kind of weird things happen to her body. She hadn't expected him back until sometime tomorrow but seeing him now, standing across the room talking to one of her brothers while slowly raking his gaze over her, was only increasing her adrenaline level. It didn't take much to recall the intimacy that had transpired between them the night before he'd left. Just thinking about it sent a quaking shiver through her body and caused heat to settle in one particular place between her thighs.

"Would you like to go outside with me for a spell?"

Rick's words invaded her thoughts, which was a good thing since she was about to melt from all the heat McKinnon's look was generating. She broke eye contact with McKinnon to glance up at Rick. "No, I don't want to go outside, Rick. I like being inside much better. Besides, I'm the guest of honor and it wouldn't look good if I went missing."

He shrugged. "Who cares about these people."

Her frown deepened. "I do. Most of them are friends of my father's."

Seeing he had ticked her off, Summers tried to backpedal into her good graces. "I didn't mean it that way…" he protested. "I can certainly understand if now isn't a good time, but before the night is over maybe we can slip—"

"May I have this dance?"

The deep, husky voice had both Casey and Rick turning around. Rick's surprise quickly transformed into annoyance. "Where did you come from, McKinnon? I thought you'd be out of town until sometime tomorrow."

McKinnon gave a smile that didn't quite reach his eyes. "See what happens when you think, Summers," he said. He turned to face Casey and held out his hand to her. "Will you dance with me, Casey?"

"No, she won't dance with you. As you can see, she's with me," Summers all but snarled.

"Is that a fact?" McKinnon asked, holding Casey's gaze.

Knowing there wasn't a decision to make, Casey placed her hand in McKinnon's. "Welcome back, McKinnon, and I'd love to dance with you." She then turned to Rick. "Excuse us, please."

Casey could feel the heat of Rick's anger burn her back when she walked off but at the moment she could care less.

And when McKinnon pulled her into his arms, threaded his fingers possessively with hers, Rick was nothing more than a very blurred memory.

It seemed McKinnon had timed it right; a slow number was playing and she couldn't imagine being anywhere but here, in his arms as they swayed slowly to the rhythm of the music. That wasn't true, she decided quickly. She could imagine being somewhere else with him—in his bed. After he'd left that night, after doing all those wondrous things to her body, she had laid there, too overwhelmed to move.

She had done a lot of thinking over the three days since he'd been gone. She wanted McKinnon Quinn. Pure and simple. There didn't have to be promises of forever-after or any pretense of something that wasn't there. At least not on his part since she knew how she felt. She loved him. All it took was waking up that next morning, remembering that special intimacy that had taken place the night before and knowing he was somewhere miles away that made her accept what she'd been trying to deny. Regardless of how he felt about her, she could admit that she loved him and unlike her mother, she wouldn't pretend about what wasn't there. Instead, she would accept what she could and be happy.

When the music came to an end, he leaned down and softly whispered, "Would you step outside with me for just a minute?"

His dark eyes were filled with so much heat that it almost singed her spine. Unlike when Rick had asked her that same question, she'd felt no hesitation when giving McKinnon her response. "Yes."

Taking her hand, he led her out the door. Once they were on the porch, he tugged her closer, slipped his hand around her waist, and he led her somewhere only he knew. This used to be his home, she thought. The place he'd been raised as a child. He knew of secret places and she had a feeling that tonight he intended to share one with her.

"This is a good spot," he said, coming to a stop on the dark side of the barn, away from prying eyes. He turned her in the circle of his arms.

"A good spot for what?" she asked as shivers of awareness and desire caressed her skin.

"For this." And then he leaned down and captured her mouth while gathering her closer into his arms. Their kisses seemed to always get hotter and hotter, more intense, bolder and more profound. Her heartbeat kicked up and her love for him increased ten fold. There was a reason she'd been so attracted to him from the first and now she understood it all.

Moments later he slowly released her mouth and she glanced up at him, her nostrils filled with his sexy scent. "That's the welcome I needed, Casey," he whispered against her moist lips. "The kind I thought about getting once I returned."

"I hope I didn't disappoint you," she said, smiling up at him.

He gave her one of those rare McKinnon smiles and said, "You could never do that." Then, moments later, he asked, "Have you given any thought to what I asked you to think about while I was gone?"

"Yes."

"And?"

She knew what he wanted to hear. "I accept your terms, McKinnon. There will be no expectations, only enjoyment."

He stared at her for a long moment before nodding. "And you can live with that?"

"Yes, I can live with it."

He nodded. "How did you get here tonight?"

"Cole came and picked me up."

McKinnon was glad it hadn't been Rick. "I'll let your brother know that I'll be taking you back to the ranch when the party's over."

"All right."

He leaned down and kissed her again before reluctantly pulling away. "I guess we need to go back inside now," he said in a tone that said he would rather stay out there with her. "And I guess it wouldn't be a good thing for me to dominate all your time tonight," he said, taking her hand.

"I wouldn't complain if you did."

A long, tense silence stretched between them and Casey wondered what he was thinking. She had no idea but she knew what was on her own mind. She would make sure that after tonight the thought of putting distance between them again would be the last thing McKinnon would want to do.

She intended to turn the tables on him and hit him with a little taste of seduction—Westmoreland style.

Never before had McKinnon thought the distance between his parents' home and his was so long. It seemed like he'd been driving for hours instead of minutes. He should feel relaxed, relieved by Casey's decision for them to get involved in a no-strings-attached affair, but all he felt was tension and a deep desire for the woman sitting beside him in his car.

After arriving from the airport he had parked his truck and decided to take his toy, an '85 Corvette he'd restored a couple of years ago. It provided him a type of horsepower that Thunder couldn't. He took a quick glance sideways at Casey. She hadn't said much since they'd left the party.

When they had gone back inside after their kiss, it hadn't surprised him that Rick Summers had tried seeking her out again, determined to stay glued to her side. But she had handled Summers by saying that as the guest of honor she had to spend time with everyone and not just him. McKinnon smiled, remembering that that hadn't gone over too well with him and he'd eventually left.

He also remembered the second dance he and Casey had shared nearly at the end, which had prompted them to leave the party as soon as they could without raising any eyebrows. The moment he held her close to him, knowing that later that night she would be his in every way that a woman possibly could, had set his loins on fire. And from the way she had shivered in his arms, he'd known she'd been acutely aware of his aroused state.

He inhaled deeply and instead of the fragrance of bitterroot, the purplish-pink flower that was abundant in the area, his nostrils were filled with the scent of Casey and he became drenched in a wave of intense yearning. He wanted her. He wanted her in a way he had never wanted any woman before, including Lynette.

His hands tightened on the steering wheel as he felt a deep ache in his gut. On the flight back to Montana from D.C., he had thought about the moment when he would hold her in his arms, kiss her…make love to her. He hadn't been able to stop his mind from going there. Whenever he closed his eyes he thought of her in his bed, burying himself inside of her so deep that—

"I was really happy to see Spencer come in," she said of Durango's brother who made his home in California. "And I found it interesting that he's in the process of buying a winery somewhere in the Napa Valley."

Her words, spoken in a soft tone, floated all around him. He wanted to glance over at her again, but if his eyes were to connect with hers he would be tempted to pull to the side of the road and put an end to his pain and agony.

"So did I, but then Spencer has always been the financial wizard and investment genius in the Westmoreland family," he said.

"And that was wonderful news that Stone and Madison shared with everyone, wasn't it?" she asked moments later. "I'm so happy they're pregnant."

"So am I. Abby is ecstatic at the thought of becoming a grandmother."

Casey smiled. "And my father will become a grandfather. Another Westmoreland baby. I think it's wonderful."

McKinnon didn't say anything for a long moment but then asked, "I take it you want children some day?"

"Of course." She chuckled. "I don't particularly want a house-full like Madison says she wants, but I'd like at least two."

Disappointment swept through McKinnon and he tried to fight it back. He couldn't blame Casey for her desire to one day want a child; a child he would never be able to give her.

"Was your trip to D.C. a productive one, McKinnon?"

Her question brought him back. "Yes, I believe it was. Jamal's friends are impressed with the American way we do things, especially in breeding horses. They've formed a partnership and want to breed champion thoroughbred race horses. They're also interested in breeding Black Sterling Friesians."

"Those are beautiful horses. My uncle bred and trained one once."

"How did it go?"

"It went okay. Uncle Sid was a very patient man. The horse's name was Roving Rogue and it suited him. He had an eye for one particular mare, and no amount of coaxing could get him to cooperate with his training until he had his way with her."

McKinnon knew what she meant but wanted her to expound anyway. "Had his way, how?"

He could feel her gaze slide over to him and the force of it was a heated caress. He wondered if she would explain, go into details, paint one hell of a vivid picture.

"I wasn't supposed to be watching that night when it happened but I sneaked out of my room and got a chance to watch anyway. I was only fourteen and I guess Uncle Sid thought the sight of horses mating would be too intense for my delicate eyes," she said, and he could hear the smile in her voice. "It was to be a private affair with only my uncle and Vick, his head trainer, watching. Uncle Sid and Vick were stationed in a hiding place, out of Roving Rogue's line of vision so they wouldn't interrupt the proceedings, but I doubt Roving Rogue would have cared if he had an audience that night. He wanted the mare that much and to finally be put in stable, with her at his mercy, was just what he wanted. I think at first, when the mare saw the intent in Roving Rogue's eyes it might have frightened her somewhat. She kept backing up, shaking her head and mane as if to say no way. And then…"

"Y-yes," he breathed in. "What happened then?"

"He seemed to be coaxing her to relax by prancing around her, whining a few times. Then I guess she felt comfortable, or she just wanted him enough that she allowed him to get close enough to sniff her out. Evidently he got a whiff of just how hot she was and before she could blink an eye, he reared up on his hind legs and took her. I had seen horses mate plenty of times before, but never like that."

McKinnon swallowed. He had seen horses mate plenty of times before too; especially since he'd been around them all his life. He couldn't help wondering how this mating had been different. To keep his mind from getting clouded with all kinds of ideas, he decided to ask.

"What was so different about it?"

"The mare evidently was in heat in a pretty bad way and was just as hot as he was. I overheard Vick call her a flirt, saying she was like a typical woman, almost driving Roving Rogue to the point of madness before she decided to give in. Good thing Roving Rogue was prime breeding material."

"What was the mare's name?" McKinnon asked, barely able to get the question out.

"Hot Pursuit."

Figures. "Continue," he said, still wanting his earlier question answered. "How was it different?"

"Hot Pursuit got just what she wanted. By the time Roving Rogue mounted her, holding her captive with his front legs while...uh...getting it on, she neighed and trembled the entire time while he thrust vigorously back and forth pumping his seed into her. I actually thought she was in dire pain, but listening to my uncle and Vick talk, they claimed she was in sheer bliss."

And after listening to her, McKinnon was hard as a rock. His entire body felt hot and solid, and he could visualize in his mind the picture of the two horses mating.

They got quiet for a while, which was all right with McKinnon since he needed to cool down. Moments later they pulled into his yard. "We're here," he said, hoping he hadn't sounded as incredibly aroused as he felt.

He couldn't wait to get her inside the house and with tomorrow being Saturday, there would be no need to get up early in the morning. That meant he could make love to her all night as well as all day. First he would take her hard and fast. Then slow and easy. Then hard and fast again. By the time Monday rolled around he intended for any encounters she'd shared with anyone else to be totally erased from her mind.

Hell, he'd never felt this obsessed before, this filled with sexual need. Even now, before bringing the car to a complete stop, he could imagine touching her breasts, widening her thighs to slip between them and then inside her, pumping in and—

"McKinnon?"

The sound of her voice jerked him erect, in more ways than one. He brought the car to a stop before turning to her. His body hardened even more from the sound of her throaty tone when she said, "Would you like to come to the guesthouse for a night cap?"

His mind raced ahead, thinking of going to her place for more than a night cap. McKinnon released a heated sigh and said, "I'd love to."

The way he figured it, he should be feeling some guilt since the only thing he would be offering her was an affair that would lead nowhere. But the decision had been hers. He'd told her what she was in for and he hadn't made her any promises. She had accepted his terms and knowing she was a Westmoreland, the only thing that had made him decide to move ahead was in knowing she wanted him as much as he wanted her.

He knew it. It was there in her gaze each time they'd made eye contact at the party. No matter who he had been conversing with, he had known every moment her gaze had sought him out. He had felt it and the heated warmth of it had sizzled his skin whenever it had slid over him.

Getting out of the car, he walked to the other side to open the door for her. After leaning down and undoing her seat belt, he tried not to notice how the hem of her skirt had ridden up, or that he could see a nice portion of her creamy dark thighs. He felt tension tighten in his belly and he tried get a grip on his control. He offered her his hand and the moment they touched, his pulse immediately kicked up a notch.

"Thanks."

That did it. Instead of releasing her hand when she stood directly in front of him, he tugged on it, tumbling her into his arms. Every part of him was ready, especially his mouth that immediately snatched the breath from hers.

The tension eased from his body the moment their tongues touched, mingled, mated. It was like a homecoming and he spread his hands wide across her bottom to illustrate his point. He needed to kiss her, feel her, touch her, and at the moment it didn't matter that they were standing in the middle of his yard in the dark while he had his way with her mouth.

The only thing that mattered to him was that she was letting him. Not only letting him, but participating in a way that had hot blood running through his veins. The kiss then got so intense he thought it was time to take it indoors before he was tempted to take her right there against his car. He slowly pulled his mouth away. His arousal had increased as a result of her wild and reckless response to him.

"Let's finish this inside." He closed the car door, took her hand and they walked toward the guesthouse.

Ten

It took every ounce of willpower Casey possessed to walk beside McKinnon on sturdy legs. She had deliberately baited him by making the tale of Roving Rogue and Hot Pursuit sound as erotic as she could. And while he'd tried keeping his gaze glued to the road, her gaze had been glued to him—at least to that area where his crotch was located.

She had watched him get aroused, larger than anything she'd ever imagined. And as she had observed the transformation, a tingling of desire had slid sensuously down her spine. What would take place once they were behind closed doors would not come as a surprise to either of them, but what would be a shocker to McKinnon was the next step in her plan of seduction.

When she had dressed for the party she hadn't a clue that he would return tonight, but her undergarments were sexy nonetheless. And from the way he had looked her up and down a few times at the party, she was well aware he liked her outer garments as well. The above-the-knee skirt had handkerchief-hem tiers of tawny chiffon with a matching fluttery tunic-style blouse. The moment she had looked in the mirror after slipping it on earlier, she'd felt feminine and sexy. And from the looks that several men had given her, they'd thought the same. But none of their interest had meant anything to her. McKinnon's awareness was the one that mattered.

Casey did her best to slow down her racing pulse when they reached the door. While she inserted the key into the lock, instead of standing back, McKinnon stood so close behind her that she could feel the hardness of his middle pressed against her bottom, letting her know how much he wanted her.

She tensed in anticipation while opening the door, and the moment she stepped over the threshold and he followed her inside and closed the door behind him, he reached out before she had a chance to go too far. "Don't you go anywhere," he whispered huskily, his arms gently tightening around her waist as he pulled her to him and turned her around. "I want you."

And then he was kissing her with more hunger than ever before, pleasuring her mouth while his tongue provided frantic strokes all around the inside. The movement of it intensified and the taste of him was delicious and so teeth-chattering good.

When he pulled back moments later, she automatically moaned out her protest and he placed small kisses along her lips and jaw in consolation. "Let's get you out of these clothes," he whispered as he proceeded to undress her, first taking her blouse and pulling it over her head, and then getting down on one knee to catch hold of her waist to tug the skirt down. She stepped out of it, leaving her exposed in just her matching thong, bra and high-heeled sandals.

Instead of standing, he glanced up at her on bended knee and, reaching out, ran a slow finger up her leg and thigh to her center, the area barely covered by her thong. "Do you know that I carried your taste with me to D.C., and it was the only thing that held my sanity together those nights I slept in that hotel bed wanting you with a desperation that kept me hard all night?" he said while sliding the thong down her legs. "I didn't know what your final answer would be when I returned, but after tasting you here that night…" he said as he caught her off-guard when he leaned forward and quickly swiped his tongue across her exposed womanly core, "…you became mine, Casey. All mine."

He tilted his head back and looked up at her. "And that's why I was filled with so much anger when I arrived at the party and saw you with Summers," he admitted in a low voice.

Almost blinded with need, Casey met his gaze. "He means nothing to me and after you finish taking off my clothes, I'm going to prove it to you."

He smiled as he stood. "I'm holding you to that," he said as he reached out and undid the front clasp of her bra. When it released, her breasts sprang forth as twin delectable globes. "I like the taste of these as well," he said, bending over and swiping both nipples with the heat of his tongue, leaving them wet as he slid her bra off.

Casey moaned. The sensations McKinnon's tongue evoked were causing every place on her body to tug at her center and she felt a deep longing all over, especially in the area between her legs.

"Now prove it," he said in a quiet yet challenging tone as he took two backward steps.

He glanced at her naked body up and down, and Casey fought for control as cool air touched her skin followed by the heat of his gaze. She had no qualms in proving anything to him. She had made up in her mind earlier tonight to treat him to a little Westmoreland seduction, and although she'd never used her tempting wiles on a man before, with McKinnon Quinn she intended to give it her best shot and then some. She might be a novice but when she finished with him he would see that she did have a lot of potential. So much that he would definitely want to keep her around.

She knew from overhearing her brothers' conversations that men preferred women who were bold and daring, and she was about to whip up as wanton as one could get.

"Did I ever tell you what a great rider I am?" she asked, taking a step forward and reaching out and pulling his shirt from his jeans.

The moment she began unbuttoning it, one button at a time, he inhaled deeply when her fingers slipped a couple of times touching his bare chest. "You didn't have to," he said huskily. "I've seen you ride several times."

She looked at him and lifted a brow. Other than that one time at her father's place, if McKinnon had seen her ride she hadn't been aware of it. As far as she'd known he had never been around when she'd mounted a horse. Did that mean he'd been somewhere watching her without her knowing it?

"Yes, that might be true," she said, undoing the last button and pushing the shirt off his shoulders. "You might have *seen* me ride before, but you've never *felt* me ride…have you?" she finished off sweetly.

She watched the darkening of his eyes and thought that now was not the time to add that no man had ever felt her ride before, but if she was an ace in riding a horse, it couldn't be much different in riding a man. And she'd had a couple of sexually active female friends back in Beaumont swear that men loved women who rode them and weren't hung up on the traditional way to make love.

"No, I haven't felt you," he said, his irises getting even darker and his breathing getting deeper.

"Would you like to *feel* me, McKinnon?"

He nodded, not taking his eyes from her as he kicked off his shoes. "Hell, yeah."

"Good. But first I need to finish removing your clothes," she said, removing his belt and tossing it aside to join his shirt. She then proceeded to unzip his jeans slowly while noticing the huge bulge pressed against them. "Ooh," she moaned seductively. "It looks like someone is ready for that ride."

She got down on a bended knee, like he'd done earlier, to tug the jeans down his hips but didn't stand back up when he kicked them aside. Instead she reached out and cupped him, testing the solidness through his briefs. "Now to get rid of the final piece," she said, easing the briefs down his legs as she got down on the other knee as well.

And when he stood in front of her stark naked, she leaned back on her hunches and admired his physique, especially one particular area. "W—wow," she said admiringly, easing the word out slowly. She then glanced up beyond his center to take in all the man. He was tall and unerringly handsome with thick, dark hair flowing wildly around his creamy dark-skinned shoulders, and had a muscular chest that was sprinkled with strands that formed a path down to the center of him. The part of him she intended to ride.

One good thing about having brothers and positioning yourself to overhear their supposedly private conversations was the ability to learn a lot about men and file that information away to use at an opportune time. She'd always thought the time would be right when she married the man destined to share her life forever. But now, she knew that man was McKinnon, even if what they shared only lasted through the night.

Her brothers had once whispered about men having certain pleasure points on their body and according to them, a man's staff was one of them. Mmm, she would see if that bit of information was true. Remembering all the wonderful and delectable things McKinnon had done to her earlier in the week, she decided when it came to love, anything was fair play.

She reached out and shamelessly took hold of him, intent on getting a taste of him like he'd done with her. Using her tongue, she started by doing swirls and swipes all over his throbbing member like it was a lollipop. But before she could close her mouth over him, he quickly pulled her up into his arms. "No more. I need to be inside of you."

Cuddling her in his arms, he headed toward the bedroom. Once there he tumbled her on the covers before joining her, pinning her down beneath him. The eyes bearing down on her flared with heat, desperation and intense need. She frowned up at him, wanting to be the one in total control, wanting to be the one who did the seducing. "I want to ride you, McKinnon," she said, pushing against him.

"Whatever you want," he said, shifting their bodies so she could be on top.

And when she proceeded to straddle his body the same way she did a horse, she smiled down at him. "I see you're ready and able," she said, placing her center right over his straight-as-a-rod erection. She made a delicious moan as she eased down, lowering her body on his. Their gazes held, locked, and she could feel the thick head of him slowly entering her wetness.

"Oh…it feels better than I ever dreamed of," she whispered, balancing on her elbows and lowering herself upon him even more.

While her eyes were still locked with his, she knew the exact moment he detected a barrier but before he could open his mouth to utter a single word, she shook her head. "No. Don't say anything, McKinnon. Get the deed done. It's what I want so just push up a little and go through it."

She saw the corner of his mouth edge into a stubborn frown as he fought to hold his body rigid. Funny thing about men, she quickly decided—they didn't like surprises, but she was determined to make this one he enjoyed. She wiggled her body and knew from his sharp intake of breath she had managed to touch another pleasure point. Then she leaned down and licked the frown from the corner of his lips and she kept licking and licking and…

"You should have told me," he growled through gritted teeth.

"I'm telling you now," she said matter-of-factly. Why did the horniest of men want to become so noble at a time like this? "Besides, it's not you who has anything to lose," she said, deliberately writhing her body while thinking of her almost-lost virginity.

"Stop that."

"Mmm, make me." Like it or not she intended to give

herself to him. A second passed, then two. Evidently he saw she meant business or maybe his willpower ran out, she wasn't sure which. All she knew was that she felt the moment he lifted his body upward a little, then a little more, breaking through the barrier. And she lowered her body down to meet his, glad he had decided not to be difficult after all.

"You're going to pay for this," he said when he was finally buried inside her to the hilt.

She inhaled deeply. Connected to him this way felt good. The pain had been minimal and now she intended to take the pleasure to the max. "And I'm about to make you glad of your decision."

Casey may not have had experience in pleasuring a man the traditional way, but if what she'd overheard her brothers whispering one night was true, then she was about to make up for it. Closing her eyes, she imagined the Montana sky over her head, flowers all around her and mounting what she considered the best piece of male-flesh to ever walk the face of the earth. He was everything she wanted in a man and more. And she loved him. She lifted her hips, lowered them, moved them around, writhing, twisting and bucking on top of him, while he tried keeping up by moving in and out of her.

Somehow he bent forward, captured a breast in his mouth and sucked while she continued to ride like the devil was on her heels, loving the way he felt beneath her as she rode him.

Moments later she felt her first electrical jolt at the same moment she remembered something neither of them had thought of. "McKinnon," she said in a strained panicky voice, barely getting the words out. "We didn't..."

Before she could finish he gripped hold of her hips and plunged deeper inside of her, roaring out her name. The intensity of the climax she felt coming from him caused her to cry out as he continued to push inside of her, deep, hard and fast, making her own body explode.

Never had she felt anything so exhilarating and mind-blowing. And she refused to stop bucking into him the same way he was bucking into her. This was one ride she wouldn't fall off. She felt crazy, she felt wild, she felt like a woman who had gotten what she'd waited almost thirty years for, and with the man she loved. And from the pleasure contorting his face, she knew he was enjoying this mating as much as she was.

She felt more spasms hitting her, hitting him, and she cried out his name once again, the same moment he cried out hers. She quickly decided that though this was her first time, it most certainly wouldn't be her last. But only with McKinnon. She may have orchestrated this seduction, Westmoreland style, but he had concocted a technique guaranteed to zap the life out of her with so many overwhelming sensations. And when the spasms finally ended and she dropped seemingly weightlessly to his chest, she didn't think she would ever be able to move again.

"You okay?"

Despite all her efforts, Casey didn't even have the strength to raise her head to look at McKinnon. She was exhausted. She could barely breathe. And from the sound of the air rattling in his chest, neither could he. But she would answer his question. "Yes, I'm okay."

She felt her head being lifted, but not under her own strength. McKinnon was raising it for her and pulling it closer to his as he kissed her deeply. He released her mouth moments later, only to be pulled back to her lips like a magnet to kiss her again, then again, like he couldn't get enough of her.

But then she couldn't get enough of him either. She sighed in his mouth when she felt his hand move to her hips, to tighten the hold on their still-connected bodies. It was then that she again remembered that important element. She pulled her mouth away from his and met his gaze. "We didn't use protection, McKinnon."

He stared at her for a long moment and she thought she saw something flash in his eyes. Finally, he leaned up and lightly kissed her lips and said, "It's okay, don't worry about it."

Don't worry about it? She lifted a brow a brow, not understanding. "I don't understand," she said, voicing her miscomprehension out loud. "Why shouldn't I worry about it?"

"Because I'm safe and I have no reason to think you aren't either."

"No, but what about an unplanned pregnancy?"

He took a deep breath and blew it out. "Is it the time of the month that such a thing could happen for you?"

She thought about it, frowned as she calculated in her head. Then she smiled with relief. "No, I should be okay."

"Good enough." And then he pulled her face to his down for another kiss.

McKinnon came awake at the first sign of dawn, grateful it was Saturday and he didn't have to stir until he was ready, which didn't say a lot for a certain area of him which was stirring already.

All it took was for him to close his eyes to remember

how, on the second go round, he had been the one doing the riding as he showed her his skill by pumping back and forth inside of her. Withdrawing, plunging forward over and over again, feeling her inner muscles contract around him as she drew him even deeper into her body. Being inside of her felt so right, a place he could have stayed forever. Each time he glanced down at her face, had seen the pleasure that took over each of her features, he'd been encouraged to double the pleasure, triple the passion and quadruple the need driving the both of them. In all his thirty-four years he had never experienced anything so amazing, so deep-in-your-gut right.

And she had been a virgin.

The thought of what they'd shared—that she hadn't shared it with another male—made it that much more special to him. She was one of the few women around who had waited until they'd been ready, and whose decisions to explore their sexuality with a partner had not been driven by society's standards, but by their own desire to abstain until they felt it was right for them. And evidently Casey hadn't thought the time was right until last night.

He glanced down at her. She was in a deep sleep and uncovered, displaying her nakedness for him to see and enjoy. He was tempted to bend forward and lick the nipples of her breasts but he knew doing so would lead to other things and he would continue licking her elsewhere which would eventually awaken her and after a night of none stop lovemaking, she needed her rest.

And he needed to think.

For a brief moment last night when she had panicked at the thought of them not using birth control, he had considered telling her the real reason why he hadn't been concerned about her getting pregnant. But all it took was for him to remember the confession he'd made to Lynette. And in knowing the risk of doing that, how he had painstakingly made the decision at twenty-three to never father a child and had ensured that fact by having a vasectomy.

He loved children; had always wanted some of his own, but it would not have been fair to bring a child in to the world knowing what medical problems he or she could be up against. He had assumed that Lynette would understand, but the letter he received weeks after she'd left had explained that she was a woman who wanted to one day be a mother and only a child born from her own body, would do. Simply stated, she could not marry a man who could not give her that.

Lynette's rejection had hurt deeply and knowing that most women probably felt as she did—and wanted to bear their own children and not entertain any thoughts of adoption—he decided to live out the rest of his days indulging in meaningless affairs, and to put an end his dream of ever meeting a woman he would marry.

Even now, as he studied Casey's nakedness, he knew he would give anything to one day see her pregnant with his child. The idea had crossed his mind the moment she brought up the fact they hadn't used birth control. But beyond that, he could see her as some child's mother, and as long as that vision stood out in his mind, there could be no place for her in his life. Other than here in his bed.

He wanted to scream out in anger, hit something in despair, but he had discovered years ago to accept any blows life dealt you and move on, not look back, not indulge in pity parties because somewhere in this universe was someone in a worse situation than you.

Casey was his present but she could never be a part of his future. He knew it and he would find a way to accept it. What they were sharing was short-term. It was that simple and he intended to keep it uncomplicated. This arrangement would work out quite nicely for him and he intended to make sure it worked out in a positive way for her as well.

He heard her sigh and looked at her face to see she had awakened. A tempting smile touched the corners of her lips. "Good morning, McKinnon," she said in a sleepy voice that was filled with enough passion to cause heat to flow up his spine and his erection got harder. "What's up?"

"Umm, funny you should ask," he said, responding with a wicked chuckle before leaning over and capturing her lips.

Eleven

McKinnon was no longer avoiding her.

That thought made Casey smile as she dismounted Prince Charming after a good day's workout. Two weeks had passed since the night of her party when he had made love to her all night long. Even now, the thought of that night sent heated shivers through her.

Of course it was a given that during the day he had his work to do and she had hers, but at night it had become a foregone conclusion that they would share a bed, whether at the big house or the guesthouse. In fact, she was becoming a regular fixture in his household. After that first almost embarrassing morning when he had talked her into another lovemaking session before leaving his bed and returning to her own—and she'd run smack into Henrietta on her way out—Casey no longer tried the sneak and retreat routine. She and McKinnon were adults, and if they decided to indulge in a lead-to-nowhere affair, then it was their business and no one else's.

But still she was grateful that no one, especially her family or his, was questioning the obvious—that the two of them were lovers. They ate breakfast together each morning and dinner together in the evenings. They even visited their families together often, and both his parents and Corey seemed to accept that they were adults to do as they pleased.

It was now the beginning of June and the sun was hotter today than usual, she thought a she walked Prince Charming back to his stall. Because of the heat, she'd decided to end her work day a little early. In a few weeks she and McKinnon, as well as a number of Westmorelands, would travel to Lake Tahoe to attend her cousin Ian's wedding, and she knew anyone who hadn't heard by now that she and McKinnon were lovers would find out since they planned to share a suite.

"Hey, beautiful. Do you want to take an evening ride with me?" McKinnon's deep, husky voice called out to her, catching her unaware. She glanced around and saw him a few feet from the corral, sitting on Thunder's back. The sun poured over him, catching the long, dark, silky-looking strands that flowed over his shoulders. Today, more of his Blackfoot features stood out and he looked nothing like the civilized man who had made love to her that morning. Now he appeared to be a fierce warrior ready to take her captive if she refused his request.

"I'd love to go riding with you. Just give me a few minutes to saddle Runaway Child." A few moments later they were headed at a brisk pace across the quiet, open range.

"It's a nice day for riding, isn't it?" Casey said when

they slowed their mounts after reaching the edge of a lake that was located on McKinnon's property.

"Sure is, and I thought it would be kind of nice to get a way for awhile. For me it's kind of a deserving treat. I sold six of my stallions today, which brought me and Durango a pretty nice profit."

"Oh, McKinnon, that's wonderful. Congratulations."

"Thanks."

As they continued to ride together, side by side, she decided to ask him something she'd been meaning to but had never got around to doing. "What made you get into the horse breeding business?" They had brought their horses to a stop and she watched as McKinnon whipped off his hat to wipe sweat from his brow before placing it back on his head.

"When I got this place I thought ranching would keep me busy enough, but it didn't," he said, tilting his head and looking at her. "Durango suggested starting the business because he thinks I have a gift when it comes to handling horses."

"Do you?"

He shrugged. "Probably, but then so do you. I consider what I have as a natural instinct more than a gift. I've discovered that if you breed quality horses there are bound to be serious buyers in all corners of the globe who're ready to do business with you. Which is one of the reasons the M&D is doing so well."

McKinnon glanced over and watched how the evening breeze ruffled the ends of Casey's hair. The urge to run his hand through and tousle it some more took hold of him and he tightened his grip on the reins. If he were to touch her, it wouldn't stop there. He would want to kiss her, pull her off her horse onto his, carry her somewhere private and have his way with her. He ran a hand over his jaw thinking that wasn't such a bad idea and he knew just the place. "Do you want to go play, Casey?"

His deep voice floated over to her and she tilted her head sideways to look at him. "Play?"

He smiled. "Yes. There's a private place not far from here where we can play."

She returned his smile. "And just what will we be playing?"

He chuckled. "How about cowgirl and Indian?"

The shade of his Stetson brim shielded his eyes but she didn't have to see them to know they had darkened at the thought of all the possibilities such a game would entail. "Cowgirl and Indian, huh?"

"Yes."

"You do recall that I'm from Texas, right?"

"Meaning?"

"I'm a true cowgirl in every sense of the word."

McKinnon didn't doubt that since he'd been the recipient of her *rides* a number of times. "And?"

"And I'm no easy prey if that's what you think."

His smile deepened. "We'll see. So do you want to play or not?"

She grinned over at him. "Yes, McKinnon. I want to play."

"Just where are you taking me, McKinnon?" Casey asked, glancing around. She knew they were still on McKinnon's land but where they were she hadn't a clue. He had taken her beyond the rolling hills and they were now going through a maze of bluffs and ravines.

"Getting nervous, cowgirl?" he asked, chuckling.

She frowned over at him. "Of course not, but hasn't anyone ever warned you that it's not good to back a woman up against a wall?"

McKinnon grinned as a vision of that very thing happening—except the woman in his mind was a naked Casey. "I beg to differ. In fact, I can think of a lot of good reasons to back a woman—namely you—up against the wall, Casey."

His voice had gone low and his eyes had darkened, so she had a pretty good idea just where his thoughts were. She forced her gaze away from his eyes to look the area over. During the past two weeks she had taken the art of seduction to a whole new level. She had come up with signals—both verbal and non-verbal—and had gotten an extreme sense of satisfaction knowing McKinnon had enjoyed being the recipient of her racy seduction each and every time. Her actions had been more on instinct than experience, which added to the aroused feelings and excitement. Sensuous shudders would pass through her every time she thought of how McKinnon had taken her from virgin to vixen.

She glanced back over at him. He was watching her intensely and for some reason she had a feeling he was about the turn the tables—he was about to become the seducer. She hated admitting it, but there was an electrical thrill floating through her veins at the thought of his sexual attentions focused mainly on her.

"We can stop riding now."

Casey halted her horse just as McKinnon took the Stetson off his head and dismounted. He then walked over, reached up with his hand and helped her off Runaway Child.

"You still aren't going to tell me where we are?" she asked when her feet touched the ground. Her pulse kicked up knowing his body had pinned her between him and the horse.

"No, not yet. Come with me. We have to walk the rest of the way." He took her hand in his and led her to an area that seemed to have been grazing land at one time but over the years the melting of ice and snow, along with the fall of rocks and boulders from the mountain, now hid it from view and made it impossible terrain for normal travel.

Casey stopped dead in her tracks when she saw what else the elements had done. A cavern had been carved deep in the surface of a huge mountain. She almost became breathless as she took in the splendor of nature's handiwork. She turned to McKinnon. "I didn't know you had a cave on your property."

He smiled. "Rango's and my secret. We came across it one day years ago while we were in our early twenties. I decided then that if this land ever went up for sale, I wanted it. As soon as it did years later, I bought it with my parents' help. In addition to a loan from them, I had to take out two mortgages to pay for it. Now I've paid my parents back and owe the bank on just one loan, but I feel I own some of the most beautiful land in Montana."

Casey nodded. She had to agree. "Do you come here often?"

"Not as much as I'd like but it's nice to get away every now and then. Come on and take a look inside."

When Casey hesitated he raised a brow. "What are you afraid of?"

"Bats. Bears. Should I go on?"

He chuckled. "Trust me. There aren't any bats or bears in there. Rango and I got rid of them long ago when we made this place into a secret hide away."

Deciding to take him at his word, Casey let him lead the way while she followed, at least until she came to the cave's opening that was protected by a pull-down metal security gate. But what caught her attention was the thick layer of tobacco dust surrounding the entrance. She stopped walking again and McKinnon turned and saw what had her attention. "That's to keep snakes and other unwanted animals out," he explained.

Casey nodded. That's what she was afraid of.

After unlocking the security gate, he called back to her, "Come on, cowgirl. You can handle it."

Casey sighed. She wasn't so confident anymore but decided not to let McKinnon know it. Once she followed him inside, her breath caught. It was definitely a cave, but McKinnon had transformed it into just what he'd said—a private hide away with a sturdy-looking made-up bed, a chair and a dresser. There were even a couple of tables with kerosene lanterns and several Native American rugs hanging on the stone walls.

She turned to him, amazed. "McKinnon, it's beautiful."

Coming to this place was hard on horseback, so she couldn't help but wonder how he had managed to get furniture in here. He smiled, evidently knowing her question. "It wasn't easy and more than once Rango and I questioned our sanity. We had one hell of a time but we managed it."

His lips turned into a mischievous grin when he added, "At the time we thought it would be the ideal place to bring female acquaintances."

She raised a brow. "Did you?"

He laughed. "Trust me, we tried to, but those we got as far as the entrance wouldn't go any further once they picked up the scent of the tobacco dust. Everyone around these parts know what it's mainly used for."

Casey snorted. "They were nothing but scaredy-cats. Evidently they weren't true cowgirls."

McKinnon chuckled. "Evidently."

Casey crossed her arms over her chest as she shot him a pointed look. "So, McKinnon, why did you really bring me here?"

His eyes glinted with a kick of satisfaction. "I brought you here to give you a taste of your own medicine."

She lifted a brow. "Meaning?" she asked, releasing a quivering sigh.

"Meaning that you've become the queen of seduction. Well today I'm going to be the king of takers and I'm going to take you, Casey," he said huskily with a half-smile that made heat form between her legs. "I plan on taking you on that bed, against that wall, on that table. Hell, I plan on taking you all over the damn place."

Casey swallowed the lump in her throat as her gaze flew around the cavernous room. The heat between her legs had intensified with his words. If he was trying to get her wet in a certain spot, it was definitely working. The thought of spending time out here alone with him was sending sparks of fire all through her.

She glanced back at him, met his dark, penetrating gaze. He was standing in the middle of the room with his booted feet braced apart. His hands were tucked in the waistband of his jeans and whether he'd wanted it to or not, his stance placed emphasis on his swollen groin area, which showed just how aroused he was.

"So you think you want to take me all over the place, do you?" she asked, holding his gaze.

"Be forewarned, Casey Westmoreland. It's not wishful thinking on my part, either. That's what I intend to do."

A flirty smile touched her lips as her hands went to her shirt. She slowly began undoing the buttons. "Okay then, King Taker. I guess we need to get started and get what you came here for, don't we?"

McKinnon crossed the room with a boy-you-are-gonna-get-laid smile on his face, and Casey decided then and there that he wouldn't just be taking her, she would be taking him as well, because she wanted him just as much as he wanted her.

He came to a stop directly in front of her. "Need help getting out of your clothes?" he asked meaningfully.

"No. You can stand there and watch or save time by getting out of your own clothes."

He grinned and began following her lead, quickly dispersing with his clothing and kicking them on the pile to join hers. When he raked his gaze over her naked body, he thought as he always did that she was an extremely beautiful woman.

He slipped his hand around her waist knowing just where he wanted to start. "So you're a woman who doesn't like getting backed against a wall, huh?" he said while walking her backward. "That's a pity because with the right person such a thing could be a very pleasurable experience."

He came to a stop when her back was pressed against the stony wall. Luckily for her this particular wall was covered with a huge finger-weaved Native American rug. He moved his hands from her waist to her hips and, grabbing hold of her rump, he hoisted her up and she wrapped her legs around him.

"Guide me in, sweetheart," he whispered against her lips.

And she did. Taking him in her hands she positioned him at her womanly entrance and met his gaze. "I need you *here,* McKinnon."

He pushed against her, easing himself inside. The moment he felt her wet heat, as well as her feminine muscles clenching him, he gritted his teeth and said, "No, baby, I'm the one who needs you *there.*"

And then he plunged deeper into her, ripping a scream of pleasure from her throat, which proved she was every bit as needy as he was. And it seemed every time he pounded into her body, her senses went on overload, her desire for him sharpened and every cell she possessed begged for more. She was struck by one sensation after another. They kept coming, he kept pounding and her muscles tightened around him with each thrust as she tried to lock him in. And when an orgasm struck, she screamed loud enough to scare off any animal nearby. But that was only the beginning, and another orgasm followed on the tail of the first.

She knew every time he detonated, she could feel the liquid heat of him shoot to all parts of her body, and like her, he kept coming and coming. And when he leaned down and captured a nipple into his mouth and began a sucking motion that she felt all the way to her womb, she let out more screams.

He gabbed her hips each time he rocked against her so not to bruise her back and although she may not be able to walk tomorrow, today she didn't care. And when he threw his head back and roared, she came again just from the mere sound of it.

Afterward she sagged against his chest as he kissed her, placing what she knew was a hickey on her neck; branding her. Although she knew it took effort since he had to be weak himself, he managed to pick her up in his arms and carry her over to the bed. He placed her on it then fell down beside her, cradling her in his arms. "We'll take a short nap and then I'm taking you in this bed."

Casey closed her eyes. She had no reason not to believe him.

"How are things going with you and your dad?"

Casey cuddled closer to McKinnon in the bed. She glanced toward the cave's opening to see it was getting dark but neither of them had made a move to get up and start getting dressed. Good to his word, he had taken her all over the place and she wondered if any part of her body would ever be the same again.

"Fine," she said, finally answering his question. "I'm discovering just what a thoughtful, kind and considerate person he is. And he's understanding to my feelings and I appreciate that. But…"

"But what?"

"It hasn't been as easy for me as it is for Cole and Clint to establish close relationship with Corey, but I'm trying. There're just some things I still need to put behind me."

"I understand. I know how I felt when I found out Martin wasn't my natural father."

She turned to him. "When did you find out?"

"At sixteen. At first I felt like I'd been betrayed."

Casey knew the feeling. "So what did you do?"

"After hearing my mom's reason for not telling me, I slowly began to accept things since what she'd done was her way of trying to protect me. My paternal grandparents had never approved of her marriage to their son, and when Martin adopted me at birth, she felt it was best to move on so I wouldn't be hurt by their rejection."

He didn't say anything for a few moments but then

added, "She did feel I should have something from my natural father, which is why she named me McKinnon, which was his last name. So in a way I have the best of both worlds as a McKinnon and as a Quinn. Each time that I see my name I'm reminded of the two men I'm honoring."

"Did you ever get the chance to meet your grandparents?"

"Yes, I met my grandmother when I was eighteen. My grandfather had passed on years earlier so I never got the chance to meet him, though. My father had been their only child and my grandmother wanted me to know what would be mine upon her death, like that was the only thing that mattered. It saddens me when I think of all those years I could have gotten to know them, developed a relationship with them, but they didn't want that because of my mixed heritage. They'd been a part of New Orleans' elite wealthy society, and my mother had not been the woman they wanted for their son. What they never accepted was that they really didn't have a say in the matter. That he was old enough to make his own decisions."

Casey nodded. "You and Mr. Quinn are so close that I can't imagine him not being your natural father. I was surprised when I heard that he wasn't."

"He's the only father I know. My mother says that John McKinnon was a good man and they had a good marriage. Short but good. They had met at one of those cultural day events at the Nation's Capital. She was there as a representative of the Blackfoot Nations and he was there representing the Creoles of Color from Louisiana."

McKinnon pulled her tighter to him. "I gather you never had a stepfather."

She shook her head. "No. Mom never dated, although

I know there were men interested in her. Her heart belonged to my father until the day she died."

McKinnon shook his head, thinking what a waste. But then wasn't he doing the same thing? Hadn't he decided to sacrifice sharing a real relationship with a woman for a reason he felt was important to him? Although he no longer loved Lynette, because of her he had turned his back on ever loving anyone again. "Ready to head back?" he asked moments later.

"Yes." She smiled up at him as she flipped on her back. "Thanks for bringing me here, McKinnon. It was special."

He leaned down and kissed her cheek. "No, you're special." Then he went for her lips. Casey sighed in pleasure the moment their mouths touched. They needed to head back and the last thing she needed from him was a long, drugging kiss, but she had a feeling that was what he was about to give her. And of course there was no way she was going to deny him.

A couple of days later, Casey got a surprise visit from her father. She had heard a knock at the door and opened it to find him standing there. "Corey? This is a pleasant surprise."

He nodded, smiling. "I dropped by to see how Spitfire and her colt were doing and wanted to check to see how things are going with you, as well."

"I'm fine. Would you like to come in?"

"Thanks."

Casey stood back and watched as he entered, not bothered that he had found her at McKinnon's home and not the guesthouse. "I was just about to sit down and eat lunch. Would you like to join me?"

He glanced around. "Where's Henrietta?"

Casey smiled. "She and her husband went to Helena for the day. She'll be back tomorrow. McKinnon and I usually eat lunch together but he met his brothers in town to help them with supplies, so I'd love the company."

"Thanks. I'd love to join you."

"Wonderful. Just make yourself at home while I get everything ready."

Back in the kitchen, Casey thought her dad's visit was perfect timing. It was time they had a talk to bury the past, something she hadn't been able to fully let go of until now. Her talks with McKinnon had helped, so had Corey's always made her feel special around him.

A few moments later she returned to the living room to find him standing at the window, looking out at the mountains. "Lunch is ready, Dad."

He quickly turned and met her gaze and she understood why. This was the first time she had ever called him "Dad." "Okay, let me wash up. I'll be right back."

She inhaled deeply when he walked toward the back room. She had a feeling that going into the back had more to do with emotions then him needing to wash his hands. She hadn't realized until that moment how calling him Corey instead of Dad had probably bothered him, although he had never mentioned it to her." He had respected her feelings and had given her time to come around on her own time and her own terms, and she appreciated him for doing that.

"So what are we having?"

She turned when he entered the kitchen. "Nothing special, just chicken salad sandwiches and lemonade," she said, sitting down at the table.

"But it's special to me, Casey," he said in an earnest

tone. "It's not everyday a man gets to have lunch with his beautiful daughter."

"Especially a daughter he didn't know he had until a few years ago," she said, watching him take the seat across from her.

"It doesn't matter. The moment I found out about you, Clint and Cole, I fell in love immediately. Just knowing the three of you were mine meant the world to me and my love was absolute and unwavering."

She nodded, believing that. "It took me time to come around," she softly admitted. "Mom and I were close and she told me these stories and I believed them. I had a vision of the two of you loving each other and it hurt to know everything she'd said had been lies and you really hadn't loved her at all."

Corey reached out and captured her hand in his. "I did love your mother but in another way. Carolyn *was* special to me, Casey, don't ever think that she wasn't. She came into my life when I was at my lowest and we had some good times together. And because she was a good woman I knew I had to be truthful with her from the start. That's the reason I told her that I could never love her completely—the way a man is supposed to love a woman—because my heart belonged to another."

Casey nodded. "And I'm sure Mom appreciated you being honest with her. Some men wouldn't have and that's probably why whenever she mentioned your name, she could do it in a loving way."

Casey didn't say anything for a long moment and then she said truthfully, "I was prepared not to like Abby, especially when I found out she was the woman you had always loved instead of Mom. But Abby is someone who's hard not to like. She's a special lady, Dad, and you're lucky to have her, and even luckier that she came back into your life after all these years. It's as if the two of you are truly soul mates. You and Abby finally being together is a love story with a happy ending if ever there was one. I can see that now. I can also feel the love each and every time you look at her and she looks at you, and I truly believe that Mom never resented you loving someone else because you gave her something special. You gave her a part of yourself, even if it wasn't your heart."

Casey smiled and tightened her hold on the hand that held hers. She gazed into misty eyes and the thought that what she'd said had touched him truly meant a lot. "You are my father and I love you and I'm proud that I'm your daughter. I find joy being a part of your life like you're a part of mine."

She stood and moved around the table and when he also stood, she went into his outstretched arms thinking it felt good to finally let go of the anger and pain she'd held within her for so long.

She felt her heart thud against her rib cage thinking there was pain still harboring there. But it was pain of the self-inflicted kind. She was in love with McKinnon and was smart enough to know that things couldn't continue between them as they were. In less than a month's time Prince Charming would be fully trained and there would be no reason for her to remain on the ranch. She had gotten lax in looking for a place in town, but she knew she needed to start again. The thought had her heart breaking but deep down she knew it was something she had to do.

She forced the painful thought from her mind that, like her mother, she would live the rest of her life loving only one man and only have the memories of their love affair to sustain her.

Twelve

McKinnon picked up the phone the moment he walked out of the bedroom. He was on his way to town for a business meeting and Henrietta had left to do her weekly grocery shopping. "Hello?"

"Yes, this is Joanne Mills and I'm trying to reach Casey Westmoreland."

McKinnon lifted a brow. He remembered Ms. Mills as the real estate agent who had shown Casey a couple of places in town. "Ms. Mills, this is McKinnon Quinn. Casey is out in the barn taking care of one of the horses. Is there something I can do for you?"

"Oh, hello Mr. Quinn. Yes, there's something you can do. You can tell Ms. Westmoreland that after talking with her last week, something has come up on our listing that she might be interested in. The seller is willing to work out a good deal since he wants a quick sale."

McKinnon leaned back against the table. Casey was considering moving off his ranch? Emotions clogged his throat, making it almost impossible for him to breathe.

"Mr. Quinn, are you still there?"

McKinnon forced himself to speak. "Yes, I'm still here and I'll give her the message."

"Thank you."

McKinnon hung up the phone as a cold chill settled in his gut. He was being forced to admit something he thought could never happen to him again. He had fallen head over heels in love.

"Damn."

He inhaled deeply knowing he had no right to even think about loving Casey. Yet he did. She was everything he could possibly want in a woman or a wife, but he couldn't have her. So maybe it was for the best if she did decide to move on. Things had to eventually end between them anyway.

He quickly headed for the door, pausing briefly to snatch his hat off the rack. If Casey leaving was for the best, why was he feeling so damn bad about it?

Durango glanced across the table at McKinnon. The two of them had just ended their meeting with Mike Farmer, who had made them an offer they couldn't refuse. Not only did Mike want to buy every foal Courtship produced, he also wanted Crown Royal's stud rights at more than half-a-million a coupling. The man was convinced the stallion's offspring would one day become a Triple Crown winner.

"What's wrong with you, McKinnon? Farmer just made us wealthy men and you're sitting there like you've lost your one and only puppy. Forget about that beer you're drinking, man. We should be calling that waiter over to our table with a bottle of champagne to celebrate."

McKinnon leaned back in his chair, remembering the phone call he'd taken right before leaving the ranch. "I don't feel like celebrating, Rango."

Durango sat up in his chair. A frown settled in. "Why not? Hey, what's going on?"

McKinnon met Durango's curious gaze. "That Realtor who's helping Casey find a place in town called and left her a message that she might have found something. With Prince Charming almost trained, Casey really has no reason to stick around, which means she might move into town."

Durango stared at him for a moment before asking brusquely, "And what do you plan to do about it? I won't waste my time asking if you love her because your attitude today has given me my answer. Take my advice about something, McKinnon."

"What?"

"Stop brooding and do what you've always done. Go after what you want."

McKinnon clearly understood what Durango was saying and a hard line formed at his lips when he drew in a deep breath. "This is different. I can't do that."

"Yes, you can."

McKinnon's anger flared and he refused to give in to the surge of emotions that was sweeping through him. "Dammit, Rango, I can't do it *because* I love her. I can't deny her the one thing she might eventually want one day."

"But you don't know for sure that's what you'll be doing. Casey deserves to know the truth, McKinnon, so tell her."

McKinnon sighed deeply, remembering the night he'd

asked her if she wanted children and what her response had been. "Why bother? Things can't be that way between us, Rango. I can't let it. She deserves more," he said grimly.

"Well, I think," Durango said softly, "that you'll be doing the both of you a disservice if it you make a decision without giving her a say in the matter. If you want her, McKinnon, don't let anything stand in your way. Tell her the truth and see how things work out. Take it from someone who knows. The love of a woman, a good woman, is the greatest gift a man could ever receive."

Durango took a swallow of his beer before he went on. "If you're so convinced she's going to leave anyway, what do you have to lose?"

Casey glanced across the table at Henrietta as the older woman peeled a bunch of apples for the pie she intended on to bake later. There was something Casey wanted to know and was hoping Henrietta would have an answer for her. "Henrietta, who is Lynette?"

The woman stopped what she was doing and glanced over at Casey, her eyes sharp. "Who mentioned Lynette to you? I know it wasn't McKinnon."

Casey nodded. "No, it wasn't McKinnon. Norris let her name slip one day saying that I was nothing like her and he was glad."

Henrietta smiled. "No, you aren't anything like her. And it's not that Lynette was a totally bad person, it's just that she didn't stick by McKinnon when she should have, especially when she claimed she loved him. The woman hurt the boy something awful."

Casey couldn't help but wonder just what had Lynette done. It didn't sound like she'd been unfaithful to McKinnon.

And how should she have stuck by him? Was this Lynette the reason he refused to open his heart to another woman? "Does she still live around these parts?" she asked.

Henrietta shook her head. "No, thank goodness. From what McKinnon told me, Lynette is married now with a child and living somewhere in Great Falls. The last thing McKinnon needs is to see Lynette and her baby."

Casey tilted her head back. Now her mind was flooded with even more questions. Why would seeing Lynette with a baby bother McKinnon? Had he and Lynette lost a baby together or something? She couldn't help but ponder Henrietta's statement. "But why would that bother him?"

Henrietta glanced over at Casey as if she was about to say something, then changed her mind and shrugged wide shoulders. "It's not my place to say, Casey. Maybe one day McKinnon will tell you all about her. About everything."

Casey doubted it. In fact, since waking that morning she'd noticed a change in McKinnon. Usually they ate breakfast together but this morning he had already eaten and left before she'd awaken. He'd been acting strange ever since mentioning Joanne Mills' call. Was he upset that she had resumed looking for a place to live? Did he think she was supposed to just continue to live here with him forever? She really didn't know what to think but she hoped it was her imagination and that McKinnon wasn't trying to put distance between them again.

"Thanks for at least letting me know who she is," Casey finally said to Henrietta.

"No problem," Henrietta said quietly. "Like I said, that woman hurt him but now you've made him happy."

Casey smiled. "You think so?"

Henrietta chuckled. "I know so. He smiles now more and

his disposition and moods aren't like they used to be, and you're the reason for it. And I know you love him, too. And I mean really love him." The older woman was silent for a few moments and then she said. "Just promise me one thing."

"What?"

"No matter what happens, follow your heart and you can't go wrong. When it comes to love, there's no way you can turn your back on it and walk away. There's no way."

Casey was waiting for McKinnon later that night when he got in. He hadn't come home for dinner, which only deepened her belief that he was trying to avoid her. She was standing by the fireplace and he looked over at her the moment he opened the door.

"McKinnon," she acknowledged when he didn't say anything. "I looked for you at dinner."

He shrugged, closing the door behind him. "Something came up and I had to stay on the range longer than expected. I'm surprised you're still up."

For some reason she got the impression he'd been hoping that she hadn't been up, and that only strengthened her resolved and made her even more determined to find out just what was going on with him. "Yeah, I'm surprised too. Especially since we've been going to bed early a lot."

There…she had deliberately made him remember how their nights had been for the past three weeks. He would rush home every day and they would get dinner, take a shower together, go to bed and make love.

"Yeah, well, like I said, I've been busy. Besides, I've been thinking."

She suddenly felt a little queasiness settle in her stomach. "About what?"

"About us. You'll be through training Prince Charming in a few more weeks and will be moving on. I even understand you're looking to buy a place in town and—"

"Is that's what this is about, McKinnon? Are you upset that I resumed looking for a place in town? Because if you are then—"

"Upset? Why should I be upset about anything? You and I both knew things between us wouldn't last and it's no problem, no big deal. You're doing the right thing by moving on."

She flinched. It sounded like he hadn't cared and she refused to believe that. She didn't want to believe it. Yes, she had known the score but at some point she'd actually believe the rules had changed not only for her, but for him as well. Although she couldn't claim that she thought he had fallen in love with her the same way she had fallen in love with him, she refused to believe she had been nothing more than a willing body to him.

"Is that what you really want, McKinnon?"

He hesitated a moment before answering. "Yes. It will be for the best."

Casey sighed deeply, intent on giving him what he wanted. She had her pride and refused to carry a torch for a man who didn't love her—like her mother had with her father. She'd thought just the memories of what the two of them shared would suffice, but now she knew that they wouldn't. And she had a feeling that at some point her mother discovered that fact as well.

At that moment she fully understood how her mother must have felt in knowing that although she had loved Corey Westmoreland, he did not love her. But he *had* given her babies, which to Carolyn Roberts were all the memories she needed. Casey was certain that each time her mother gazed into her children's faces, which so closely resembled the man she had loved, she was content. And that contentment had lasted until the day she had died. In realizing that, Casey's love and admiration for her mother increased.

Now Casey was faced with a similar decision. During all those times she and McKinnon had made love, they'd never once used protection. The first couple of times had been during the wrong time of the month, but the recent times had not. That meant she could possibly find herself in the same situation her mother had. Single and pregnant by a man who didn't love her. But unlike her mother who'd kept silent, she intended to let McKinnon know it.

"Fine, I'll leave and find someplace else when my business here is finished, and if I'm pregnant you'll know it. There were a number of times that we engaged in unprotected sex."

For a moment he looked as if she'd slapped him. After a few seconds of silence he finally said, "You aren't pregnant."

She laughed softly to hide her pain. "Oh, so you're a doctor now, McKinnon?"

He leaned back against the closed door and placed his arms across his chest. His face was rigid and stern. "No, but I know you aren't pregnant. There's no way you can be."

Casey frowned as she stared at him. "And what makes you so certain of that?"

Here we go again, McKinnon thought. Tell her so she can do the same thing Lynette did. Lynette didn't waste any time packing up her stuff and hauling ass because you could never give her the children she wanted. So go ahead and tell Casey the truth and see how fast she leaves.

He would never forget how he had arrived back at the ranch or his meeting in town with Durango and Mike Farmer. He'd been determined to follow Durango's advice and confront Casey, tell her the truth and let the decision be hers. But when he'd walked in on her in the barn, she'd been talking to Dawn Harvey, the wife of one of his ranch hands who'd had a baby a few months earlier. She had brought the baby by and Casey had been holding it, smiling down at it, teasing the infant by making funny sounds—baby talk. He had known after seeing the glow on her face that he could never deny her from being a mother. He loved her too much to deny her something like that.

He sighed deeply as he lowered his arms and moved away from the door to start crossing the room toward Casey. When he came to a stop in front of her, he tried to recall the exact moment he'd fallen in love with her and couldn't. Chances were it had been the first time he's seen her at Stone and Corey's weddings. But he *could* recall when he had first accepted that he loved her in his heart. It had been that night they had made love for the first time and she had deliberately seduced the hell out of him. Not only had he surrendered his body to her, but on that night he had surrendered his heart to her, too.

"McKinnon? What makes you so sure that I'm not pregnant?"

He looked down at her, deep into eyes that had the ability to turn him into putty in her arms; eyes that he enjoyed gazing into each and every time he had entered her body. The eyes that would take on a darker shade just seconds before she came.

"The reason I know you aren't pregnant is because I can't get you pregnant." Ignoring the confused look on her face he continued. "About the same time I found out Martin wasn't my natural father, I found out that my real dad had had a rare blood disease that neither he nor my mother knew about. In fact, it was only discovered after he'd been in that car accident that eventually took his life. Although there's no health risks to me, the disease makes me a carrier, which I can pass on to any children I have. I couldn't do that to a child, so I made the decision around eleven years ago to have a vasectomy."

She shook her head, not sure she'd heard him right. "You've had a vasectomy?"

"Yes. So now you know why there can't ever be a future for us."

She looked stunned and then moments later said, "Excuse me. Maybe I'm a little dense or something but I really don't see your point."

"You will eventually and if you'll excuse me I need to take a shower. And I think it will be for the best that you stayed at your own place tonight…in fact from now on."

And without giving her a chance to say anything, he turned and walked toward his bedroom, closing the door behind him.

For the longest time, Casey just stood there, seemingly rooted in place as her mind replayed all that McKinnon had just told her. Was a similar announcement is what sent Lynette running? For goodness sakes, if that was true then the woman really hadn't loved McKinnon at all.

A part of Casey, the stubborn Westmoreland part, wanted to follow McKinnon right now, beat on his bedroom door and have it out with him. Surely he didn't think his inability to have children meant she couldn't love him, or didn't love him? But after thinking about it for a few moments she knew he did think that way; mainly because another woman had done that very thing.

Her heart went out to him. Had he and Lynette not discussed other options such as adoption? Had Lynette not wanted to go another route? No wonder Henrietta had said it was a good thing the woman didn't live around these parts since seeing her and her child would probably bother McKinnon. Now Casey understood. Seeing that child would be a reminder of what he hadn't been able to give the woman he'd loved.

He had walked off, letting her know he preferred being alone tonight and for once she would grant him his wish. Mainly because she needed to think things through to determine what would be the best way to handle McKinnon. How could she make him understand that it didn't matter to her and she would be willing to adopt a child one day, or even consider artificial insemination.

She sighed as she headed toward the back door to return to her own place. Tomorrow she intended to put her plan into motion. Before, it had been seduction. Now, it was all about satisfaction, and she wouldn't be satisfied until McKinnon understood that she was the one woman who would always be by his side, no matter what.

Early the next morning Casey found Norris in the stables and requested a day off work. There was someone she needed to see and talk with immediately. McKinnon's mother.

The moment she pulled into the yard, Morning Star Quinn stepped out of her home wearing a huge smile. Not for the first time Casey thought the woman was absolutely stunning with her huge dark eyes in an angular face, high cheekbones and long, straight black hair that flowed past her back. It was apparent she was Native American and she looked more in her thirties than in her fifties.

"Casey, this is a pleasant surprise," Morning Star said, giving her a hug. "Is everything all right?"

Casey shook her head. "No, but I believe eventually everything will be. First I need to talk to you about something important."

"Sure. Come inside and join me in a cup of coffee."

Casey followed the older woman inside and the moment she stepped foot across the threshold, she felt a special warmth. She followed Morning Star into the kitchen and sat down at the table. "Is Mr. Quinn at home?"

Star glanced up from pouring the coffee, smiled and said, "No, he and your father went hunting today. I don't expect either of them back until later. Do you need to see him as well?"

"No, you're the person I came to see. I'd like to talk to you about McKinnon."

Morning Star's dark brow lifted as she joined Casey at the table. "What about McKinnon?"

"I'm in love with him," Casey came right out and said, thinking she needed to let Mrs. Quinn know how she felt upfront. She began to relax when she saw the huge smile that touched Morning Star's lips.

"I saw it happening," Morning Star said, taking a sip of her coffee.

Surprise lit Casey's face. "You did?"

"Yes. It was there in your eyes whenever you looked at him and I saw the same look in his."

Casey sighed as she took a sip of her tea. If he loved her that was definitely news to her. "We've been together ever since the night of my party," Casey said, pretty sure she didn't have to paint a picture of what she meant by that. "And last night McKinnon sort of broke things off. He told me about his health issue and for some reason he's convinced that—"

"Because of it the two of you couldn't have a future together even if you wanted one," Morning Star finished for her.

Casey met the older woman's eyes. "Yes."

Morning Star didn't say anything for a long moment, but then she met Casey's gaze and said, "We all have Lynette Franklin to thank for that. She took off right after McKinnon confided in her."

Casey nodded. She had figured as much. "But that was her. What does how she reacted have to do with me?"

Morning Star smiled. "Because you are a woman. McKinnon sees you as a person who would probably make some child a wonderful mother, a child he can not give you. He really thinks he's being noble in cutting you loose."

"Well, he's not. Of course I want children, but we can adopt. Giving birth to a child isn't such a big deal to me."

"It is to some women and he knows it." Morning Star sighed deeply before continuing. "Making the decision to have a vasectomy was probably one of the hardest things my son had to do because he loves children and always wanted to settle down one day, marry and have some. He was torn about what to do until one particular day when he had to go to the hospital for his annual tests."

"What happened?"

The older woman stood and walked over to the sink. Then she turned around and Casey could see the love and pain for her child etched on her face. "While in the waiting room, McKinnon met a man who was also a carrier. The man shared with McKinnon how he'd unknowingly passed the disease on to his six-year-old son, and the rough time his son had had before dying the year before. It's my understanding that from that conversation, McKinnon swore that he wouldn't have any children and risk passing anything on to them."

Casey wiped a tear from her eye, sadden by the stranger's loss and even more sadden that McKinnon's dream for a family had died that day, too. "I refuse to walk away and let him go through life alone with this, Mrs. Quinn."

"He's pretty much made up his mind that he will never let another woman into his life."

Casey stood and met Morning Star's gaze with a defiant look in her eyes. "Well, we'll just see about that. I love McKinnon and I won't let him turn his back on what we can have together. I simply refuse to let him do that."

Morning Star smiled. "And I'm happy to hear it. No matter how difficult he gets, don't let him push you away. Fight him with your love."

Casey nodded. She intended to do that very thing.

McKinnon spotted Casey the moment he turned the corner of the ranch house. She'd sent a message by Norris that she needed to see him and not knowing if it could wait, he had put his work aside to look for her.

On his way he'd seen Henrietta leaving and wondered why she had ended her work day early. Since it was Friday, chances were she probably had something to do and had forgotten to mention it to him.

He inhaled deeply. Casey was standing in the courtyard by the flower beds, the same place she'd been standing the night they had shared their first kiss. He muttered a curse. That was the last thing he needed to think about now. But hell, how could he not when she looked so beautiful standing there in jeans that cupped her bottom so deliciously, and a short silky-looking blouse that showed what nice breasts she had; breasts he had touched and tasted so many times. He let his gaze flick over them one last time before putting his control in place.

"Norris said you wanted to see me, Casey," he said, trying to stop his heart from hammering away in his chest.

She looked up at him. "Yes. I thought we could finish our discussion now." She watched as his body moved into that stance she loved—arms crossed over his broad chest and booted feet braced apart. The man certainly had the body to fill out any pair of jeans he put on. Today his hair was pulled back in a ponytail, making him look very sexy.

He blew out an impatient breath. "We finished our discussion last night. There's nothing to add or subtract."

"I think there is and would like for you to hear me out."

His lips pressed into a firm line and he inhaled deeply. "Okay, say whatever it is you have to say so I can get back to work."

She nodded and slowly crossed the courtyard to him. He nervously rubbed his hand across the back of his neck when she came to a stop. She was too close for comfort and she smelled too damn good.

"I just want to get a few things straight in my mind, McKinnon. Let's do scenario number one. If I had come to you the other night, and told you that I had a female condition that stopped me from ever giving you a son or a daughter, would you have ended things between us for that reason?"

"Of course not!"

"Okay, let's move to scenario number two. If, for any reason, I wanted to adopt a child, would you have had a problem with that?"

McKinnon frowned, wondering where she was going with this. "No, I would not have had a problem with it."

"And what if I wanted to try artificial insemination to get pregnant, would you have a problem with that?"

"No, I wouldn't have a problem with that either."

"That's good to know." Then she placed her hand on her hips and glared at him. "Then what the hell is *your* problem," she snapped, all but screaming at him. "What kind of woman do you think I am to expect more from you than I'm willing to give myself? Just like I wouldn't expect you to walk out on me if I couldn't produce a child, I would think you would have the decency not to expect the same thing from me. But do you? Hell no! You expected me to be like that other woman—who evidently didn't know a good thing when she had it—and run off. There're plenty of babies out there who need a loving home, a home that we can give. I think it's a crying shame that you think so little of me."

"Casey," he said in a low tone, so low it almost sounded like a whisper. "It's not that I think so little of you, it's because I think so much of you that I want you to have more. I love you. I love you so much it hurts and knowing I can't give you the one thing you might want one day is killing me."

Casey inhaled slowly and deeply, taken back by his words of love. "If you love me as much as you say you do, then listen for a moment to what I want, McKinnon. I want *you*. The man who tries so hard to hide that easy grin and those kind eyes. The man who showed me just what real love is about, made me see what a wonderful human being my father is and helped me to understand why my mother was willing to live the rest of her life on memories. Well, unlike her I can't be that content, McKinnon. I want you. If I never gave birth to a child it wouldn't matter as long as I had you. I love you and to me, to us, that should be all that matters. We will handle the rest when the time comes."

She reached out, locked her fingers with his, felt the tenseness slowly ebbing away in them. "I want you to be there for me, McKinnon, to hold me close in the middle of the night, to make love to me, to wake up with me. I think these past three weeks have shown us how good we are together, and if it's only just you and me, then that's how things will be. But since you like kids and so do I, I can see a child in our future, a child we will make ours—a child we will watch grow in our love. Martin isn't your biological father but I know you don't love him any less. The same will hold true with our child, our children."

She took a step closer and after releasing his hand, she lifted hers to cup his chin. Misty eyes stared into his. "Let go, McKinnon. Stop protecting your heart. Place it in my care for safe keeping and I promise it won't ever get broken again."

Before Casey could take her next breath, McKinnon's arms closed around her, brought her to the solidness of his body, and he lowered his mouth to hers. This kiss was like the others, full of passion. It made her world tilt, the ground shake and every bone in her body melt. But then it was different. It was a kiss of love and devotion. Not only was he giving her his heart, he was giving her his body and soul as well.

He then swung her up into his arms and gazed at her. "Will you marry me?" he asked in a voice filled with emotion.

"Yes!" she said, smiling brightly. "I've gone through seduction, satisfaction and now the next step has to be a wedding—Westmoreland style. One that will last forever."

He leaned over and placed another kiss on her lips and whispered, "Yes, sweetheart. Forever."

Epilogue

McKinnon glanced over at his fiancée sitting beside him in the church. He knew weddings made some people cry but Casey was taking it to a whole other level. He put the handkerchief back in his pocket deciding it was useless for dabbing her tears. He knew of only one way—to shut her up. So, ignoring the wedding proceedings at the front of the church, his parents and her father and stepmother who were sitting beside them, he leaned over and kissed her.

And as he'd known she would, she melted right into his arms, so he pulled her from her seat and settled her into his lap. She wrapped her arms around his neck and leaned close into his body. "Thanks, I needed that," she whispered contentedly in his ear.

"Make sure you tell that to your brothers and cousins after the wedding," he whispered back. "They're staring, giving me dirty looks."

Moments later, everyone stood to their feet when the preacher presented Ian and Brooke Westmoreland as a married couple. Cheers and applauses sounded inside the Lake Tahoe church that had accommodated over three hundred guests.

It had been a beautiful day for a wedding and all the Westmorelands were present. Even Delaney who looked like she would deliver anytime. Jamal's jet was ready to return them to Tahran immediately after the reception. He was determined that their second child be born in his homeland as well.

McKinnon and Casey hung back while everyone departed the church for the Rolling Cascade, Ian's casino and resort where a huge reception would be held. "Okay, why so many tears today?" McKinnon asked, pulling her into his arms.

She glanced up at him with tear-stained eyes. "Because I could feel Ian's and Brooke's love, and because I have so much to be thankful for myself. Next month around this time I'll be the bride and you'll be the groom. For a moment I could picture you standing there, pledging your life to me. And also, the ceremony was beautiful."

McKinnon nodded as he took her hand and led her out of the church. "Yes, it was." They had decided on a November wedding that would take place on Corey's Mountain. Savannah would have delivered her baby by then. He was thrilled to be the father of the bride, and to say McKinnon's mother and Abby were excited about planning a wedding was an understatement.

He thought about the party the two women had thrown together last month and shook his head. He and Casey expected their wedding would be on a much larger scale, although they'd let it be known they wanted a small affair. But Morning Star Quinn and Abby Westmoreland didn't know the meaning of small.

"Do we have to stay at the reception for a long time?" Casey asked, stopping on the church step and getting on tiptoe to bring her lips closer to his.

"No, not for long," he said, wrapping his arms around her waist.

Their lips met in a kiss that held promises.

Moments later she stepped away from him and smiled. "I've decided where I want to spend our wedding night, McKinnon."

"You have? Where?"

"Our cave."

He lifted a brow. She looked serious. He smiled, actually liking the idea. "You sure you don't mind finding yourself backed up against a wall?"

She smiled and took his hand as they walked down the church steps. "Not as long as you let me demonstrate my horsemanship to you later."

He chuckled and leaned down and whispered. "Baby, you can ride me anytime."

* * * * *

Happily ever after is just the beginning…

Turn the page for a sneak preview of
A HEARTBEAT AWAY
by
Eleanor Jones

Special? A prickle ran down my neck and my heart started to beat in my ears. Was today really special?

"Tuck in," he ordered.

I turned my attention to the feast that he had spread out on the ground. Thick, home-cooked-ham sandwiches, sausage rolls fresh from the oven and a huge variety of mouthwatering scones and pastries. Hunger pangs took over, and I closed my eyes and bit into soft homemade bread.

When we were finally finished, I lay back against the bluebells with a groan, clutching my stomach.

Daniel laughed. "Your eyes are bigger than your stomach," he told me.

I leaned across to deliver a punch to his arm, but he rolled away, and when my fist met fresh air I collapsed in a fit of giggles before relaxing on my back and staring up into the flawless blue sky. We lay like that for quite a while,

Daniel and I, side by side in companionable silence, until he stretched out his hand in an arc that encompassed the whole area.

"Don't you think that this is the most beautiful place in the entire world?"

His voice held a passion that echoed my own feelings, and I rose onto my elbow and picked a buttercup to hide the emotion that clogged my throat.

"Roll over onto your back," I urged, prodding him with my forefinger. He obliged with a broad grin, and I reached across to place the yellow flower beneath his chin.

"Now, let us see if you like butter."

When a yellow light shone on the tanned skin below his jaw, I laughed.

"There…you do."

For an instant our eyes met, and I had the strangest sense that I was drowning in those honey-brown depths. The scent of bluebells engulfed me. A roaring filled my ears, and then, unexpectedly, in one smooth movement Daniel rolled me onto my back and plucked a buttercup of his own.

"And do *you* like butter, Lucy McTavish?" he asked. When he placed the flower against my skin, time stood still.

His long lean body was suspended over mine, pinning me against the grass. Daniel…dear, comfortable, familiar Daniel was suddenly bringing out in me the strangest sensations.

"Do you, Lucy McTavish?" he asked again, his voice low and vibrant.

My eyes flickered toward his, the whisper of a sigh escaped my lips and although a strange lethargy had crept into my limbs, I somehow felt as if all my nerve endings were on fire. He felt it, too—I could see it in his warm brown eyes. And when he lowered his face to mine, it seemed to me the most natural thing in the world.

None of the kisses I had ever experienced could have even begun to prepare me for the feel of Daniel's lips on mine. My entire body floated on a tide of ecstasy that shut out everything but his soft, warm mouth, and I knew that this was what I had been waiting for the whole of my life.

"Oh, Lucy." He pulled away to look into my eyes. "Why haven't we done this before?"

Holding his gaze, I gently touched his cheek, then I curled my fingers through the short thick hair at the base of his skull, overwhelmed by the longing to drown again in the sensations that flooded our bodies. And when his long tanned fingers crept across my tingling skin, I knew I could deny him nothing.

* * * * *

Be sure to look for
A HEARTBEAT AWAY,
available February 27, 2007.

And look, too, for
THE DEPTH OF LOVE
by Margot Early,
the story of a couple who must learn that love comes in many guises—and in the end it's the only thing that counts.

HARLEQUIN
Driver cameo:
Carl Edwards
NASCAR
SPEED DATING
Nancy Warren
USA TODAY bestselling author
99

Receive $1.00 off
SPEED DATING
or any other Harlequin NASCAR book.
Coupon expires December 31, 2007. Redeemable at participating retail outlets in the U.S. only. Limit one coupon per customer.
RETAILER: Harlequin Enterprises Ltd. will pay the face value of this coupon plus 8 cents if submitted by the customer for this specified product only. Any other use constitutes fraud. Coupon is nonassignable. Void if taxed, prohibited or restricted by law. Void if copied. Consumer must pay for any government taxes. Mail to Harlequin Enterprises Ltd., P.O. Box 880478, El Paso, TX 88588-0478, U.S.A. Cash value 1/100 cents. Limit one coupon per customer. Valid in the U.S. only.
113854
5 65373 00076 2
(8100) 0 11385
NASCPNUS